BLACK & WHITE

BLACK & WHITE

A Parker City Mystery

Justin M. Kiska

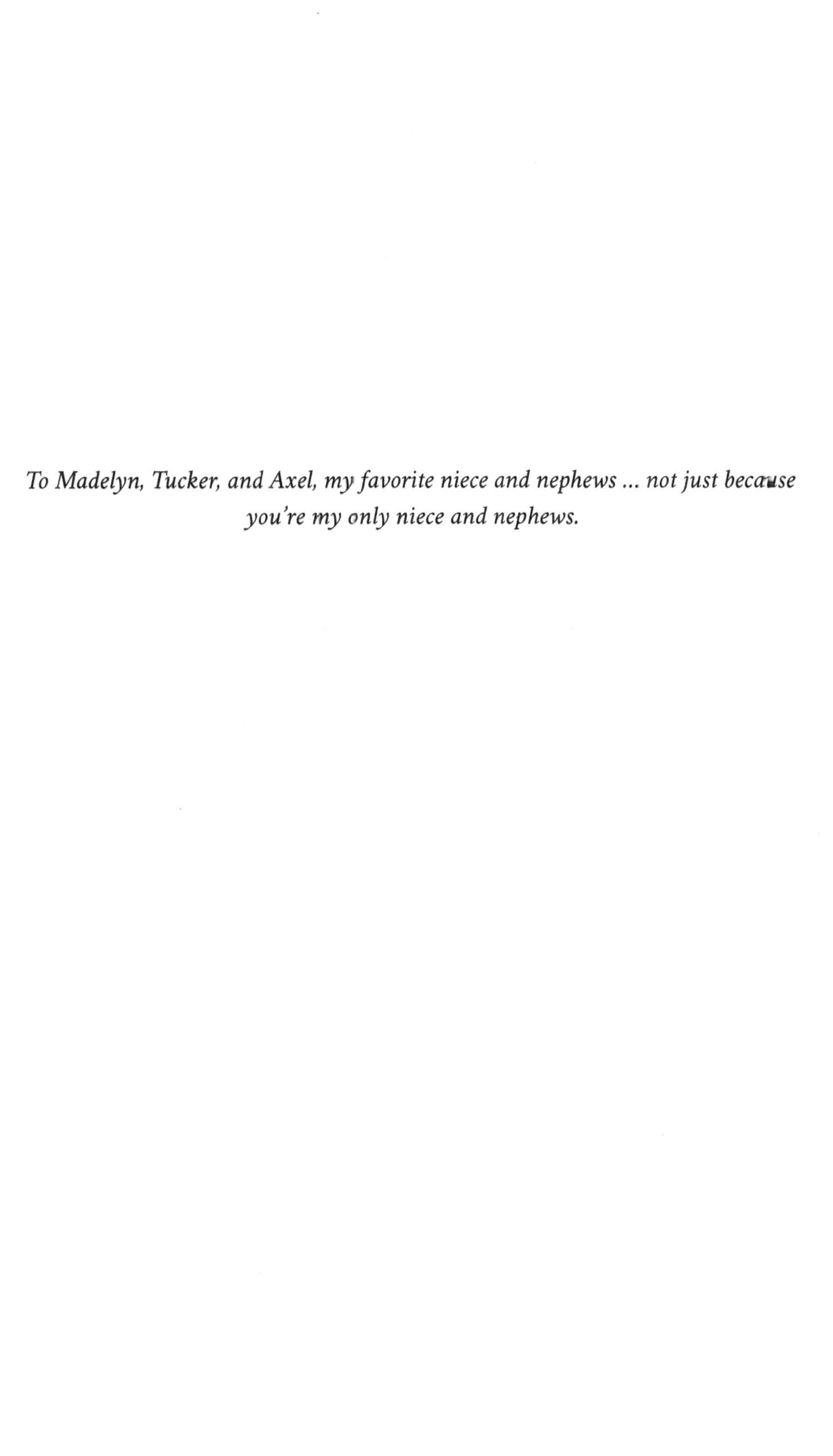

To Madelyn, Tucker, and Axel, my favorite niece and nephews ... not just because you're my only niece and nephews.

Praise for Black & White

"An intriguing murder case, or is it? *Black & White*, Justin Kiska's latest novel, is a well-crafted and propulsive mystery set in a small Maryland town where nothing is what it seems. From the aftermath of WWII through the mid-1980s, three different investigators race to unravel clues to solve a crime that bridges the decades. A fantastic read!"—Bruce Robert Coffin, award-winning author of the Detective Byron mysteries, and The Turner and Mosley Files

"Kiska keeps the tension high in this intricately plotted mystery. Sins of the past come to haunt the present making *Black & White* a crackling page turner."—James L'Etoile, award-winning author of *Dead Drop* and *Face of Greed*

Chapter One

Spring 1985...

Detective Sergeant Ben Winters pulled the unmarked Crown Vic off the paved road onto the dirt and patchy grass of the expansive field. The tires crunched loose stones and twigs as he pulled up next to the pair of Parker City Police squad cars already on the scene. They, in turn, were parked on either side of a mustard yellow pickup truck emblazoned with the city's Public Works Department logo on its doors. Easing to a stop, through the dust-covered windshield, Ben saw two uniformed officers about a hundred yards further on. With them was a man he could only assume was the city engineer who'd reported the disturbing discovery.

The day had begun beautifully with a bright blue sky and white cotton candy clouds lazily drifting overhead. It was almost too picturesque to be real. The kind of day you only saw in movies and paintings. As Ben made his way across the parking lot from his apartment building to the car, he heard the birds chirping in the trees and smelled the sweet scent of the freshly blossomed flowers lining the sidewalk. Yes, the day was picture-perfect. Not normally one to stop and smell the roses, he found a little extra bounce in his step that morning. With his suit jacket slung over his shoulder–giving him the distinct appearance of a young model out of the J.C. Penney catalogue— he thought even the temperature couldn't be any better. Not too hot and not too cold. Goldilocks would undoubtedly have approved. Whether he was simply allowing the brilliance of the moment to cloud his judgment, or it truly was, he felt it would be hard to describe a perfect spring day.

Stopping for a cup of coffee and a bagel on his way into the station, even the sometimes-surly waitress behind the counter welcomed him with a warm smile and cheery greeting. And could that be a new butterfly clip in her hair? Seeing a copy of the *Herald-Dispatch* left by a previous customer lying there, Ben scanned the headlines on the front page as he sipped his coffee and listened to the random conversations surrounding him in the small coffee shop.

"They're opening against the Blue Jays next week. What do you think of that Ripkin kid? I hear he makes a million a year," one elderly gentleman was saying to his friend across the table between bites of pancake.

Next to him at the counter, Ben overheard a woman telling the waitress, "My sister just doesn't know how to make ham for Easter. It was so salty. I gave her my recipe for how to make it the right way, but every year, it's always the same. Too salty."

He wasn't exactly eavesdropping, but in his line of work, it never hurt to keep one's ear to the ground. In his experience, he'd learned many cases were solved because of something someone saw or heard and didn't think much of at the time. How much more innocuous could a conversation over a cup of morning coffee be? Thankfully though, Ben didn't overhear anyone plotting a bank heist or talking about knocking off a business partner. By the time he finished his bagel and headed for the door, Ben was convinced it was going to be smooth sailing for the rest of the day.

As was his routine, he fully intended on arriving at the station early. But with no pressing cases open at the moment, he was in no rush. All he really needed to do was take care of some paperwork that was sitting on his desk. Even that wasn't time-sensitive, but Ben's personality didn't allow him to get too behind on his paperwork. A self-avowed workaholic, he wanted to make sure his reports always landed on the desks of his superiors in a timely fashion. Whether those reports were read in as expedient a manner was something he had no control over. He could only control his part in the flow of information.

Arrived at the outdated police headquarters with its leaky roof, horribly worn floors, and institutional-colored walls, he was delighted to see the splendor of the day had also found its way inside the PCPD. Instead of the sour expressions he was accustomed to seeing on the faces of the officers coming off the night shift, he was taken by the broad smiles and laughter he encountered as he made his way to the small office the Detective Squad occupied on the second floor.

It was going to be a good day.

And it would have been if, several hours later, he and his partner hadn't been rolled out to take a look at a body found in the middle of a field. It was a large piece of property the city owned on its outermost edge on the north side of town. An area expected to soon see a large amount of construction, according to those in the know. Homes in Parker City's suburban neighborhoods were filling up quickly, which meant new developments were needed for those looking for houses. What was planned for this particular parcel of land would be the largest residential development the city had seen in some time.

For at least the last decade or so, Parker City had been struggling. The once-booming town fell on some pretty hard times throughout the '70s. The population dwindled, and businesses fled. The final nail in the coffin came with the Great Flood of 1978 that devastated the city, leaving many parts of the downtown completely abandoned.

It was the election of a young, energetic mayor who vowed to restore Parker to its former glory that began the city's turnaround. While the Downtown neighborhood still had a way to go before it was returned to its once bustling grandeur, the new developments popping up around the edges of the city were a sure sign there was momentum behind Parker's revitalization. It was looking as though the city was on the right track after a long period of decline.

Stepping out of the car, the weather was so pleasant that Ben left his suit jacket lying in the backseat where he'd tossed it before leaving the station. But, as he always did when he was about to enter a new crime scene, he placed his hand on the Smith & Wesson on his hip. The weight of the cool metal helped to center him so he could focus on whatever he was about to be confronted by. It reminded him how important his work was and the duty he believed so much in. It was thinking like that that earned Ben a reputation of being a Boy Scout. An idealist who truly wanted to protect and defend the people of Parker City. He always wondered how some people could make that sound like a bad thing.

Maybe after a few more years as a detective, Ben would become more jaded and start to be more cynical. It happened to so many police officers, after all. But Ben hoped he'd never turn that corner. In the few years he'd been a detective, he'd seen some disturbing behavior and knew the depth to which society could sink. But he still tried to look for the positive. That was the only way to fight against the drag that inevitably carried some members of law enforcement into a dark place. No matter how much *bad* he saw in the world, there was still *good*.

Some of the older members of the department liked to live in a gray area of the law, while Ben tried his very best to always do what was right. It's when what was right fell into those gray areas that Ben needed to rely on his partner to help make sense of what needed to be done.

Trying to imagine what they'd been called out for, he knew no two crime scenes were ever the same. Sure, elements could be similar. There was always a tragedy overshadowing them, but each was unique. Which is why Ben walked into each with a completely open mind and a keen pair of eyes, trying to take in every single detail. It was always the details that cracked a case. Which meant one never knew how important the smallest piece of evidence could really be. If something was out of place, it was important until it wasn't. That's how he thought. And sometimes—and this was often the more confusing part—the absence of something was just as important. If not more.

"Not putting your jacket on?" The voice of Ben's partner, Tommy Mason, came from the other side of the car. "I didn't realize this was a casual crime scene."

Ben raised an eyebrow and rolled his eyes.

The two were always taking shots at one another. It's what they did. It's what made their friendship so strong. When it came to what to wear as police detectives, there was a continuing debate between the two. Ben felt a suit and tie was most appropriate. Not only did it look more professional and attract a certain level of respect but, with his clean-cut babyface, it helped him look a little older than his thirty years. Though not much. Tommy, on the other hand, saw nothing wrong with wearing jeans and a T-shirt under a leather jacket. While he might look like a cop on one of the popular crime shows on television, Ben always pointed out that that was *Hollywood's* version of a police detective. And since Ben technically was his supervisor and commanding officer, Tommy begrudgingly put a tie on every morning. Most days, though, he usually left it loose with his collar wide open. Ben still took it as a victory.

Blowing a ring of smoke into the air, Tommy dropped what little remained of his cigarette on the ground and stamped it out before taking his corduroy jacket off and tossing it back into the car. If Ben didn't have to wear his jacket at the crime scene, he sure as hell wasn't going to wear one.

"Doesn't this feel much less constricting," he asked with a grin. "And it's so much easier to get to our guns in the event we're in danger."

"Shut up," Ben said as he started toward the cluster of men in the field.

"I'm just saying. If your life was in danger, it would be so much easier for me to shoot someone to save you—which you know I would do—if I didn't have to worry about my jacket getting in the way. Those few precious seconds could save your life one day. Natalie would agree would agree with me."

Stopping and turning to look at his partner a few steps behind him, Ben asked, "Why exactly do you think it would have to be *you* saving *me* and not the other way around?"

"Because that's just the way it is," Tommy answered very matter-of-factly. "Think about how many times I've saved your life?"

Ben's forehead wrinkled, a puzzled expression appearing on his face. "What the hell are you talking about? I'm the one that saved *you* at least two times that I can think of in the last year alone."

"Clearly, we remember things very differently."

"You're a pain in my ass. You know that, right?"

Smiling the thousand-watt smile for which he was known, Tommy answered, "I like to think that I keep you grounded."

So was the way of Detectives Ben Winters and Tommy Mason. More often than not, they sounded like an old married couple bickering about one thing or another. Completely devoted to one another, they were closer than brothers. They'd grown up together, gone to school together, joined the academy together, and when the order was given for a new Detective Squad to be created within the Parker City Police Department, they were tapped for the job.

As it was, for the last four years, they were the *only* two members of the department's official criminal investigation team. Though Parker City was by no means a hotbed of criminal activity, they'd been involved in several major investigations that rocked the city. Two of which even attracted the national spotlight, making the pair famous for a few minutes. Most police officers could go their entire careers without being involved in the types of cases that had kept them up at night, but the two young men had earned their detective shields through trial by fire.

Catching his foot in a clump of thick weeds, Ben knew if he tripped and landed in the dirt, Tommy would never let him hear the end of it. Thankfully, he was able to quickly regain his balance and keep himself upright.

His hope that Tommy didn't see the awkward contortion the lower half of his body performed to avoid hitting the ground was dashed when, from behind him, he heard the sarcasm-laced comment, "As graceful as a gazelle." Which was then followed almost immediately by the unmistakable sound of something hitting the dirt. Hard.

"Sonofa…"

Ben turned in just enough time to see Tommy jumping to his feet and dusting off his pants.

"Not a single word," Tommy admonished, vigorously shaking his head. "I'm well aware Karma's a bitch."

Deciding to take the high road, Ben valiantly stifled the laugh, fighting to burst free.

"You've got a little bit of something there on your…" Ben started, pointing to his partner's pant leg.

"Shut it!" Tommy said. At which point Ben couldn't contain himself. The laughter won and overpowered him.

As the two detectives reached the other men standing in the field, they recognized one of the patrolmen as a new officer who'd just recently joined the department, and the other was one of Tommy's least favorite people on the planet, Buck LuCoco. An overweight, lazy throw-back to the days when the police in the city did as little as they needed to. Neither Ben nor Tommy understood how he was still on the force. Or why he wanted to be with his attitude.

"LuCoco, Brown," Ben said, giving the uniformed officers each a quick nod of his head.

"How is it, Buck," Tommy began, "whenever a body drops in this town, you're the first man on the scene?"

"Just lucky, I guess," LuCoco said, mopping his sweaty brow with a wrinkled handkerchief from his pocket. "It could also be that the scumbags in this city do their dirty work at night, and since I'm the first one outta the door in the morning, I get the call. Either way, it's crap. I tell ya!"

"Being that it's after lunchtime already…" Tommy began to say before Ben placed a hand on his arm, giving him the signal to let it go.

Then, turning to the younger officer, who appeared quite eager to give his report to the department's chief detective, Ben asked, "What have we got?"

"This is Sam Ruppert," Brown introduced the man, referring to his notebook. "He's one of the city's engineers. He was doing some routine work out here this morning when he found the body of a young female. D.O.A."

Turning to Ruppert, a tall, beefy guy in a flannel shirt, jeans, and work boots, Ben took his own notebook from his shirt pocket. "Morning, Mr. Ruppert. I'm Detective Ben Winters. You're with the city?"

"Public Works Department," he said in a gravelly voice. "Almost fifteen years now."

"What brought you out here today?"

"The city's getting ready to do some work in this field, and I needed to take a few quick measurements. We've been out here every day for the last week. I thought I'd be here and gone in a few minutes. Then I found…" His voice trailed off as he looked away toward something another twenty or so feet away.

"What did you find?"

"A body. She wasn't there yesterday. I know that for a fact because I was here all day with a couple other guys. We were all over this place. We'd have seen her for sure."

Pointing at the mound the engineer was staring at, Tommy asked, "Is that the body?"

"Uh-huh."

"Did one of you cover her up, or did you find her like that?" Ben asked, referring to the tattered, green-checked blanket.

"She was like that," Ruppert said, taking a deep breath. "At first, I thought it was someone in a sleeping bag or something. Thought maybe they'd slept out here last night. Sky was clear. They could see the stars. But when I got close and hollered, there was no… She didn't move. When I got up close, I saw… Geez. I've never seen anything like it. This isn't how I thought my day was gonna go."

Other than the occasional funeral, it was true; the average person didn't have much exposure to dead bodies. But there was something in the way the man was acting that made Ben think there was more to the story. He was too shaken up. If one could be *too* shaken up after finding a dead body on the job. Judging by the look on Officer Brown's face, Ben could tell there was something still to come. The young policeman seemed giddy. Or nervous. He anxiously shifted his weight from foot to foot. Either he had another interesting piece of information to share, or he needed to find a restroom.

"What is it you've never seen before?" Ben inquired, interested to hear the conclusion to Ruppert's story.

"Oh, I think you should just see for yourself, Detective," LuCoco said, interrupting, a twisted smirk on his fat face.

"What is it, LuCoco? Just tell us." Tommy had no patience for the man.

There was a time he used to hide his contempt; now he didn't even bother. Not that LuCoco was very observant. Or he just didn't give a damn.

"Sirs," Officer Brown interrupted, "let me show you."

Walking the group over to the covered body, Brown knelt down and, using a handkerchief he'd had in his pocket, pulled the blanket back, revealing the naked body of a beautiful young woman with dark wavy hair. But something wasn't right. Not that the naked body of a woman in the middle of a field was right. But in this instance, it was her skin.

"What the hell?" Tommy's reaction matched what Ben was thinking. "She's blue."

Blue wasn't entirely accurate, but it was pretty close. The skin was a pale hue, almost white. And there was a frosty sheen to it, with small ice crystals visible around her eyes and mouth. Little droplets glistened on her eyelashes.

"She's frozen," Brown said, looking up at the detectives.

"It was cool last night," Tommy said, kneeling down himself to get a better look, "but not cold enough to freeze to death."

"No. I mean, she's frozen like a block of ice."

Laying the back of his hand on the woman's cheek, Tommy quickly pulled back. "She's frozen solid. Like...rock hard."

"I told you you needed to see this for yourself," LuCoco said. "I've seen a lot of crazy shit in my time, but this...a frozen body in the middle of a field...I'm glad it ain't my job to solve this one, Benny-boy."

"That's *Sergeant* Winters to you, LuCoco," Tommy snapped, always eager to defend his partner's stripes...and put LuCoco in his place. More often than not, it was the latter.

"Officer LuCoco," Ben began, wanting to get him as far away from Tommy as possible before he said something that would make the situation any worse and probably end with an internal investigation, "would you please go radio in and tell them to send the medical examiner and the state Crime Scene Unit? And a few additional patrolmen to help secure the scene."

They all watched as the hefty officer lumbered off toward the patrol cars, mumbling something to himself.

"What the hell, Ben?" Tommy asked, not able to take his eyes off the woman's frozen form, his voice betraying his utter confusion.

"I'm not sure what we have here," Ben admitted, looking down at the body at their feet. "But we need to do what we always do. Start at the beginning. Once everyone gets here, we'll let the ME do his job, CSU will do theirs…"

Tommy looked around the open, empty field. There was a line of trees only a few yards away. "Isn't that the city-county line?" he asked.

The engineer squinted and pointed to a patch of bushes just short of the trees. "Right there is where the city ends. Officially."

"And if this body had shown up just a few feet that way," Tommy said, pointing toward the bushes, "this would be the sheriff's problem?"

Ben nodded.

Tommy looked down and tilted his head. "Okay, you get the legs; I'll get the shoulders."

"Stop it," Ben said, raising an eyebrow. "This one's ours."

"I know," Tommy grumpily agreed. "I just have a bad feeling about this."

Chapter Two

1945 . . .

There is nothing like a spring wedding, so people say. And Parker City was abuzz with talk of the upcoming nuptials of Ambassador Conrad Martin's eldest daughter, Lillian, and her handsome beau. The entire city had become enthralled with what was expected to be the biggest and most elaborate social event of the year…or decade. Depending on whom one asked. Everyone who was anyone in Parker society would be in attendance. Even though the Martin family was not originally from Parker, once they'd arrived following the ambassador's retirement, they were welcomed with open arms by the city's wealthy elite.

For the last several weeks, every morning, articles ran on the front pages of the *Blue Ridge Herald* and the *Chronicle Dispatch,* updating residents on the latest wedding news. Not that much seemed to change from day to day, really, but readers were interested in light, feel-good articles. Just as much as the publishers and editors were interested in increased circulation, which is what they were seeing each day, a story about the wedding ran on the front page above the fold. Maybe he was too thick to understand, but Fitz thought there were a lot more important stories the papers could be covering. There was still a world war going on, after all. Or if they wanted something closer to home, the president had just died. He thought that was rather newsworthy. But maybe people needed a distraction, and news about a joyous occasion like a wedding served as a happy diversion for readers.

It was considerably more cheerful, if nothing else. Though the fact Allied forces were moving closer to Berlin should have rated at least a few inches on the front page. Or something about Harry Truman's first few days in office, perhaps. But Fitz was the furthest thing from a newsman, so what did he know?

Folding the *Chronicle* and laying it aside, Fitz slid a couple of dollars from his wallet and laid them on the table to cover the bill for his breakfast, making sure to leave a very generous tip for the kitten who'd been batting her eyelashes and waiting on him all morning. He was a sucker for a pretty face, and hers was the prettiest he'd seen in a while. She had the kind of smile a guy could get used to.

He'd spent the last several mornings having eggs and bacon at the little diner instead of taking breakfast at his hotel. It was a quaint little greasy spoon with good food and a pleasant staff. Each morning, he'd been greeted as if he'd been a regular part of the breakfast crowd for years. Fitz liked being out with the people and soaking up the atmosphere. Parker was always a friendly town. At least, that's what he remembered growing up there. So, he figured he'd enjoy it while he could. Before he headed back to the big city where people weren't always so congenial.

Shrugging into his trench coat and placing his hat at just the right angle on his head, he tucked the newspaper under one arm and started for the front door. Stopping momentarily, he used the reflection of the glass to adjust his tie before stepping outside. Far from vain, he saw nothing wrong with making sure one always appeared presentable. He was a gentleman, after all. And while he wasn't the most physically fit he'd ever been in his almost forty years, he wasn't in bad form either. Even with the salt and pepper hair and a couple of extra lines around his eyes, he was happy he could still catch the eye of a pretty little thing like his waitress. If nothing else, his square jaw with its cleft chin always drove the birds wild.

His personal favorite was when one dame said he was better looking like than Cary Grant. True, she was trying to use her feminine wiles to get some little-known information out of him at the time, but he was certain one thing had nothing to do with the other.

Glancing up and down the sidewalk, then stealing a look at his watch, Fitz saw he had fifteen minutes before the meeting. Plenty of time to stroll down Commerce Street and do some window shopping. Unlike the large department stores he usually frequented, Parker City had a variety of unique shops and boutiques along its Downtown Shopping District.

He remembered walking through the shops with his brothers when they were children, begging their parents for a few pennies so they could buy a piece of candy. Life was much simpler back then, he thought. Or he was just idealizing a time when he didn't fully comprehend what was happening around him. He was just a kid. What did he actually know? Whether his parents were shielding him, Bobby, and John from the harsh realities of life during a world war–supposedly the war to end all wars–or not, he and his brothers had a pretty good childhood. There were no complaints from him on that count.

Preparations for his impending meeting had taken time that morning. Longer than he would have preferred. So, after a late breakfast, all the shops were already alive with activity. Women were popping in and out of the stores carrying bags filled with their retail conquests as men in dark suits hurried to and from their offices. Parker City was a hopping place, Fitz thought to himself. But it couldn't hold a candle to the bustling avenues of Baltimore, where he spent most of his days. He was just in Parker City, back on his old home turf, on business. When he was finished with his current task, he'd visit John and his new bride, have supper with them, and then it was back to Baltimore in the morning for his next assignment.

At the corner of Commerce and High Streets, Fitz paused to allow a woman pushing a stroller to pass in front of him. He took the opportunity to surreptitiously glance around to see if anyone may be following him. Not that he expected anyone to be, but it was a force of habit from his years overseas. His work had been highly sensitive, which required a great deal of caution and even more secrecy. Now, he couldn't help but to always be on his guard. It was a part of his life. As natural to him as breathing. And a little caution could go a long way.

Satisfied no one had their eyes on him, and everyone on the street was wrapped up in their own lives, he casually strolled the few blocks it took to reach the small park in front of City Hall, pausing only once to admire a charcoal gray fedora in the window of Parkertowne Haberdashers. He was set to meet an executive with the Worthington Trust Company, one of the area's most lucrative financial firms. The park was filled with just enough people to allow him to blend in and not be noticed. He looked like all the other men in suits hurrying from one place to the next. He could easily have been someone on his way to an appointment at City Hall.

Considering the nature of the rendezvous, one might think meeting in front of City Hall was daring. But Fitz liked the idea of using the public as camouflage. This was something he'd done a number of times in the past. Which was why he was an expert operative and his services were so highly sought after. Not that he ever allowed his ego to interfere with his actions, of course. But he knew his reputation preceded him. At least in certain circles. Which was another reason he was always looking over his shoulder.

Casting his eyes over the idyllic spring scene of mothers sitting and chatting as they bounced their baby carriages and the city employees taking an early break to soak up the sun, he saw the money man he was set to meet, Wendell Kittman.

This would only be their second face-to-face encounter. The first time Fitz had laid eyes on him, he was rather surprised. He'd expected a scrawny, non-descript dud of a man. The sort of fellow who'd been put down all his life and never got the respect he thought he deserved. The type of guy never given a chance to get ahead in the world. Instead, he'd shaken hands with a tall, athletic gentleman with jet-black hair with just a hint of gray at the temples. His self-confidence was unmistakable. Almost as suffocating as his cologne. It was obvious the man was doing well by his expensive attire. Not that Fitz had anything against indulging one's taste for haute couture. His own suit had come from a high-end shop on Lexington Street, while his shoes were imported Italian leather. Who was he to critique another man's wardrobe? King Arthur's Knights of the Round Table had their suits of armor; Fitz's battle gear just didn't weigh as much.

Nonchalantly striding across the park, whistling a little tune, Fitz slid onto the bench next to the executive. "Mr. Kittman, nice to see you again. I trust you have what we discussed."

"As we agreed," he answered out of the side of his mouth, a cigarette dangling from the other corner. "I like a man that gets right down to it. No sense in wasting time."

"My employers are extremely happy about the arrangement we were able to come to. You really have no idea."

"Of course I do. This sort of information can make a man a fortune. If your bosses use it the right way, maybe they'll even share the spoils with you."

"I'm but a humble courier, Mr. Kittman. If they tell me to deliver an envelope, I deliver an envelope," Fitz said, taking one from his inside jacket pocket and laying it next to himself on the bench. "If they tell me to retrieve an envelope," he said, eyeing Kittman carefully, "I retrieve an envelope."

On cue, the man withdrew an envelope of his own and laid it next to the one Fitz had produced. This was going to be duck soup, Fitz thought, taking Kittman's envelope and peering inside to confirm the contents. As expected, there were some sheets of paper with information on them that could be valued at hundreds of thousands of dollars if used properly.

Happy with what he saw, Fitz stood and said, "That's for you, Mr. Kittman. You want to count it before I go?"

With the arrogant sneer of a man who always thought he was the smartest person in the room on his face, Wendell Kittman looked past Fitz toward the entrance to City Hall and casually said, "In this business, it's all about trust. I'm an excellent judge of character. I trust you, Mr. Hampton. If I didn't, I would have *never* met with you in the first place."

Fitz smiled as he watched the financier place the envelope he'd left on the bench in his jacket pocket and stand. The men shook hands, concluding their deal. Just as Kittman was about to pull his fleshy palm away, Fitz dropped the newspaper, which had been tucked under his arm the entire time since he left the diner. As it fluttered to the ground, he tightened his grip, making it impossible for Kittman to bolt. A shrill whistle sounded, and policemen from various points around the park—some hidden behind trees, others disguised in suits sitting on wrought-iron benches–rushed toward them. The two were suddenly surrounded by Parker City's finest, all brandishing their revolvers.

"Wendell Kittman, don't move. You're under arrest," said one of the policemen as he lowered his gun and approached with a shiny pair of handcuffs.

Kittman's eyes grew to the size of golf balls as he registered what was happening. "You're a copper, Hampton?" he spat, his cigarette tumbling to the sidewalk.

"Oh, no. I'm with the Stride Detective Agency. The name's actually Fitz Mason. It's a pleasure to meet you," he said, genially tipping his fedora and offering a broad smile that would make the Devil himself blush.

Chapter Three

"I don't like that we needed to bring in an outsider," Chief Walt Buchanan said, lowering himself into the chair behind his desk, his large frame causing an excruciating moan to emanate from the old wooden chair. Fitz wondered just how much longer it would be before it collapsed in protest of the exhausting task. Opening the top drawer of his desk, the chief withdrew a pack of Camels, offering one to Fitz then selecting another for himself. "My boys could have handled this just fine," he said, striking a match.

The man's raspy voice sounded somewhat annoyed, but also resigned to the fact that what was done, was done, and there was nothing that could change it. So, why should he worry about it anymore? A stack of folders was piled high on his desk, each another matter that required his attention. He had plenty of work to deal with. No reason to waste any more time on this.

Accepting the cigarette, Fitz used the engraved golden lighter he'd been given by a diplomat during his time stationed in Europe to light up. As the tip flared, Fitz inhaled the glorious tobacco essence. Letting the smoke fill his lungs, a momentary feeling of euphoria washed over him. It could only have been better if he had a tumbler of scotch to go with it. But he didn't think asking the chief if he kept a bottle tucked away somewhere in his office was a wise idea—even though he was most certain he did. He was already something of an uninvited guest, no reason to make himself a true nuisance.

Taking in the room around him, Fitz wasn't very impressed with the chief's office. Not that he was all that impressed with the chief himself. But he believed one could learn a lot about a man by observing his surroundings. An old, battered desk took up most of the room, behind which sat Buchanan in his splintering banker's chair. Behind him, bookcases that looked as though the books hadn't been touched in decades ran along the wall. And the walls themselves, were painted a shade of green Fitz couldn't even begin to think how to describe. But it complimented the yellow haze clinging to the windows quite nicely. A dusty yellow that seemed to somehow match the chief's ruddy complexion.

Watching the smoke from the two cigarettes drift into the air, Fitz recognized the cause of the grime on the windows and wondered if that was also what made the color of the walls so indescribable. Realizing the damage was already done, Fitz blew a puff of smoke toward the ceiling as he pulled a wobbly guest chair up in front of Buchanan's desk and took a seat.

"I have no doubt your men could have managed and dealt with this situation," Fitz said, trying to leave things on a positive note. "But you must admit, Parker City is not exactly a metropolis, Chief. If you'd've sent a man in there that Kittman recognized, the whole scheme would have gone down the drain. And then where would everyone be? I don't think it's that Mr. Worthington didn't trust you, but we at the Stride Agency are something of experts when it comes to this sort of racket."

Fitz was absolutely correct. While the Pinkerton Detective Agency made a name for itself, getting physically involved in labor disputes, the Stride Agency built its reputation, placing agents in corporate offices and helping to protect company secrets from being sold to competitors and those looking to bring down the capitalist system. Handling business intrigue wasn't the firm's only source of income of course, but you'd certainly never find a Stride man trying to catch some poor schmo under the covers with a cheap dame who wasn't his wife. Those were cases left to the independent gumshoes. So, when Henry Worthington–Parker's most prominent financier–thought someone was selling company secrets, he knew where he needed to turn.

"I'm sure Mr. Worthington is going to be very pleased with your work, Chief," Fitz said, trying to assuage the man's ego. "I'll be sure to put in a good word for your men when I turn in my final report. After all, your men are the ones who arrested Kittman. I merely delivered him to you."

The chief's eyes narrowed, forcing his eyebrows to practically come together as one over his nose. He didn't much like Fitz Mason. The private detective certainly seemed to have the steel and be made of the right stuff, and he had unbegrudgingly worked in cooperation with the department on catching Kittman in the act, but there was an air of superiority about him. Maybe it was the fact he was so confident in himself and his work. Either way, something about the slick guy from the *big city* rubbed Buchanan the wrong way. He felt the sooner he was on his way back to Baltimore, the better. And if the door hit him in the ass on the way out, so be it.

Fitz was right about one thing, though. If Henry Worthington was pleased with the outcome, that's all that mattered. Worthington was a very powerful man. Which meant it was always a good idea to stay in his good graces. If the chief wanted to keep his job, he couldn't have Worthington as an enemy.

"How much longer do you plan on sticking around in Parker, Mr. Mason? I'm sure you must have other pressing matters to attend to. I could have a car take you to the train station if you'd like."

"I get the feeling my welcome's been worn out."

Buchanan didn't respond, his dark hooded eyes just stared at Fitz.

Seeing a coffee-stained copy of the morning's paper folded on the desk, Fitz pointed and said, "That wedding's going to be a big deal tomorrow, isn't it?"

Spreading the paper out in front of him, Buchanan tapped the photo of the Martin house with one of his large, sausage-like fingers. "This place is going to be as secure as Fort Knox for the wedding tomorrow. You can count on it. We don't need any private dicks sticking their noses where they don't belong. I'm overseeing the security personally. As a favor to the ambassador."

"Conrad's something else, wouldn't you agree? Not many words you can use in polite company to describe him, if you know what I mean."

"You know Ambassador Martin?" the chief asked, not able to hide the surprise in his voice. Or the irritation.

"I was stationed at the embassy in Rome before it was shut down. He was one of the big muckety-mucks there at the time. A real tough so-and-so."

Buchanan pushed the newspaper aside and leaned back in his chair. The wood gave another wail.

They sat without speaking for a moment, the silence turning awkward in the blink of an eye.

"Well, Chief, if ever I can be of assistance, don't hesitate to get in touch," Fitz said as he stubbed his cigarette out in an overflowing ashtray on the desk. "I'm sure you can find my number. I won't bother to leave a card."

The chief remained silent. He just waved his hand in the direction of the door.

Fitz tipped his hat and eased out into the hallway, making sure to close the door behind him.

The chief's secretary was not at her desk, so Fitz took the opportunity to place a call to his office in Baltimore. No reason Chief Buchanan couldn't pick up the tab for the call, he thought as he gave the operator the number he was trying to reach.

After more rings than expected, the line was answered by a voice that sounded like it was coming out of a carnival barker's megaphone. "Archibald Stride here." He was the grandson of the firm's founder and Fitz's boss.

"Archie. It's Fitz. We got our guy out here in Parker City. It was a cakewalk. I passed off the lettuce, and the schnook handed over the goods. Next time, you've got to give me something a little more challenging. I'm a little insulted you put me on this one. Walford or Brody could have handled it."

"I know the assignment must have seemed like small potatoes to you, Fitz. Not like that San Francisco affair. But I thought you were the right man for the job. Parker City being your hometown and all."

The thought of the San Francisco case and that leggy blonde who'd played a pivotal role in his assignment put a smile on Fitz's face. Those memories would carry him through the night. And possibly into the morning. At least until he saw the doll at the diner again.

"Well, take the night off and get back here as soon as you can. An interesting file just came across my desk. I may need to send you down to Miami for a while."

"I'm seeing my brother for supper, then I'll catch the train back to Baltimore first thing in the morning. I should be back in the office by lunchtime. Unless something catches my eye in the window of Hutzler's."

"How many suits does one man need?" Stride asked, only half joking.

In his usual droll manner, Fitz answered, "I think that's just another one of those mysteries of life that will have to go unanswered, Archie."

Chapter Four

The next morning, after a hearty dinner at his brother's, Fitz woke and started packing up his things for the trip back to Baltimore. Two valises sat open on the bed as he circled the room, making certain he hadn't forgotten anything. He'd taken the room the week before under the name Mr. F. Hampton, an alias he used frequently. One of many, but his favorite while on assignment when he needed to conceal his identity. He laid his false identification card on top of his neatly folded shirts, along with the Worthington case file and his ankle holster and spare pistol.

Locking the cases and sticking the key in his vest pocket, Fitz heard the unmistakable wail of police sirens passing under his window. Pushing the pale blue curtains aside, he watched two police cars speed down the street, then disappear around a corner several blocks on.

"Hmmm. Interesting." Looking at his watch, Fitz said, "Too early to commit a serious crime if you ask me."

Fitz took one last look at the room he'd been using as his temporary base of operations. Far from the Savoy in London, he'd had a comfortable stay in what was considered Parker's fanciest hotel. The staff was pleasant and attentive, and the room bright and inviting. But it was the Parker House's restaurant that made his stay so enjoyable. He'd had some delicious meals the last few nights he'd been a guest.

Placing his hat on his head, he was just about to depart for the train station when the telephone sitting on the stand next to the door sprang to life.

Lifting the receiver, he listened to the operator on the other end.

"Yes. Put him through. Thank you."

After several clicks, Archibald Stride's voice boomed, "Fitz! Something's come up. You've been requested."

"Good morning to you too, Archie. I was just getting ready to leave for the train. I should be back—"

"No," Stride cut him off. "You're staying in Parker a little longer. Conrad Martin is sending a car for you."

Fitz wasn't sure if he'd heard correctly. "Pardon?"

In the next moment, there was a hammering on the door, sharp wraps that startled Fitz, making him instinctively reach for the pistol strapped under his jacket. As loud and thunderous as they were, he wondered if someone was using a sledgehammer to knock.

He opened the door with the telephone still in hand to find a short, square man standing there. A thin, well-trimmed mustache brushed his top lip as a few strands of hair covered his otherwise exposed head. A tense expression was plastered on his face.

"Whadaya know, Joe?" Fitz asked the man he'd last seen standing in the U.S. Embassy in Rome four years ago.

In a voice that let everyone know he was not a man who put up with nonsense and little things like small talk, Joe Grainger, Ambassador Conrad Martin's valet, said, "The ambassador has sent me to collect you."

"So I understand," Fitz said, looking back at the receiver in his hand. "Archie, my car has arrived. Any chance you'll give me a hint as to what this is all about?"

"The ambassador wants to see you. That's all you need to know for now. He asked *specifically* for you."

"I guess I should be flattered." Fitz didn't know whether Stride had heard the comment because all he could hear from the receiver was the buzz that accompanied an ended telephone call.

"I guess I'm in your hands, Joe. Take me to Conrad."

Chapter Five

The ambassador's man was just as tight-lipped as Fitz remembered. He didn't say a single word during the entire car ride from the hotel. Twice on their way, they were passed by a police car with its siren blaring. A sinking feeling in the pit of his stomach began to form as Fitz realized they were following the direction of the cop cars. Whatever was causing such a ruckus that morning appeared to have something to do with Conrad Martin. And knowing today was the day of his daughter's wedding, Fitz was starting to wonder if it was related.

The Martin estate was a farm on the outskirts of the city. While Fitz had no delusion that Conrad Martin had gone from diplomat to working farmer, he understood why the man bought the property once they passed through the front gates and the beautiful colonial manor came into view. Rising from behind the manicured hedgerows, the white façade glistened in the sun. Unlike any "farmhouse" Fitz knew of, this one had a large set of marble stairs leading from the front door down to the circular drive, in the middle of which sat a water fountain.

The sprawling grounds would no doubt have been even more breathtaking without the small army of cop cars in front of the house. Between the number of city police and state boys, Fitz couldn't even begin to imagine what had happened that required this kind of turnout.

Stepping from the long, black Cadillac Fleetwood limousine, Fitz tossed his cigarette into the grass and looked around at the uniformed men walking around the grounds, searching the bushes and shrubs circling the house. The valet was suddenly at his elbow, silently directing him toward the front door. With each step, Fitz could feel the sense of urgency increasing. He didn't like being kept in the dark, especially when it was obvious whatever he was being dragged into was causing such an uproar.

As they approached, a Maryland State Trooper held up his hands, stopping the two men in their tracks. "Sorry. No one's allowed in."

"I am Ambassador Martin's valet," Grainger said, leveling a withering gaze at the state officer. "Please step aside."

"His what?" the trooper asked, a genuine look of puzzlement on his face.

"He's a fancy butler," Fitz said, pulling an official identification card from his pocket. "The name's Fitz Mason. I'm with the Stride Detective Agency. The ambassador sent for me. And if you don't want to get into a scuffle with Joe here, I suggest you let us in to see the ambassador post haste."

"Post what? Hold on. I should check with–" the trooper said before Joe Grainger pushed past him.

"There is no time for this," he snarled.

"You got off easy." Fitz quickly followed the ambassador's man into the house. "But I probably wouldn't let anyone else in if I were you," he said over his shoulder.

Fitz was immediately taken by the elegance and grandeur of the foyer where he now found himself. Memories of the palazzos in Venice and Nice came flooding back to him in waves. The artwork, armchairs, credenzas, marble-topped side tables, and wall coverings were unquestionably Italian… and completely out of place for Parker City. The pieces just in the entry–not even including the art hanging on the walls–were worth tens of thousands of dollars if they were all authentic. Knowing Conrad Martin as he did, Fitz knew they were all the genuine article.

"I don't mean to be nosey, but is that a Caravaggio?" Fitz asked, noticing the painter's unmistakable signature trait of contrasting light and dark in his work.

"You know the ambassador has always been a fan of the masters," Grainger said without stopping to look at the piece in front of which the detective paused.

Fitz would have sworn on a stack of Bibles the last time he'd seen that painting–at least he thought it was that particular painting–it had been hanging in a museum in Rome shortly before the embassy was closed down in '41.

Not knowing Martin's personal collection was so extraordinary, he wondered if he'd been called upon because of a theft. Something of that nature would easily explain why the ambassador would have called upon the Stride Agency. But Fitz didn't see any bare spaces on the wall, not that he imagined these were the only treasures in the house.

Following the valet down a long hallway lined with even more antiques and masterful works of art, muffled voices could be heard from behind the closed door at the end of the corridor. Grainger opened the door without knocking and stood aside so Fitz could enter the room. Which he did with some trepidation, not certain of what he'd find on the other side. All eyes turned to him as he stood in the open doorway.

The room, a formal library—or possibly an art gallery of some sort judging by the paintings–was much like the foyer and hallway he'd just passed along, decorated in a classic European style with expensive furniture throughout the space. It did not look particularly comfortable and inviting, but to each their own, Fitz thought. The style definitely suited the man he knew from his days stationed at the embassy.

"Pardon the intrusion, but I believe I've been sent for," Fitz said with a smile he could have stolen from the Cheshire Cat.

"What the hell are you doing here?" Chief Walt Buchanan growled as he saw the Stride agent standing there. The silver badge on his broad chest rose and fell with every uneven breath the man took. Judging by the pallor of his face, the erratic breathing, and sweaty brow, Fitz feared the chief might be on the verge of a heart attack.

From behind the seriously troubled-looking police chief, a smaller, rounder man emerged. Not as tall or broad as Buchanan, his appearance being dwarfed by the chief made him no less fierce. Impeccably dressed in a formal cutaway suit with a silver silk vest, the crown of dark gray hair ringing the man's head was not enough to conceal the red that had flushed his scalp. A shade of red that matched his mood.

"I asked for him," the man barked at Buchanan.

"Mr. Ambassador, there's no reason to bring in a private detective before we even know what we're dealing with," the chief protested. "This could all be a simple misunder—"

"My daughter has gone missing *on her wedding day*. I think it is exactly the right time to call in a *professional* detective."

Chapter Six

1985 . . .

"Τ his one's completely new to me," the assistant medical examiner said to the detectives as his men loaded the frozen female into the van. "Until we get her thawed out and really have a chance to look at her, all I can say for certain is that it appears she has a contusion on the lower right side of the parietal bone."

"In English, Doc, please," Tommy begged.

"It looks to me like she was hit on the back of the skull," he said, raising an eyebrow and pointing to the corresponding spot on his own head. "As a detective, I would've thought you'd have picked up some of the medical terminology?"

"You'd think, wouldn't you? But with an expert like you around, I didn't think we *both* needed to know all the bones in a person's head."

"Is he always like this?" the medical examiner asked Ben. Making his first run to Parker City, he was new to the job and had never met Ben or Tommy before, so was unaccustomed to the latter's sense of humor. The young assistant examiner didn't give the impression he was the type to play along. He seemed much too straight-laced and, by the book, to indulge in having a sense of humor.

"Believe it or not, he's actually behaving himself right now," Ben answered. "But you were saying?"

"Ah, yes. Your victim appears to have a contu... received a blow to the back of the head. Did that kill her? I have no idea. How long has she been dead? I have no idea. Is she in rigor? Is she out of rigor? I have no idea. She's frozen solid. I can't even get a body temp because I can't get the thermometer into her. She's *frozen*."

"But you're sure she's dead?" Tommy asked, trying to get a rise out of the guy.

Ignoring the question, he pointedly turned and looked directly at Ben. "Sergeant Winters, my boss is definitely going to have to be involved with this one. Chances are, his boss, too. Once we figure out the best way to defrost her without doing any sort of damage, I will let you know. I wish I could be more help right now, but we're going to have to…I don't know. Do a little bit of research once we get back to Baltimore."

It was times like this when Ben wished Parker City had its own medical examiner and the bodies they came across—infrequently as that was—didn't have to be transported to Baltimore, where they were put into the queue with all the other bodies from all the other jurisdictions around the state. With this case, though, odds were pretty good that the naked frozen woman dumped in a field was going to get bumped to the front of the line for examination and autopsy. Once they figured out how to thaw her out.

As they watched the black van, now carrying their Jane Doe, pull away, Ben was just waiting for Tommy to suggest one of his outlandish theories as to how the frozen woman ended up where she did. To his surprise, and mild disappointment—though he'd vehemently deny it—no conspiracy theory was offered. That was very unusual for Tommy.

Turning their attention to the Crime Scene Unit techs who were scouring the area around where the body had been discovered, Ben was happy to see all familiar faces. Like many police departments in Maryland, those that did not have crime scene investigators relied on a team from the state police to collect evidence and any forensics they were lucky enough to find. All of the members of the CSU team were Maryland State Troopers, under the supervision of Lieutenant Clover, whom Ben had become friendly with over the last several years. A man as thin as a piece of spaghetti with an unkempt mustache and glasses two sizes too big for his face, Clover was a master of forensics. Stationed at the Parker County State Police Barracks, he'd been involved with all of Ben and Tommy's big cases.

"Have your guys found anything useful?" Ben asked, hoping the trooper would say they found the calling card of whomever dumped the body lying right there under it along with a photograph of him in the act–but not holding his breath for that answer.

"Umm."

Definitely not the response Ben was looking for, but one he expected.

"Well," Clover began, pushing his glasses back in place, "we have the blanket she was wrapped in. It's pretty ratty, but there could be some fibers that don't belong or other materials, particulates we can trace. That may give us something. As for the body itself, well…"

"Let me guess," Tommy said, "it was frozen?"

Clover looked at him, clearly not understanding that the detective was trying to be funny.

"Yes, it was. I mean, is. Which only allowed us to do a rudimentary examination. The ME didn't want us touching it too much. Said they'd take care of a more thorough exam once they did whatever it is they're going to do to…thawed her out."

"Okay, bear with me on this one," Tommy began.

"Oh, God," Ben said under his breath, preparing himself for whatever was to come next. He was certain this was going to be the hair-brained theory he was waiting for. During their last high-profile case, his partner first suggested that the person who killed one of the city's most popular priests was a Russian assassin. He couldn't wait to hear what he thought this time.

Before he continued, Tommy gave his partner a dirty look, then turned back to Clover. "It looked like there was a thin layer of frost on the body. Do you think it's possible to get fingerprints off her? If there are any."

"Hmmm." Clover closed his eyes and appeared to be having an internal conversation with himself.

"What do you mean?" Ben asked, realizing this wasn't Tommy being a smartass but being completely serious.

"I'm not sure how to say this, but sometimes, when something is at its normal temperature, like a glass that's been sitting on a counter, you touch it and don't see your fingerprints. But if that glass has been in the fridge and it's chilled, when you touch it, your fingerprints are very noticeable. I realize a glass isn't the best example because we can always get prints from that, but…well, look."

Tommy took Ben's hand and put his thumb on the back of it.

"See, nothing there. But your skin is its normal temperature and texture. But if it was rock hard because it was frozen and there was a layer of frost on it and I put my thumb there…"

"I see what you're saying," the CSU supervisor said, shaking his head. "I'm not entirely certain about it, but it sounds feasible. I've never seen anything like this before, but I'll call the Medical Examiner's Office and have them take a look for any visible prints like you're suggesting. An alternative is, I could also see that as the body begins to thaw, prints could start to present themselves. Like bruises do. If there'd been enough pressure on the frozen skin. Like I said, I'll talk to the guys in Baltimore and make sure they know what to look for when they examine the body."

"This is all very interesting," Tommy said, a genuine sense of awe in his voice. "It's possible we could find a print from the person who carried her into the field."

"What the hell?" Ben stared dumbfounded at his partner. "When did you… I mean, you've never understood… You didn't even know what a contusion was a minute ago, and now you understand thermal physics?"

"I don't actually think that's what thermal physics is." Tommy stood shaking his head with a deeply knit brow.

"It's not," confirmed Lieutenant Clover. "Thermal physics is the study of thermodynamics. It has to do with energy."

Ben was stunned into silence. Tommy's eyes usually glazed over when they were talking to the crime scene guys about forensics or the ME about lividity and time of death. But now, all of a sudden, he was Mr. Wizard.

"It was just a thought I had," Tommy explained with a shrug of his shoulders. "You seem surprised."

"We're going to talk more about this," Ben promised before turning back to Clover. "Did your guys find anything else, Aaron?"

"There don't appear to be any footprints leading up to or away from the area. I have everyone working a grid out from here, but so far, we haven't found anything that is getting me too excited. Right now, we have the body and the blanket. That's about it."

"That's what I was afraid of."

"Detective, this one's pretty weird," the lieutenant said, lowering his voice. "I mean… Actually, I'm not sure what I mean."

"No. You're right," Tommy said, agreeing with the trooper. "It's a woman frozen solid in an open field. That's weird."

"We have to figure out who she is," Ben said, mentally creating a list of things that needed to be done. "You were able to get fingerprints at least, right? *Off her fingertips* to try and ID her," Ben was careful to say, not wanting to go down the scientific rabbit hole again.

"We were able to pull some prints, yes," Clover confirmed by checking his clipboard.

"It's something. Since she had no identification on her, and it doesn't seem like we're going to find her purse just lying around, we start there." Ben was trying to put a positive spin on what little they had to work with. Besides the fingerprints and dozens of photographs the CSU guys had taken, there wasn't much else. Which meant he needed to search for the silver lining.

"We'll start working on the prints as soon as we get back to the barracks," Clover said, trying to sound reassuring. "And I will get copies of the photos over to you as soon as I can. Tomorrow morning at the earliest. I should be able to push those through the process pretty quickly. I have a feeling this case is going to get flagged as a priority."

"You think?" Tommy asked only half sarcastically.

"My fear is that this may just be the beginning," Ben said, thinking out loud.

"What do you mean?" Clover asked.

"What if this is some sort of serial killer thing? A guy who kills women and freezes them. It sounds just crazy enough. Doesn't it?"

Tommy stared at Ben for a long moment before saying, "I thought I was supposed to be the one who came up with the outlandish ideas? I don't like this version of you."

"I'm uncomfortable with the smart, science version of you. Now we're even. I'm just bracing myself for the worst possible scenario. That's all. Look at the cases we've dealt with over the last few years. Not exactly normal. It seems to be the way it works for us."

Tommy couldn't argue. In their short four years as detectives, they'd already been faced with the types of cases you only saw in the movies, not in small, idyllic communities like Parker. Tommy was hoping this was one of those rare occasions when his partner and best friend was completely off the mark and this was going to be an isolated, yet very odd, incident. Not that that made it any better. But at least it would be *something* in their favor.

Chapter Seven

By the time the State's forensics guys finished their work, afternoon had turned into evening. As feared, nothing of any significance was found as the search grid was carefully expanded outward. There was a brief moment of excitement when a partial tire track was discovered. Unfortunately, it was quickly matched to Sam Ruppert's city-issued pickup, which had been at the site over the last several days. After discussing the matter with Lieutenant Clover, Ben decided there was no reason to try and cordon off the area for an extended period of time. He'd had a quick conversation with the department's operations commander, who said they didn't have the resources available at the moment to lock the site down if there wasn't a solid reason. Especially considering the crime scene was a massive open field constituting a large number of acres. It would require more officers than he could spare. This was one time Ben wasn't going to try and squeeze the chief for additional support because no one thought there was anything left to uncover. So, why waste a favor?

One thing that made Ben extremely happy was that it wasn't until activity at the site was beginning to wrap up that the first news reporters appeared. Thankfully, the press hadn't picked up on what was going on until it was too late for them to get in the way. Those who did show up from the *Herald-Dispatch* and the local radio stations were kept at bay by Officers LuCoco and Brown, who'd been stationed at the road to keep any looky-loos from trying to get a peek at the official police activity in the field. Ben felt bad for assigning Brown to such a mundane task when he knew this could have been a good opportunity for him to gain some crime scene experience. But he knew someone needed to make sure LuCoco didn't let anyone slip past him. In the end, Ben and Tommy were also able to get away without having to answer any questions, which made them both happy. To date, they have not had the best of luck with the media, so they prefer to avoid them as much as possible.

As always, all information would come directly from the department. Leaving everyone to be reminded not to speak to any member of the press. Once Ben was able to brief the chief back at the station, they'd decide what details to release for public consumption.

The press was always a thorn in the side of the police, Ben felt. Not just in Parker but in every jurisdiction. He understood they had their role to play, but his personal experience with them over the years was not always positive. He'd let the few bad apples who would do anything for a sensational headline tarnish his opinion of the news media as a whole. He specifically blamed Roger Benedict. He was the reporter for the *Herald-Dispatch* who'd covered his and Tommy's first big case and always seemed one step ahead of them. For a time, Benedict was even at the top of the list of suspects for the Spring Strangler–a name for the killer he also happened to coin. Benedict had moved on from Parker, and even though he was another police department's problem now, he still lingered in the back of Ben's mind. And he'd never dare bring the name up in front of Tommy, who'd once asked Ben if he could shoot the reporter. *In the foot.*

After arriving back at the station, Ben called Natalie, his fiancée, and left a message on the answering machine letting her know he was probably going to be late that evening. He was not too worried about his absence, though. He knew she had wedding planning with one of her bridesmaids, so she wouldn't even know he was running late. But he preferred to leave a message just in case. Their wedding was coming up in a couple of months, and she was feverishly finalizing all the details. Ben had offered to help with whatever he could, but Nat had a plan and an army of friends helping her arrange everything. Other than answering a few questions here and there about the flavor of the cake, menu options, and where to hold the reception, Ben's job was pretty much just showing up for the big day. And to make sure Tommy didn't lose the rings…or sleep with any of the bridesmaids. Nat loved Tommy, but under *absolutely no circumstances* was he to sleep with any of the bridesmaids.

Hanging up the telephone, Ben couldn't help but think one more time how lucky he was to have found Nat. She never complained about his long hours. Never tried to talk him into leaving the force for a safer job. She understood how being a police detective was more than just a job to him. In fact, one of the things she loved most about him was his belief in duty and willingness to serve the city.

Ben's reveling was quickly interrupted.

"You have that dopey grin on your face again," Tommy noticed.

"I know," Ben answered, taking out his notebook and starting to look at what he'd written down at the scene. "By the by, have you decided who you're bringing to the wedding?"

"*By the by*. Seriously. Who talks like that? Man, you have got to loosen up. And…for your information…I have narrowed down the list to a few lucky ladies."

"I kind of thought you'd bring Shirley from down in Dispatch. She always seems to be your go-to gal."

"No. Shirley and I are now just friends," Tommy said, searching through his desk drawers for something. "She has a *boyfriend* now, and she thinks he *might be the one*. I think they've been on two dates."

"Sorry to hear that," Ben said, leaning back in his chair. "I know how much you liked her."

"Let's be honest," Tommy said, sounding oddly serious. "Shirley and I were never going to end up like you and Nat. You and I both know that. She and I were just having a good time. No strings and lots of flings."

Ben was surprised that Tommy was being so open about his love life—or lack thereof at the moment. He'd always been a ladies' man and never once given even the slightest hint of an impression that he was interested in settling down. Bearing a striking resemblance to the star of television's *Magnum P.I.*, mustache and all, didn't hurt his chances with the ladies. But there was something in his eyes that made Ben wonder if his friend was beginning to change his tune. Maybe seeing how happy he and Natalie were together was beginning to influence Tommy.

"But there is a chick I just met the other night that has legs that go on for days and a butt you could bounce a quarter off. She's been helping me get over Shirley," Tommy confessed. "And what she can do with an ice cube..."

And the moment passed, Ben thought.

Chapter Eight

"She was frozen?" Chief Nicholas Brent asked, the apprehension in his voice clear beyond a reasonable doubt.

"Solid," Ben added.

"Frozen solid? No clothes?"

"That is correct, sir."

"She *did not* freeze to death. She's actually frozen?"

"Well, we don't know what the cause of death is yet, Chief. But for purposes of this conversation, that's correct." Ben was doing his best to walk the chief through what little information they had on the mystery woman in the field.

Brent, a law enforcement veteran, was having difficulty imaging their victim's state. Like everyone else involved with the day's unusual discovery, he was struggling to wrap his head around the facts. In his fifty-five years, he'd seen a lot. As a Naval officer during the Vietnam War, he'd witnessed some pretty nightmarish events. Then, as a police officer rising through the ranks in Buffalo, he realized it wasn't just in war that humans could do such terrible things to one another. But nothing he'd seen or heard before was so puzzling. He would rather cases be cut and dry. It was more efficient that way.

As Ben had been catching him up on the events of the day, the chief paced behind his desk. He was already an imposing figure, but with Ben seated, Brent towered over him like a Grizzly bear observing a chipmunk in the woods. It wasn't just his large, bear-like frame that gave him such a commanding presence, though. It was also his personality and demeanor. There were times Ben felt his stare could burn a hole through a solid steel door. Lucky to have never been on the receiving end of one of Brent's disapproving glares, he had witnessed them firsthand on several occasions.

Even with such a fierce personality, there was not a single person in the department who wouldn't walk through fire for Nick Brent. The admiration the members of the PCPD felt for the man was unquestionable. And he for them. Brent led by example. He didn't talk down to anyone or bark orders just because he had stars on his collar. He gave his people a chance to do their jobs, all the while helping to point them in the right direction if he felt they were straying too far off course.

In their early days as extremely green detectives, he'd been Ben and Tommy's most vocal cheerleader. He'd made certain they were given every chance to succeed in their new roles while so many were rooting for them to fail—including the chief at the time. Over the last several years as the city's top cop, he'd proven to Ben why he was the right man for the job and why he absolutely deserved the respect of the department.

"I remember one particularly bad winter up in Buffalo," the chief said as he took his seat, finally giving the well-worn path behind his desk a reprieve, "when we had a number of homeless people die from exposure in one night. But none of them came in as a block of ice."

Brent scratched his ginger mustache as he thought back to that cold day in upstate New York when he was still just a beat cop.

"The ME is going to need to figure out the best way to thaw the body so they can perform an autopsy. I don't think they can just use a bunch of hairdryers," the chief said without a hint of humor behind his words.

"Tommy actually asked the assistant examiner about that," Ben said with a sigh.

"Of course."

"Not only did he think that wouldn't work the way Tommy was thinking, it could compromise a…post-frozen, for lack of a better term, examination. We still need an official cause of death."

"So how are they going to do it? Defrost her?" Brent asked, leaning forward in the chair, placing his elbows on the desk so he could rest his chin on his tightly clasped hands.

"He said they were going to need to do some research on the best method," Ben answered. "We're going to have to trust them on this one."

"Maybe CSU will get a hit on the fingerprints they took."

"It would certainly give us somewhere to start. Otherwise, we don't have much to go on right now. No identification, no clothing, no witnesses, no cause of death. We're batting a thousand. It's pretty much the worst-case scenario."

The chief began absentmindedly shuffling some papers that were sitting on his desk. Pushing them aside, he placed a large binder that had been sitting on the corner of the desk in front of him. Tapping his fingers on the cover, he said, "I'm scheduled to present my reorganization plan to the mayor and City Council tomorrow morning. They're all wrapped up with the budget, so I was ready to talk dollars and cents. But I have a feeling they may have some questions about the frozen woman in the field."

"There's not much to say about it at this point, so hopefully, they'll listen to your plan and won't be too distracted."

"You keep thinking that, Detective. But a frozen body mysteriously turning up on the outskirts of town is a lot more interesting than listening to how we can reallocate funds to expand the size of the force and increase readiness."

Ben knew the chief had been working feverishly on his reorganization plan since taking over the department several years earlier. He wanted to turn the PCPD into a modern law enforcement agency. That meant there were going to have to be a lot of significant changes. As he was working on his plan, he'd come to use Ben as a sounding board. The two had already formed a good, solid working relationship built on respect and understanding, so it was no surprise Ben became one of the chief's most trusted confidants, even if he was only a sergeant. There were a few lieutenants and a captain between him and the chief on the organizational chart.

As the head of the department's Detective Squad, though, the chief felt Ben's thoughts were vital if a newly beefed up Criminal Investigation Division was going to play as important a role in the future as both men were anticipating. There was no doubt in Brent's mind that it was Ben and Tommy's age and innovative thinking that helped them solve the tough cases.

The chief liked that they didn't do things the same way they'd always done in the past. Though sometimes Tommy needed to be reined in, he and Ben were making a big difference. And their successes were going to help sell the reorganization plan.

With it looking like Parker City was going to begin to see the seeds of the mayor's revitalization plan come to fruition, that meant, inevitably, the crime rate would also begin to tick upward. That was just the way it worked. More people equaled more crime. More business equaled more crime. And with new residential developments sprouting up, and businesses starting to relocate into the city, the chief saw the writing on the wall and hoped his plan was a step in the right direction to putting the department on a path that would prepare it for what was ahead.

Ben was never much for the politicking and all the budget wrangling he knew the chief was faced with. Having to deal with the City Council was something he couldn't even fathom. He was happy to focus on the work and said as much as he collected his notes. "As soon as either the medical examiner or CSU delivers their initial report, I'll let you know."

"Thank you, Detective. If there's nothing else you feel you can accomplish tonight, you don't have to stick around. Go home and start fresh tomorrow."

"Will do, Chief," Ben agreed, looking at his watch. "I'm just going to put my notes into the computer, and then I'll head out. Assuming Tommy hasn't thrown the thing against the wall while we've been in here. I asked him to start up the new case file."

"You're tap dancing through a minefield there, Ben," the chief said with a smile. "Even I know how much Tommy hates computers."

Ben grinned. "He does. But I feel forcing him to use the thing helps build character."

Chapter Nine

It didn't take long for Ben to add his notes to complete the file Tommy had begun, as there weren't many more details that could be included. The basic information was all there–location, state of the body when discovered, observational notes. There were still a lot of blanks to be filled. When he'd returned to their office, as expected, Ben found his partner swearing up a storm. His anger and frustration were directed, also as expected, toward the large IBM computer that Ben insisted was going to help with their cases. Tommy was yet to see how, but he wasn't going to argue the point any further. The two had already gone dozens of rounds over it. In the end, Tommy knew Ben had an uncanny way of understanding technology that he never would. Not that he cared to. He was willing to trust his friend. That didn't mean he wasn't going to complain about it, though.

Ben always found it amusing to watch Tommy use his index fingers and his index fingers only as he hunted and pecked at the keys he needed to fill out the form pages on the screen. When he wasn't watching, Ben would hear *click click* "dammit," *click click* "sonofabitch." Then, there would be a long sigh, and the typing would begin again. Usually, to save time and his partner's sanity, Ben was the one who did the team's work on the computer. Tonight, Ben just wanted to get even with Tommy for the whole thermodynamics conversation earlier.

When Tommy was finished, he said good night and headed out to have a nightcap with his new female friend with legs that didn't quit. If the night went as Ben would assume, his partner would be in a great mood the next morning…and, quite possibly, the same shirt and tie.

After Tommy said goodbye for the night, Ben took his seat at the computer as silence fell over their small, makeshift office. Every few minutes, however, a slight rattle from the air vent in the ceiling interrupted the quiet, but it was a sound they'd grown accustomed to hearing. Once a storage closet in the middle of the second floor, the space had been converted into the official workspace of the Detective Squad. There was just enough room for Ben and Tommy's desks, a couple of file cabinets, and one trash can. It was cramped, but they'd made it work. Like the rest of the building, the walls were in desperate need of a fresh coat of paint and a new floor—the old linoleum was so worn and scuffed Ben couldn't tell what its original color was. But it must have been something that at one time went with the institutional gray-green of the walls. He hoped.

As far as the case was concerned, with so little information, Ben's contribution to the file was more observational notes from the scene. His goal was to include as much information with each file as possible. There'd also be the physical file with all of their handwritten notes and photos, et cetera, that would eventually be stored in the basement, but on the computer, they could access key details and pieces of information much quicker.

Finished with his portion of the report, he shut down the computer for the day and collected his things. Deciding there was no need to carry his briefcase home, he grabbed his suit jacket from the back of his chair, flipped off the lights, and headed out into the now deserted second floor of the PCPD. During the day, the entire building buzzed with activity. But in the evenings and into the morning hours, what little personnel was needed to keep the department operating was all found on the first floor. The shift commander worked out of a small office next to Dispatch so he could easily check in with the units on the streets and keep tabs on calls. In addition, there were usually a couple of patrol officers assigned to desk duties overnight in case extra hands were needed at the station. Or, as a reserve, to be deployed if no one else was available. Other than that, the rest of the night shift was out on patrol.

This was just one of many nights Ben was the last to leave, turning off lights as he went. Down the hall, though, he could still see a glow coming from under the chief's door. That was no surprise. Brent usually worked late and arrived early. Just like Ben. Each morning, it was a toss-up as to which one would make it into the office before the other and start the day's first pot of coffee in the small second-floor break room.

It was in the mornings, over coffee and talk of baseball, that Ben and the chief solidified their friendly working relationship. They tried not to discuss too much official business first thing in the morning if they could avoid it. Rather, opting to discuss sports and local news. They both found it helped them ease into their day. The caffeine didn't hurt either.

Descending the stairs to the ground floor, there wasn't much more action happening there than upstairs. As he made his way down the hall that led out to the parking lot behind the station, Ben saw the duty sergeant in the watch commander's office flipping through a stack of forms and a patrolman escorting a boozer to the drunk tank for the night. As he passed the door, Ben gave a quick nod to the sergeant, and walked out into the cool night air. At first, the crisp chill was refreshing, but by the time he'd crossed the pavement to his car, the cold was seeping into his shoulders.

Pulling out of the lot, he turned the radio off so he could enjoy the solitude of his drive across town to the apartment he shared with Natalie. At this time of the evening, traffic was nonexistent, so he'd be home in ten minutes. Less if he made all the lights.

Short as it was, he used the drive to collect his thoughts. Even though he should be trying to clear his head and forget about work, he couldn't help but think about the case. It was a curse. He was never able to turn his brain off and completely forget about his day. When he was in the middle of a big case, or something far outside the norm was his primary focus–like a woman turned into an ice cube, for example–he would fixate and have a hard time leaving his work at the office.

The frozen body of a young, unidentified woman was hard not to think about. She looked to be in her twenties, if that. For her to be frozen through the way she was, she'd been missing long enough for someone to have noticed. Which, in theory, meant someone should have reported her missing.

Ben made a mental note to pull the recent missing person reports first thing in the morning. If CSU could ID her off her fingerprints, so much the better. But it gave them a place to start otherwise.

He felt the need to be *doing* something to help further the investigation. Not just sitting around waiting for others to bring him information. Ben didn't enjoy taking a passive role this early in a case. But deep down, he knew he needed to let other people do their jobs so he could do his. Natalie always tried to remind him that he couldn't do it all alone. He needed to realize there were times when things would be out of his hands and accept it. Grudgingly or not. But accept it nonetheless.

The second issue nagging Ben, on top of everything else, was exactly what type of investigation this was. Was it a homicide case? Or, if she died in some natural fashion, was it a body dumping case? If there was such a thing, Ben wasn't exactly certain what the criminal statute they'd be working under. Ben made another note to call the state's attorney's office and talk to someone about that. This case was already stumping the PCPD, the State's forensics guys, and the ME's Office, why shouldn't the county prosecutor share in the fun too? Regardless of everything else, until they knew the official cause of death, they couldn't even say what sort of crime they were dealing with.

Easing the Crown Vic into his usual parking spot, Ben shut off the engine, closed his eyes, and forced himself to take several deep breaths to clear his head of all thoughts of the case and the work still ahead of him. The remnants of the day he couldn't dismiss were quickly knocked away as he opened the door, and a blast of freezing air assaulted him. In the time it took him to drive from the station to his apartment, Ben would have sworn the temperature dropped at least ten degrees. If not more. His beautiful spring day had turned into a frigid night.

Chapter Ten

1945 . . .

"Fitz, please come in," Ambassador Conrad Martin barked, stepping around the police chief and crossing the exquisite Persian rug to greet the private investigator he was so desperately hoping would be able to locate his missing daughter. "I've never been so glad to see you."

Martin wasn't a tall man, but his personality made up for it. Some called him a bull, others a bulldog. How he'd ever become a diplomat, Fitz was not certain. Admittedly, all of their interactions had been in the midst of high-stress situations, but Conrad Martin never presented himself as the type who valued tact and negotiation. Force and arm-twisting were his preferred methods of diplomacy. Which could have explained why he'd been stationed at the embassy in Rome as the war in Europe was heating up. Maybe the thinking in Washington was that his sheer force of will would get Mussolini under control.

The ambassador's thundering baritone echoed off the painted canvas-ladened walls, reminding Fitz of those final hours in Rome as the embassy was being shut down. As his unit was securing documents and clearing the complex of any sensitive material, Martin could be heard behind closed doors shouting orders at his staff. It hadn't exactly been a frenzied evacuation, but tensions were running high, and people were moving with a fevered urgency.

Taking Fitz's arm in a vice-like grip, Martin guided him to a pair of large leather club chairs next to the fireplace. Practically pushing the detective into one of the seats, the ambassador took the other for himself. Fitz would have found it an extremely comfortable place to light a cigar and enjoy a fine snifter of brandy under different circumstances.

"Fitz, Lillian, my oldest girl, is missing."

Before Fitz could respond, Martin charged ahead, adding, "Today's her wedding day. She was in her room with her mother and sister, getting ready. They stepped out, and when Lucy—her sister, my youngest—went back in to find her, she was gone. Vanished."

Hesitating a moment, not wanting to sound completely impertinent, Fitz cautiously asked, "And you've checked to make sure she didn't just go for a walk around the grounds? Maybe to clear her head. Get some fresh air? A wedding is a stressful event. So I'm told. It can stir up all sorts of emotions and nerves in young women."

"Of course, we checked the grounds!" Chief Buchanan declared empathically as he made his way over to where the pair were sitting. "She's not on the property. But like I've been saying, that doesn't mean something has happened to her. As much as I hate to admit it, Mr. Mason, here, does have a point."

"Thank you," Fitz said with a smile, knowing how much it would irritate the chief.

"Sometimes girls get nervous on their wedding day. It happens all the time. The wedding itself isn't for a few hours. Maybe she did just want to go somewhere to collect herself. It's not difficult to imagine. Women can be like that."

It was painfully obvious to Fitz that Buchanan wanted this to be a case of a bride getting cold feet and not something worse. Because if it was, and he'd made it clear he was personally in charge of the security for the wedding, he knew he was in serious trouble. On the other hand, the ambassador seemed to have already decided something terrible had happened to his daughter without any cause. Not that Fitz had any children, but he understood how protective parents could be. The Conrad Martin he knew did not overreact and jump to conclusions, though, lending credence to his theory of foul play.

"Mr. Ambassador, Conrad—if I may—why is it you think something has happened to your daughter and that she isn't just somewhere trying to settle her nerves?"

"Because she hasn't shown one stitch of nervousness about the wedding. And she'd never just disappear hours before the ceremony without telling someone. Her mother or her sister, at least. Lillian doesn't just run off. She's not the type. She's solid. Perfectly stable. She doesn't suffer nerves. Neither of my girls do. They're strong. Like me."

One of the other two police officers who'd been quietly standing with the chief spoke up, thinking he was being helpful. "Her car's still parked in the garage out back."

"Thank you, Sergeant Stanley," Buchanan said through clenched teeth, "but I can handle this. Why don't you two go help the boys outside? I'm sure you'll be of more use out there than in here."

Fitz broke the moment of awkward silence as the officers left by asking, "Where are Mrs. Martin and Lucy now?"

"In the sitting room," the ambassador answered, leaning back in his chair, running a hand over his bald scalp as if it would somehow help him think of where his daughter could be. Fitz couldn't remember ever seeing the man so out of sorts before. Even when the news came across the wire that the Japanese bombed the naval base at Pearl Harbor and everyone knew the United States would be forced to enter the war, Martin was unflappable.

"And the last place Lillian was seen?"

"Her bedroom. She was getting into her wedding dress."

"Then...I think that's where I should start. Would someone be so kind as to lead the way?"

Chapter Eleven

A s Martin and the police chief led the way through the house, Fitz was struck by the amount of artwork the ambassador had accumulated. Everything from paintings to sculptures to tapestries. Though he wasn't an art expert, he knew enough to recognize that some of the pieces he was seeing were unquestionably original works by some of the greatest artists in history. Masterpieces hung on every wall around them. The Martins' house was more of a museum than a home. Definitely the perfect backdrop for a ritzy party, which Martin always loved. Playing host was one of his favorite duties. The soirees he would throw at the ambassador's residence in Rome were just short of legendary. He'd spare no expense. Letting Uncle Sam pick up the tab, he served the finest food and drink to his guests, all in the name of foreign diplomacy. He believed this was the best way for him to represent the United States and show off its vast resources. Even though the country was just coming out of the worst economic depression it had ever experienced. But with no one willing to step in and temper his appetite for extravagance, Conrad Martin kept the champagne flowing, so to speak.

At the top of the stairs and down a long hallway, Fitz counted a number of bedrooms. Lillian's was at the end of the hall. At the other end, on the other side of the house, was her parents' room. Fitz wondered if there was a reason her room was so far away from her parents. Or, if she just enjoyed watching the sunset through her windows in the evening, that was the best room in the house to do so.

Stepping into Lillian's bedroom, Fitz was slapped in the kisser by a color pallet of pink on top of pink with an accent of pink on the side. If it weren't for the fact the girl's four-poster bed was painted white, it would have blended in and been camouflaged by the pink bedspread that was identical in color to the carpet.

Other than the choice of color, Fitz noticed how large the room was. In addition to her bed and a pair of large dressers, there was room for a writing desk and a small sitting area near the windows. It was the room of a princess, all right. The ambassador's princess.

While Martin and Buchanan stood in the doorway, eyeing him carefully, Fitz slowly circled the room, allowing himself to take it all in. The usual female trinkets and bobbles were scattered throughout. On one dresser sat a collection of small figurines and a music box; perfume bottles and a large jewelry case took up most of the surface of the other. There was nothing sitting out on the writing desk. No paper or pens. No magazines. And there were no photos in the room. In fact, unlike the rest of the house, there was only a single painting hanging on the wall over the antique desk. A simple arrangement of flowers looked back at Fitz as he stared at the piece hanging in front of him.

Everything had its place in this room. Even though he was certain the Martins had a household staff that did the cleaning for them, he could still tell Lillian didn't like clutter. She was an organized young lady. Even her closet, which Fitz found himself thoroughly impressed by, was arranged not only by type of dress but by color as well. As expected, all of the clothing was expensive, some with designer names that Fitz knew quite well from Europe.

But just as he was about to close the closet doors, he paused and scanned the garments hanging there one more time. Something was missing. Turning around, he looked once more at the room and saw an empty hanger on the bed. He figured he'd missed it when he first entered the room because he was so surprised by the aggressive amount of pink. It was still a little distracting, but he was adjusting.

"Remind me again what Lillian was doing when her mother and sister stepped out and left her alone?"

"Lucy said she was putting on her wedding dress. The photographer was coming early to take photographs of the family. That's why we were all dressing early."

"I see," Fitz said, walking over to the little sitting area by the window. "And there was no one in here with her except Mrs. Martin and Lucy?"

"No. The other bridesmaids haven't arrived yet."

"None of your household staff?"

"No. They've been preparing for the reception. The wedding is at Saint Joseph's, then the party will be…was supposed to be here."

"Chief," Fitz said, quickly shifting his gaze and addressing Buchanan, "did your men search this room when they arrived?"

"Yes. But you can see nothing looks out of place. Nothing was taken. The jewelry box is full of expensive necklaces and earrings. Nothing is broken or upended. There doesn't appear to be any signs of a struggle. *Yes*, my men searched the room. Why?"

Buchanan's patience had been lost long before the group entered Lillian's room. And now, the vein on his temple pulsated as he stared down the detective. Fitz knew he wouldn't like what he had to say next.

"Mr. Ambassador, I'm very sorry to say, but I do believe something has, in fact, happened to Lillian. I do not share the opinion of Chief Buchanan that she simply went out for a walk. Something hinky happened here."

"Oh, what are you on about, Mason?" the chief blurted, not able to contain himself any longer. "My boys looked in this room and didn't see a single thing that led any one of them to believe anything happened to Miss Martin."

"That's exactly it, chief. They didn't see it," Fitz said. "And because I *don't* see it, I'm suspicious."

"Don't see what?" Buchanan asked, looking around the room. The ambassador was also straining to see what *wasn't* there.

Casually walking to the bed, Fitz picked up the empty dress hanger. As the hook dangled from his finger, he said, "The wedding dress."

"Ambassador Martin told you. Lillian was putting her dress on the last time she was seen. She's wearing it, wise guy."

"Really?" Fitz asked, walking back to the sitting area. "Wearing what I am sure is an expensive, white wedding dress to go out walking around? In the grass that is still damp because of the time of day. With her veil on? Because that's nowhere in sight either. I find that hard to believe, Chief."

Buchanan stared at him, his eyes ablaze. Fitz thought he should take a few steps away from the chief so he was out of striking distance. "That doesn't prove anything, Mason. You're just trying to cause a ruckus so you can swoop in here and get the ambassador to hire you and your fancy detective firm to find his daughter who's gonna ankle it through that door any minute now."

Without a word, not taking his eyes off the exceedingly frustrated officer, Fitz slowly backed away and lowered himself into the chair next to the window. "There's one other thing. I noticed it the minute we walked into the room. The one thing that was obviously out of place," he said, reaching down to the floor and retrieving a handkerchief that was partially obscured by one of the chair legs. Passing it by his nose, then holding it out in front of him between his index and middle fingers, he said, "I see no reason whatsoever that young Lillian would need to chloroform herself after putting her wedding dress on."

Chapter Twelve

"How could you have let this happen!? You assured me… You *personally* assured me you would have everything in hand. I wanted to bring professional security people in, but the mayor promised your department could handle things."

The color of Conrad Martin's face was as red as the rose in his lapel. Which, incidentally, was also the color of Chief Walter Buchanan's face. But for completely different reasons. As the ambassador stood in the middle of the library dressing down the city's police chief, Fitz sat quietly in the chair next to the fireplace, legs crossed and arms folded. He was taking no pleasure in seeing Buchanan verbally eviscerated but was not about to stick his head into the lion's mouth and try to intercede. Once Martin ran out of steam, then he'd talk to him about what steps they should next take to locate Lillian.

Finding her was going to begin by figuring out what happened to the girl while she was happily–he assumed–preparing for her nuptials. Fitz took the time to start thinking about all of the possibilities. Was Lillian kidnapped because of something she'd done or something she knew, or was this an attack on Conrad Martin, and they were just using his daughter to get to him? Or worse? Was it a random kidnapping? If it were simply a random act and the perpetrator had no connection to the family or the victim, it would make everything exponentially more difficult. However, Fitz's gut told him that wasn't the case. Parker wasn't that big of a city. Everyone would know who the Martins were and where they lived. Some run-of-the-mill goon off the street didn't just *happen* to sneak into the house of a former ambassador on his daughter's wedding day and kidnap her, not noticing the police presence outside.

That brought up another point. How did someone get in without being noticed by the police guards? They could have been disguised. Looked like household staff. There was no way the officers watching the house could know all of the individuals who worked there on sight. Unless they'd been given pictures, which Fitz wouldn't put past Martin. But then they would need to trust that the police officers took the time to study the pictures. Fitz wasn't willing to place a wager on that.

Instead of focusing on how the kidnapper, or *kidnappers*, got in, he thought it might make more sense to figure out how they got *out* of the house with a woman in a puffy white wedding dress without being spotted. Regardless of the police's knowledge of the staff, the detective hoped that if one of them had seen an unconscious bride being carried out of the house, someone would have done something. That shouldn't have been too much to ask.

Fitz was running through the possible scenarios in his head when he heard the door to the library close with a loud thud. Looking up, he saw that he and the ambassador were now alone.

"I told the chief to search the house again. From the attic to the cellar," Martin huffed, walking over to the bar in the corner and pouring himself and Fitz a drink.

Taking the tumbler of dark amber liquid, Fitz could tell just by the smell that it was the good stuff. He knew how much scratch this scotch must have cost, so he was going to savor every sip. Even if it was still well before noon.

"Look, Fitz," Martin said after draining his entire glass in one long gulp, "I know you and I butted heads from time to time in Rome. But you were the best officer MID had in Italy. I need you to use those skills to find my daughter. I don't care what it takes."

Fitz's military service in Europe had been the reason for the two men crossing paths in the first place. He'd been a member of the U.S. Army's Military Intelligence Division. His unit was stationed in Rome, working out of the embassy. Not that anyone would confirm that. Very much as it sounded, he was an intelligence officer charged with uncovering other nation's secrets while safeguarding America's. And as the war was threatening more and more to drag the United States into active combat, his team had its hands full.

As commanding officer of the Rome unit, Major Francis Mason found himself in the room with many of the most powerful and influential people, not only in Italy, but throughout all of Europe. He'd overseen countless operations that positioned the U.S. for what was its inevitable entrance into the fight. Working regularly with "Wild Bill" Donovan, he kept the information flowing, knowing full well some of his reports would make it onto the desks of the country's top brass.

When the order was given to shutter the embassy after Italy declared war on the United States in 1941, he was one of the very last to leave.

For the next two years, he continued working out of the London Embassy, making him one of the most senior and experienced intelligence officers the United States had on the ground in Europe. But after an inexplicable near-deadly automobile accident on Westminster Bridge following a meeting with members of the British Parliament, he returned to the States to recover. Fitz was never able to prove beyond a reasonable doubt that the accident was a cleverly concealed attempt on his life, but it did achieve one objective if it had been an assassination attempt. It ended his military career.

Back in the United States, he took with him the skills he'd honed and a network he'd helped build over nearly ten years of serving in Europe. Very honorably discharged, and because of his specialized experience, it wasn't long before Archibald Stride of the Stride Detective Agency came calling. For the last year and a half, Fitz was one of Stride's top operatives, now helping to keep the wheels of commerce spinning and the nation's technological secrets secure. The assignments weren't nearly as exhilarating as finding oneself behind enemy lines using an alias, knowing if you're caught, it would mean certain death. But as Fitz was getting older, he found the work much easier on the knees and less harmful to his wardrobe.

Sitting across from Martin was bringing back a flood of memories.

"If I may ask, Mr. Ambassador. How did you know I was in Parker City today?"

Martin exhaled, waiting for the scotch to help relieve the frightful tension in his chest. That moment when the alcohol would allow his muscles to relax ever so slightly. "I may be retired, but I still know what's what and what's going on. But…if I am going to be perfectly honest with you…"

"I wish you would."

"I didn't know you were *actually* here already. I just knew you were with Stride. And I wanted someone I knew could handle something like this. Clearly, I cannot rely on the bumbling police in this town to get Lillian back. I know you, Fitz. And I know what you're capable of. I want you to do whatever it takes. I don't care what it costs. And when you find whoever did this…"

"Conrad," Fitz interrupted, his tone even and cool. "I will do what I can to find your daughter. But I will *not* cross any lines. That's not my style."

"You always did rate, Fitz. One of those right guys," Martin said, leaning back in his chair and closing his eyes, the first feeling of relief beginning to wash over him. Whether it was from the scotch or the fact he knew he now had a first-rate detective on the case, he didn't care.

Chapter Thirteen

L ucy Martin looked very much like her sister. That's what Fitz thought sitting there with the ambassador's younger daughter after seeing a photograph of Lillian in Martin's library. Only eighteen, the girl presented herself with a great deal of confidence. Even under the terrible circumstances. She'd obviously been crying, her eyes were puffy, and her make-up was smeared in several places. At least on the side of her face he could see. Her dark hair was loose and flowing down over one eye, giving her a distinct Veronica Lake appearance. If she'd been wearing her bridesmaid dress earlier, she'd now changed into a simple day dress. An empty cup of tea sat on the coffee table in front of her.

"Why is it when something upsetting happens, people think tea will make it better?" she asked, her eyes fixed on the expensive piece of Royal Doulton China. Her voice was calm and surprisingly deep for a petite young lady. "What magical properties does tea have?"

"I think it goes back to the British," Fitz said with a smile. "Or possibly the Chinese."

"I don't even like tea, really. I just thought I would have a cup with Mother to help calm her. I'd prefer something stronger."

"Did it work? For your mother, I mean?"

"Mother's upstairs lying down."

Fitz wanted to proceed cautiously. The last thing he wanted was to upset Lucy any more than she already was, but he needed to ask some questions about her sister. He needed information about Lillian. Information the ambassador said Lucy could provide.

"I'm terribly sorry to have to bother you right now, but if I'm going to find your sister, I need to know a little bit about her. Your father said the two of you are close."

Lucy smiled. "We are. We usually tell each other everything."

"That's very nice. I have two younger brothers. We haven't always gotten along."

"I would expect that of boys."

"Well, we get along now," Fitz added, not sure why he was trying to justify his relationship with his brothers to an eighteen-year-old girl. Returning to the subject at hand, he said, "Tell me about your sister. What is she like? What interests does she have?"

Lucy smiled again, a peculiar twist to her lips. There was something in her eyes that made Fitz wonder if he was about to hear the truth or a version of the truth. "Everyone loves Lillian. She's smart and funny. And very kind. She's always talking about how important it is to help those who aren't as fortunate as we are. I remember one time when she tried to talk Daddy into donating thousands of dollars to a group called the American Brotherhood for the Blind. Daddy wasn't too keen on the idea. But she was always going on about one cause or another. I'm sure if women didn't already have the right to vote, Lillian would be out there carrying a sign and marching every weekend with the Suffragettes."

"She sounds very charitable. What about you?" Fitz asked, studying the girl's face, watching for her reaction.

"Me? I prefer to sit by the fire and read Shakespeare. My sister's the one that wants to change the world. I support her in everything she does; I'd just rather not get my hands dirty. Lillian has enough social consciousness for both of us."

"And your parents? Do they support your sister and her activities?" Fitz was curious to hear about this young, civic-minded woman. He was beginning to wonder if some cause du jour in which she'd become involved could be the reason she was taken. It could open a new line of inquiry that he wasn't originally expecting.

"Daddy is very busy and doesn't believe much in charity. But you said you know him, so that shouldn't surprise you. He's more interested in art than people sometimes. And mother, well, she will attend the right charity events but would rather donate to the church or the Red Cross and let them deal with the world's problems."

"Were any of the groups your sister was involved with the kind that could have gotten her into any sort of trouble?"

"She wanted to help people who were *blind*, Mr. Mason. She wasn't the secretary-general of the American Communist Party. But I can just imagine Daddy's reaction if she were."

For the briefest of moments, a wicked smile flashed across Lucy's bright red lips.

"I certainly wasn't trying to accuse her of any wrongdoing. It's just that in my line of work, I've seen innocent people get mixed up in things that ended up going bad. Sometimes without them even knowing. Situations can go queer without anyone even realizing."

"I can assure you, Mr. Mason, my sister's interests never crossed into anything *nefarious*. None of the groups with which she's involved is in any way a threat to anyone. Lillian isn't a rebel."

Fitz wondered if perhaps Lucy was, but instead said, "This is all very helpful, Lucy. And you can forget the *Mr. Mason* business. You can call me Fitz. All my friends do."

"Are we friends?"

"I was hoping we could be. I'm friends with your father."

"I didn't think Daddy had any friends."

Lucy Martin was something else, Fitz thought, sitting there staring at the young beauty across from him in the sitting room. He was having trouble getting a good bead on her. Other than the fact it *looked* as if she'd been crying, she wasn't showing the type of emotion he expected. This Jane was a cool customer.

"You know, *Fitz*, you aren't like any police detective I've ever seen before."

He couldn't help but smile. She was trying to read him as much as he was her. "There's a good reason for that, Lucy. I'm *not* a police detective."

"I didn't think so. Not dressed like that. Your shoes are too expensive.

And you aren't writing everything I say down in a little notebook."

"I have a very good memory."

"If you aren't a police officer, why are you here? Who are you? Are you a private detective? Did Daddy hire you? Is that how he knows you?" Lucy asked, leaning forward with great interest.

"Your father and I worked together in Rome. I was stationed at the embassy for a time. Now, I'm with the Stride Agency. I'm sure you've heard of us."

"Everyone's heard of the Stride Agency," Lucy said, raising an eyebrow. "You arrived on the spot lickety-split, didn't you? You really are good."

"I hate to ruin the illusion, but I happened to be in Parker City on another assignment," he answered, shrugging his shoulders.

The corner of Lucy's lips twisted into a slight smirk. "How very fortuitous."

While Fitz was enjoying the verbal jousting, he wanted to get the interview back on track. Broadening his questions a bit, he thought he'd take a slightly different approach.

"Do you know, was your sister…was Lillian having any sort of trouble with anyone? Was she in a jam of any kind? Has anyone been threatening her?"

For the first time, Lucy Martin didn't have an immediate answer prepared. She looked as though she was genuinely trying to think if her sister might have had any enemies. Someone, anyone who would be willing and capable of snatching her from her own home on her wedding day.

"Lillian's former boyfriend wasn't too keen on the idea of her getting married. He didn't take the breakup well. Not like a man anyway. I remember after he found out she was going with a new guy, he made a scene at church. Can you imagine? Causing a scene at church! Lillian was mortified."

"What exactly did he say?"

"I honestly don't remember."

In Fitz's experience, when someone said, "*I honestly,*" or "*to be honest with you,*" more often than not, they weren't being very honest. But he could tell by the tone in her voice, Lucy was not an admirer of the fellow. There was definitely a smoldering anger there.

"And what is this former beau's name?"

"Sonny Baker. He's state Senator Wilson Baker's son."

Of course. Why not throw a powerful politician into the mix, Fitz thought.

"Do you think Sonny was angry enough to try and hurt Lillian?"

Lucy laughed.

"Oh, please. Sonny Baker? First of all, he doesn't do anything for himself. He has someone cut his steak for him. And second, as much as I hate to admit it, I think he really did care for Lillian. I can't imagine him wanting to hurt her."

"Then why'd they break up?"

"Because he wanted someone who would cut his steak for him! Lillian wanted someone who wasn't a layabout. Someone who was going to do something with his life. Not just live off his family's money."

"Admirable," Fitz offered. "What about the groom?"

As if on cue, a loud commotion in the hallway drew Fitz and Lucy's attention toward the door. Raised voices could be heard coming from the entry. Fitz stood and walked toward the door, opening it so he could hear what was being said.

He hadn't realized Lucy followed him until she startled him when, standing just behind him, she said, "That would be Sid Mercer. Lillian's fiancé."

Chapter Fourteen

Sydney Mercer was an extremely handsome gentleman, Fitz noted, giving the fellow a once over as he entered the sitting room where he and Lucy had been speaking. Tall, athletic, with a firm jaw, he looked like a collegiate boxer on his way to becoming a bank president. No wonder Lillian Martin went for him.

"Sydney, this is Fitz Mason," the ambassador said, introducing the two men. "He's the very best the Stride Detective Agency has to offer. He's here to find Lillian. Fitz, this is Lillian's fiancé, Sydney Mercer."

Extending his hand, Fitz was taken by the surprising lack of strength in Mercer's grip. Maybe he was one of those men that didn't feel the need to show off, Fitz thought.

Pleasantries out of the way, Mercer dove right in, asking no one in particular, "Where's Lillian? What's going on? They called and said I needed to come right over. That Lillian was missing."

"They?" Fitz asked.

"The police."

Raising an eyebrow, Fitz acknowledged, "That probably could have been handled better. I find face-to-face is best when dealing with sensitive matters."

The ambassador began pacing in front of the large window, looking out over the garden, trying to keep his anger under control. "So far, the Parker City police have shown themselves to be as incompetent as the Keystone Cops! I'm going to have words with the mayor about all of this. They were supposed to be keeping an eye on things today. And now Lillian is missing…kidnapped! And they didn't even know that until you came along, Fitz!"

"Kidnapped?!" Mercer repeated. All color drained from his face.

Compassion was not something with which Conrad Martin was very deft. Lillian may have been his daughter, but blurting out that she'd been kidnapped in front of her fiancé wasn't very tactful. How he'd risen so high in the diplomatic world, Fitz would never truly understand. Because being diplomatic was also something with which Martin had difficulties when his temper was flaring, and the situation was tense. Which was the exact time you wanted a diplomat to be…*diplomatic.*

Wanting to clear up as much as possible for Lillian's fiancé, Fitz ushered the boy to the chair he'd previously been using and carefully explained to him what had been discovered. They didn't have very many details to work with, but he wanted to tell Mercer everything. Because, as he was doing so, he was also keeping a keen eye on the fellow's reactions. At this point, Fitz had no idea who he could trust in this affair, so everyone was a suspect until they weren't. He wasn't giving anyone the benefit of the doubt.

Mercer's reactions seemed to be what one would expect if they were told the woman they were supposed to marry in just a few hours vanished from her room while getting ready, and a handkerchief laced with chloroform was found in her place. Either he was genuinely stunned by what he'd been told, or he was a practiced thespian. After speaking with him a little further, Fitz would be able to tell. He just needed to watch for the subtle tells humans always tried to control. An almost imperceptible twitch of the lip or shifting of the eyes could give him away.

Fitz perched himself on the edge of the chair opposite Mercer, leaning forward so that he could focus his attention on the man.

"Mr. Mercer, I would like to get a little background if I could. I never met Lillian, so it will help me get to know her. How did the two of you first meet?"

Rubbing his temples, Mercer took a deep breath and said, "It was at a party this past Christmas."

"A whirlwind romance," Lucy offered from the other side of the room where she was sitting and listening to the exchange, her tone biting.

Ignoring her, Mercer continued. "I was friends with the host's son. We'd attended Georgetown together. When he found out I was going to be around for the holidays, he invited me to the party. Lil was there. She was stunning. She looked like an angel. Her smile lit up the room, and her emerald eyes sparkled brighter than the lights on the Christmas trees. I fell for her the minute I laid eyes on her."

Fitz thought he heard a distinct scoff come from Lucy as Mercer was describing his first encounter with Lillian. He was getting the impression Lucy was not very fond of her would-be brother-in-law.

The story he'd told sounded romantic, like a fairytale. Unfortunately, Fitz knew not all fairytales had happy endings.

"Who is this friend? Who's party was it?"

"Sonny Baker. It was his father's annual Christmas party. Senator Baker."

"Did I forget to mention that?" Lucy asked.

Fitz looked at Lucy, noting how different her demeanor was since Mercer's arrival. He still couldn't quite figure her out. One minute, she was her sister's best friend, and she worried about her. The next, she was acting like this was all one big game, taking shots at the man who was about to marry her sister.

Turning back to the groom, he cautiously said, "I understand at one time, Lillian and Sonny Baker were an item. Were they still—"

Mercer leaned forward now. "Look, I don't make it a point to steal other fellows' girls. But when Lil and I met…I don't know. We just… Something happened that night."

Another sound came from Lucy's corner of the room. This time, Mercer shot an ice-cold glare in Lucy's direction.

Fitz waited for a moment before asking, "And how long after that night was it before Lillian broke up with Sonny?"

"I believe it was actually that night," Lucy gleefully chimed in.

"Lucy!" both Conrad Martin and Mercer snapped.

To the sudden rebuke, Lucy slouched down in the chair with her arms crossed over her chest. Her face was a combination of anger and…what was it in her eyes Fitz was seeing? Sadness? No. Pain.

"Being a fella who's had his heart broken a couple of times," Fitz said after a moment of awkward silence, "I can imagine that Sonny wasn't too happy when the two of you started going together."

"I didn't hear a question, Mr. Mason?" Mercer was now on the defensive. Not where Fitz wanted him.

"Sydney, I'm not saying that anyone did anything wrong here. I'm just trying to determine who might be angry enough with Lillian to kidnap her and what their reasoning might be. I have to look at all the possibilities. And believe me, love can make a man do desperate things. What about you? Were you seeing anyone at the time who might be upset that you and Lillian had—"

A sudden flash of anger flared in the young man. "I don't think sitting here dredging up the past is very useful!" he snapped, slamming his fist on the arm of the chair. Fitz remained silent, allowing Mercer to get his temper under control. "I'm sorry. I just think we should all be out there looking for Lil. We need to be *doing* something."

"All of this is going to help. You need to trust me." Fitz let that sink in before continuing. "Tell me about how Sonny reacted when he found out about the two of you. Because I'm definitely going to want to talk to him. So, the more I know, the better."

Mercer sighed and slumped back in his chair.

"He was pretty angry at first. He saw Lil and me at the pictures one night. Started yelling at us in the lobby of the theater. Some ushers had to throw him out. But he did apologize eventually. We haven't spoken since, though."

That's the second time someone related a story in which Sonny Baker had caused a scene in public. He was quickly becoming the person with whom Fitz most wanted to speak. The trouble was his father was a very powerful man. And Fitz had gotten into tight spots before when he went after someone who was well connected. He was going to need to play this one straight. Before he could do that, he needed to finish up with Sydney Mercer, for the time being.

"Mr. Mercer, what is it you do?"

"I'm a manager in my family's business."

"What kind of business is that?"

The question was met with a puzzled look as if Fitz should already know. "Real estate."

"Sydney Mercer? As in Mercer-Avery? One of those Mercers?" Now Fitz understood.

"That's my father. Alvin Mercer. And my uncle–my aunt's husband–Roger Avery. You're familiar with them?"

"I live in Baltimore. I see your family's buildings all over the place."

Yet another possibility now presented itself.

"To your knowledge," Fitz asked, "is there anyone who has a problem with you or your family? Or Mercer-Avery? Some business deal that went wrong? Someone who might want to harm you by taking Lillian?"

Mercer thought for a moment, then shook his head. "My family and our company is above reproach. We have a sterling reputation. One that has been cultivated for decades through hard work and honest business dealings. But…wealthy people always have enemies. Some people just don't like us because we have money. Other people don't like my family because they don't think we should be building office buildings with more than three stories. But no one has been threatening me, my family, or Lillian."

Chapter Fifteen

itz paced along the drive outside the Martin home, watching as the city's police officers combed through the yard, looking for anything that could help them track down where Lillian Martin may have been taken. The more time that passed, the less likely they were to discover anything useful. As the moments ticked by, a sinking feeling settled in the pit of his stomach. Holding his cigarette out in front of him, he watched the wisps of smoke circle up into the sky. After a few more puffs, he stamped the butt out in an elaborate waist-high ashtray just outside the front door. There was no smoking inside the Martin home, he'd been told. The ambassador said the smoke would do too much damage to the paintings.

The interviews he'd conducted so far were not sitting well with him. At first blush, Lillian didn't appear to have any enemies. No surprise there. He didn't expect anyone to say anything unflattering about the missing bride. Lucy, her sister, was a bit of an enigma. She was strong-willed. Intelligent. But he felt as though there was something she was holding back.

Sydney Mercer was like so many men he came across in his work. The son of a wealthy businessman now working in the family firm, taking advantage of his good fortune. Mercer-Avery was a big name in Baltimore, but he couldn't remember ever hearing anything questionable about the outfit. He'd make a couple of calls and see if the company was on the up and up.

The incidents with Sonny Baker were what interested Fitz most. If Mercer stole his girl and Sonny was holding a grudge, there was a chance he could be the one behind this. Maybe he thought if he could just get Lillian alone and profess his undying love, he might still have a chance. Love made people do inexplicable things. But would he have gone as far as chloroforming her and carrying her away? If he were as lazy as Lucy suggested, would he have really gone to that extreme? Odds were he'd have paid someone to do the job. Either way, he was at the top of Fitz's list. Even if he was the son of a state senator.

As Fitz considered lighting another cigarette to help clear his head, Chief Buchanan stepped out of the house looking worn and beaten down. For a big man, he was looking significantly smaller right at that moment. Feeling sorry for the guy, Fitz offered a cigarette, which the chief grudgingly accepted. The two smoked in silence for a few moments. Fitz wasn't one to kick a fellow when he was down, so he had no intention of pointing out the fact Buchanan said he was personally overseeing the security for the wedding. That would have been ungentlemanly.

Before stubbing out his cigarette, Buchanan said, "My guys are in there talking to the family now. But the ambassador said he wants you runnin' the show. Says he doesn't trust us." After an awkward pause, he went on. "I telephoned the mayor to let him know what happened."

"That was probably an unpleasant conversation," Fitz said without looking at the chief.

"That would be one way of putting it. He let me know, in no uncertain terms, that if Lillian Martin wasn't found, I should consider retiring."

"That could be nice. Spend some time down on the Chesapeake fishing."

Buchanan looked directly into Fitz's eyes. "I hate fishing."

Before Fitz could respond with a quip to lighten the mood, a whistle sounded off in the distance. Both men instinctively turned in the direction of the signal and saw a pair of patrolmen running toward the tree line where the whistle had sounded.

"They found something," Buchanan said, starting in the direction his men had gone.

Fitz followed suit, hoping that whatever the officers searching the woods found was going to be helpful. And that they weren't about to come upon Lillian Martin's lifeless body. He hated that he even thought that way, but there could be some comparison to the Lindbergh baby, and everyone knew how that ended. Shaking the horrible thoughts from his head, Fitz carefully waded into the trees with the chief. Not a terribly huge fan of the outdoors, Fitz was not enjoying trudging through the damp leaves and mucky soil. He didn't dare look down to see what it was doing to his shoes.

Reaching the end of the trees, Fitz found himself, along with the chief and several police officers, now staring out into an open field. According to one of the policemen, the treeline ended at the boundary of the Martins' property and the field belonged to their neighbor.

One of the officers—the one who'd summoned everyone with his whistle—drew everyone's attention to a patch of mud he was standing over. A set of tire tracks were plainly visible in the wet dirt. The group followed the tracks for several yards before they tapered off as the ground cover became dryer and thicker, obscuring any signs of a vehicle.

"Which direction is this?" Fitz asked, pointing off in the distance.

Buchanan looked around, gaining his bearings, and said, "Well, if they headed straight that way, the way the tracks are going, they'd run right into Highway 40 eventually. From there, they could go east or west and get off anywhere."

Looking around, it was abundantly clear to Fitz that this was not an area where any vehicle should have been. Which could only mean one thing in his mind. It was the getaway car. Someone had driven here, snuck through the trees onto the Martins' property, gotten into the house, knocked Lillian out, managed to get her out of the house and back to the car, then drive off. Thinking about it, that version of events would have been much more difficult than it sounded. Fitz was still caught up on how anyone could have gotten Lillian out of the house without being seen. Something wasn't right. This wasn't some typical kidnapping. There must have been some planning involved. Something else was going on. He just didn't know what.

Before he could even begin to piece things together, an officer emerged from the trees, mud splattered all over his pants, holding a torn wedding veil. "I found it in a bush."

Chapter Sixteen

1985 . . .

Ben woke to the sound of rain beating against the bedroom window the next morning. A loud clap of thunder only served to punctuate the complete difference twenty-four hours had made. The gorgeous spring day that greeted Ben the day prior was long gone, replaced by the complete antithesis. Through the slightly parted curtains, all Ben could see were gray thunderclouds filling the sky. He hoped it wasn't a sign of the day to come.

Rolling over and looking at his alarm clock, he saw there were still twenty minutes left before it was set to go off, and he needed to get out of bed. Wide awake, though, he decided to start the day early and get moving. Ben wasn't one to just lay around in bed when there were things to do. It was one of his flaws. He recognized that. But he had a difficult time doing nothing. He needed to be on the move.

Out in the living room, he could hear Natalie collecting her things for the day. She'd been asleep when he got home the previous evening, so he was glad they'd have some time together now before he needed to head back to the office.

"Good morning," he said, tying the knot on his robe and walking into the living room.

Natalie, her hands full of papers on the American Revolution written by her students, gave him a kiss as he passed her on the way into the kitchen.

Most days, she looked like she could pass for one of her high school students. But that morning, Ben thought she looked like the stereotypical History teacher. She was wearing an oversized cardigan sweater, her big glasses, and had her usual flowing brunette hair pulled back into a ponytail. Definitely not her sexiest outfit, but she was still the best-looking History teacher Ben had ever seen.

"I just made some fresh coffee," she said with a smile.

"Have I ever told you you're wonderful?"

"Not nearly enough," she answered with a wink. "Would you pour me a cup? What kept you out so late last night? I didn't see any big headlines in the paper this morning."

In the message he'd left on their answering machine saying he didn't know when he'd be home, he hadn't gone into specifics about what they'd discovered in the field. He didn't have a problem telling Nat about his cases–what he was able to tell her about, at any rate–but he didn't like leaving details on the answering tape. Especially about a poor woman who'd suffered some sort of yet-to-be-explained indignity.

"Nothing about a body being found?" he asked as he poured what he was certain would only be his first cup of coffee that day.

"Unless I missed it," Nat said. "You found a body?"

"Yeah. In that big field off Lincoln Pike heading out of town."

Natalie joined him in the kitchen and happily accepted the cup Ben offered. "Murder?"

"Funny thing," Ben began, "we're not sure yet."

She gave him a puzzled look over the rim of her mug. "What exactly does that mean?"

"Right now, we don't actually know how she died. It was a young female."

"Why don't you know?"

"That's the interesting part. She was frozen." Ben popped a couple pieces of bread into the toaster.

"So, then she froze to death."

"No. I mean, she was *frozen*. Like a block of ice. Like she'd just come out of a freezer."

Natalie stared at him, a blank look on her face. Ben had to smile.

"That's the exact same reaction the chief had."

"Well, it's not every day you come across… She was frozen?"

"Yep. The ME said he was going to have to figure out the best way to thaw her out so that he could perform the autopsy to determine cause of death. It's going to take a few days."

"You couldn't ID here?"

"You really are sounding like Brent. No. She had no identification on her. In fact, she didn't have anything on her except an old blanket. Like I said, young girl. Probably in her twenties. I'm going to pull missing person cases when I get in this morning."

"Hmmm. All I have to do is give a pop quiz today. Want to trade?"

Nat and Ben first met several years earlier when he'd been investigating the death of a pair of her students. The circumstances were not ideal, but after the case was closed and some time passed, their relationship began to blossom. Now, in just a few months, they'd be married. As unfortunate as the conditions of their first meeting were, they'd eventually found happiness together.

"Do you think it will be another late night?" she asked.

"That will all depend on what happens today. If we don't get an ID and we have to wait on the medical examiner to do his thing, I should be able to get out normal time. Unless, of course, some sort of crime spree kicks off today. But, judging by the weather, it should be a quiet day."

"Criminals don't like breaking the law when it's raining?" Natalie asked.

"No. It's a proven fact," Ben joked. "They only commit crimes when the weather's nice."

Chapter Seventeen

y the time he'd showered and dressed and was on his way to the
station, the rain was falling in solid sheets. The downpour was now
so loud, it nearly drowned out the incessant rumbles of thunder
accompanying it. If not for the streaks of lightning racing across the sky
every few minutes, there would be nothing more than a black abyss hanging
over the city.

Storms like this were not unheard of, usually occurring more in the
summer months. But since the city's Great Flood, whenever there was a long
period of rain—heavy and violent like now—Parkertons grew concerned.
Back in '78, it rained for days and nights on end. The storm hit so hard that
the waters of the Tasker River, which ran straight through the center of the
city, burst over the banks and flooded the entire downtown area, leaving
buildings under feet of water. Already suffering from economic hardships,
the storm decimated the few businesses still struggling to survive. When
the raging waters finally receded, a swath of devastation was left in its wake.

Since the devastating flood, with so many buildings being boarded up
and abandoned, the affected area, once the heart of Parker, had become
the epicenter of crime in the city. More incidents were reported on a
regular basis there, in what used to be a thriving commercial corridor, than
anywhere else in Parker.

As he drove along Commerce Street toward the station, Ben thought
about one of his first night shifts on patrol in Downtown. He'd seen drug
deals being made openly on the street and prostitutes working their corners
without a care that a PCPD squad car was passing by. Not that there were

many people even out during the nighttime hours downtown. But when the only businesses that still operated in the dilapidated buildings were seedy bars, the clientele that did venture out was not that savory.

Ben was happy to see that the mayor's plan to revive Downtown looked like it was taking hold. Formerly vacant storefronts now displayed permit signs in the windows indicating that work was underway and new shops would be opening soon. The Harlequin Theatre, the jewel of Downtown, was preparing for a major renovation. And thanks in large part to the PCPD's Drug Task Force, the illegal trade had suffered a massive blow. Things were getting better. There was still a way to go, but things were on the right track.

Crossing through one intersection, Ben's Crown Vic wheeled through a pool of water so wide, the car sent waves as high as its roof off in both directions. The windshield wipers were having a difficult time keeping up with the pelting rain, making it more and more difficult to navigate the sodden roadways. A couple of times, Ben could feel the wheels spinning on the slick surface, not able to gain any traction due to the slick surfaces.

Finally, pulling into the station's parking lot, a line of officers suited up in rain gear were exiting the building and heading for their cars. There would no doubt be a number of accidents requiring responses and, if power went out anywhere in the city, traffic control. Ben was happy he was no longer in uniform. But if things got bad enough, there was always the possibility he and Tommy would be asked to lend a hand in some way. He didn't even want to think how Tommy would react if he was sent out in the storm. Though, it would be amusing. Ben could only try and imagine some of the things his partner would have to say.

Mentally preparing himself to jump out of the car and make the run for the station's back entrance, Ben pulled the collar of his raincoat up around his neck. He was thankful he'd left his briefcase the night before so didn't have to worry about carrying anything and could focus solely on avoiding any puddles, which could more accurately be described as miniature lakes at that point.

He noticed he wasn't the only person making the mad dash from their car. A few steps in front of him was someone he'd planned on speaking with that morning when he got in and one of his favorite people who worked for the department. He didn't know how long Betty'd been in charge of the Records Department for the PCPD and dared not ask. It would come too close to asking her age, which would only get the person asking the question a biting remark from the Baltimore native and institution of the Parker City Police Department. Needless to say, Ben figured both numbers were on the high end of the double digits.

"It's wetter than a dolphin's chin out there today," Betty said to Ben as they stood just inside the door, shaking off the drops of rain clinging to their coats.

As innocuous a statement as it might have been, Ben couldn't help wondering if dolphins actually had chins. He'd never thought about it. Not that he'd ever had a reason to.

"Would you be a dear, hun, and hold this?" Betty asked, handing him her oversized purse so she could unwrap the plastic rain cap from around her hair. After which, she removed her pink rain slicker with giant sunflowers all over it. There was no way anyone could miss her coming, Ben thought.

Betty always wore some of the brightest colored clothing he'd ever seen. Sometimes, the colors even coordinated. Today, however, was not one of those days. Not one to care very much for style or what other people thought of her choices, Betty wore what made her happy, which were usually brightly colored items, stylish a decade earlier. The woman was bold, brassy, and a force to be reckoned with. She was not the woman whose bad side you wanted to be on.

With the raincoat now hanging over her arm, she dug around in the purse Ben was still holding until she found her pack of cigarettes and lighter. Betty was the only person he knew who smoked more than Tommy. But even Tommy accepted the fact he wasn't allowed to smoke inside the station any longer. This was a rule Betty flagrantly ignored, which always troubled Ben due to the fact she worked in a room full of old paper documents.

"How many of those do you smoke a day?" Ben asked, trying to sound lighthearted, like he was just making conversation to pass the time.

With a cocked eyebrow, Betty shook her head and answered, "I'm gonna tell you the same thing I tell my husband. These cigarettes are the only reason I've lived as long as I have."

"I don't think I understand."

"All the tar keeps these old bones together," she said, then broke out into a full-throated laugh that echoed off the pasty green concrete walls. Ben couldn't help but join her. She was irascible, and he just loved her. Everyone did.

Lighting one of her unusually long cigarettes and tossing the lighter back into her bag, she collected her purse from Ben and started down the hall toward the Records Room. Ben tagged along behind as she shuffled her way to the door with the word RECORDS stenciled on it in black paint that had been chipping for so long that the 'O' was only a shadow at that point.

"I take it you need something from me, hun," Betty said, her Baltimore accent heavy that morning. "Or are you just stoppin' by to flirt with me?"

"You know Tommy does all the flirting for both of us."

"I do like him," Betty said with a wink as she unlocked the door. "Come on in. Let me turn the lights on and get situated, then you can tell me what you need."

Other than Betty's cluttered desk with the giant IBM computer sitting in the center of it, the room was filled with row after row of file cabinets. Every record the department had was stored in them. Ben wasn't sure how far back the files went, but he knew Betty had her system and could find whatever someone needed. For someone as advanced in years as she was, he was always happy to know that Betty wasn't afraid of technology and was doing her part to computerize the records system. Why she was able to understand that computers were going to be a useful tool and his partner couldn't, Ben wasn't able to figure out.

Sitting behind her desk and pulling a notepad from under a stack of papers, she announced, "Okay! The shop's open. What are you looking for today?"

"Missing person cases. Young females."

Betty looked up at him over the rim of her glasses, the lenses of which were thicker than Ben's thumb. "Do you remember what happened the last time you went poking around in the missing person cases?"

"I do. But we had a set of bones we needed to try and identify. And we ended up solving the case."

"Yeah, but you needed the files from fifty years ago."

"I don't think we need to go that far back this time. The girl was maybe twenty...?"

"Is this about the body you found yesterday? Out in the field off Lincoln Pike?"

"Yep. So far, we have nothing to go on. So, we're thinking she might have a file already."

Betty leaned back in her chair and started tapping the tip of her nose with a pen. "I'll see what I can find. I can't say that we have any open missing young girl files down here right now. I don't need to tell *you* that. Hell, you're the head detective around here."

"Right," Ben agreed. "So, let's go back before '81. Say, ten years."

"That will definitely narrow it down." Betty thought for a moment. "But I think I'd remember if a young girl had gone missing and the case was still open. At least if it was recently. Even ten years back. That's the kind of thing you don't forget."

"Until I have a better lead, it's somewhere to start."

"Did you think about the fact she might not be from Parker City?"

Betty was right. Just because they'd discovered the body inside the city limits didn't mean she'd lived in Parker City. If she'd lived in any of the towns around the county and gone missing, it would be the Sheriff's Department that would have gotten the call. While they would have sent out information to other local law enforcement agencies in the area, the cases wouldn't necessarily be top of mind if they weren't active in their own department.

Before Ben could say anything, Betty made him an offer. "I'll tell you what I'll do, hun. Since I'm so helpful, I'll get in touch with Bernie over in the Sheriff's Department and see if they have anything that might fit with what you're looking for. It's a pretty big county. This could be one of their cases."

"I appreciate that, Betty. You're the best. Tommy's right. You're not just a pretty face."

Crossing her arms and shaking her head, Betty asked, "Now, who's the one doing the flirting, Detective?"

Chapter Eighteen

"I wasn't thinking our Jane Doe might not be from Parker City," Ben admitted to Tommy as they sat in the office, each with a fresh cup of coffee in hand.

"Really? I'd thought of that. I just assumed you did, too. I guess you're not infallible," Tommy said, punctuating his jab with a sip of coffee and an innocent shrug of his shoulders.

Ben shook his head and went back to flipping through the morning's paper. He was specifically looking to see if there was any reference to yesterday's discovery. They'd been able to get most of their work done before any press arrived, but whenever the medical examiner's van is spotted, questions are bound to be asked. Surprisingly, the brief article that did run in the paper did not speculate on what had happened in the field. The whole piece was more of a passing reference to official activity than anything else.

In Ben's experience, when the press didn't have all the details, they tended to embellish as much as possible to fill however many column inches were available. This time however, they hadn't done that. The *Herald-Dispatch* was evidently showing some restraint for a change.

However, the lack of information in the paper did explain the three telephone messages he'd received from reporters. The messages were waiting for him when he arrived that morning.

At some point, they'd have to make a statement. And if CSU didn't hit on the fingerprints, they were going to end up needing to go public to try and get help identifying the girl. Ben didn't want to return any of the calls until he'd had a chance to speak with the chief. Unfortunately, he was tied up at

City Hall, so was unavailable.

For the time being, he and Tommy would wait on all the reports. He was just hoping either the ME or Lieutenant Clover would get back to them sooner rather than later. Until they did, there wasn't much more that could be done.

Ben's nervous energy forced him to stand and start pacing back and forth in the small office. He didn't like feeling so helpless, like there was nothing he could do. Even going back out to look around where the body had been discovered just to see if they missed anything was out of the question because of the rain. If there had been anything left behind, it was long gone now, washed away by the downpour. Which, judging by the continued thunderclaps and flickering lights, was still going strong.

"Dude, would you sit down," Tommy said. "Don't you have some paperwork you could be doing? You like paperwork. It'll take your mind off whatever's making you so anxious. Because what you're doing right now is making me anxious."

"I'm anxious because we have nothing on Jane Doe right now," Ben huffed, stopping and perching on the corner of his desk. "I don't like that we don't know where to start to start."

"I get it," Tommy said, sitting forward and leaning his elbows on his desk. "But two things. First, it isn't that we don't have somewhere to start. There's just nothing we can be doing right now until other people do what they do. The ME and CSU are doing their thing. Betty's doing hers. We aren't super cops. Sometimes, we have to wait for other people to do their jobs so that we can do ours."

Ben began to argue, but Tommy cut him off by holding up a hand.

"And second…until we have a cause of death, we don't even know there *was* a crime."

"But we'd still need to figure out who dumped the body," Ben protested.

Tommy sighed. "Okay, yes. But…if it's not a murder, I don't consider it that big of a crime. You just need to relax. Is something else bothering you? Wait. Are you worrying about the wedding?"

"What are you talking about?"

"I've just never seen you act like this."

Ben sighed, walked around his desk, and sat back down. "I'm just frustrated. I want to be able to *do* something. Not just wait for other people. And for the record, I'm not at all worried about the wedding."

"Lookit," Tommy said, shifting his weight and leaning on the arm of his chair. "I know you like it when everything is organized, and you can make a plan. When you can make a list and check things off. I get it. I do. But think about how bad some of our previous cases were. Those took a lot out of us. So, don't sweat this one. At least not until we know something more definitive."

Sitting with his head in his hands, Ben mumbled, "I really don't like when you're the levelheaded one."

He was willing to admit he was feeling off. There was no way it was wedding jitters. He knew he wanted to spend the rest of his life with Natalie. There was no questioning that. Plus, they'd been living together for the last couple of years, so not all that much was actually going to change once they exchanged rings. Was it really all the unknowns of this current case that were bothering him? Tommy was one hundred percent correct. He liked to be in control and right now, he wasn't. That's what had to be bothering him. Right?

Chapter Nineteen

Taking Tommy's advice, Ben spent the miserable morning doing paperwork. He didn't think the average person realized how much of police work was just filling out reports. It wasn't like on television, where there was a major crime spree every week, and the detectives were always out on the street, finding themselves in the middle of a shootout or high-speed chase. Detective work could be very mundane. Especially when you were a supervisor. Even with only two of them in the squad. Ben could only imagine what kind of paperwork he'd have to do if Parker City had the kind of crime they saw in Baltimore and other big cities, and he commanded a large team of detectives.

By one o'clock, the heavy showers were finally subsiding, leaving behind a mist lingering in the air. Now cool and damp, it was going to take days for the city to dry out. From the breakroom on the second floor, Ben looked down at the parking lot behind the station. Half of the pavement sat under water. Nothing like what had been seen during the flood, but enough to create a giant pond behind the building. And it was right at the entrance to the lot, so every time a squad car pulled in, water sprayed up all around it.

"The rain didn't cause as much trouble as I expected," Ben heard from the doorway behind him.

Turning, he saw Chief Brent standing there, an armful of files and the large binder with his reorganization plan held to his chest. For a moment, Ben was surprised to see the chief out of uniform, instead wearing a dark gray double-breasted suit. Brent was intimidating in a uniform, but something about him dressed in a suit was downright menacing. Dressed like this, he looked more like one of the guys out of *The Godfather*–if all the mobsters were Irish. Ben felt it was better to keep that to himself.

"I thought I would dress up for the council meeting," Brent said, acknowledging the look on Ben's face.

"Can I pour you some coffee? It's a new pot."

"Fantastic. I would be very grateful. After that marathon session, I need a pick-me-up. Is anything happening with our frozen Jane Doe?" Brent laid everything he was carrying on the counter and began rubbing his eyes. Spending the last several hours talking to a group of politicians proved exhausting.

As Ben poured a fresh cup of steaming hot coffee for the chief, he told him how they were still waiting on all the reports to come in and how Betty was pulling together open missing person cases. So, in essence, a lot of waiting.

"It must be driving you crazy," Brent said after drinking half his cup in one gulp. The scalding temperature did not faze him in the least.

"Is it that obvious?"

The chief smiled and took another sip.

"How did your meeting go?" Ben asked, motioning toward the binder.

"Surprisingly well. Mayor Oland is behind the plan, and I think a majority of the City Council may be, too. Now it's up to them to come up with the money to fund everything and then give me the go-ahead to start shuffling things around. They'll vote on the budget this summer, then I can start the wheels in motion, and the department could be operating under the new plan by the beginning of the year. Best case scenario, of course. But when does anything go according to plan?"

"Well, if they–"

"Ben! Where are you?" Tommy shouted from down the hall, then walked through the door a moment later. "CSU sent some things over."

Ben crossed the breakroom in two long strides and eagerly took the large envelope emblazoned with the Maryland State Police seal from his partner. Opening it and pulling out the contents, he found photos and a number of documents summarizing their activities at the scene yesterday. There was also the initial report on what the techs had been able to gather from the body before it was taken away by the ME's people. Ben wanted to get back to his desk as quickly as possible and spread everything out so he and Tommy could start combing through it all.

"Chief, if you'll excuse us. We've finally got something to work with! If there's anything here, I'll let you know."

"Go do your thing," Brent said, finishing his coffee and walking over to the old, oversized brewing machine to pour himself another cup to take back with him to his own office.

Walking down the hall, Ben was flipping through the photos. So engrossed in them, he didn't see Betty coming from the other direction.

"Whoa! Hang on there, big boy." Betty put her hands out to stop Ben from running into her.

"I'm so sorry. We just got the report from the Crime Scene Unit."

"Yeah, Ben's been climbing the walls waiting for it," Tommy added.

"It's good that you've got that to start with then because I came up with a big zero in my search. The PCPD has no open missing persons cases that would fit what you're looking for. I went back fifteen years. Nothin.'" Betty paused to clear her throat. "But I called over to Bernie, and he's going through the sheriff's cases. So, there may be something there. Sorry I couldn't be more help with this one, kiddo."

"You've been very helpful, Betty. Thank you," Ben said, walking into the office and laying the stack of photos on his desk.

Being the naturally curious person she was, Betty sat down at Ben's desk, making herself comfortable, and picked up the enlarged photos. Flipping through them, she saw the wide shots of the field, then the closer pictures of the body wrapped in a blanket. When she got to the close-up photographs of Jane Doe's face, she paused, thinking her eyes were playing tricks on her. With Ben's nose in the CSU's summary report, it was Tommy who saw Betty's face go white.

"Everything alright there, Betty?" Tommy asked. "You look like you've seen a ghost."

Ben looked over at her and registered her troubled expression as well. "What's wrong?"

"These are the photographs of the girl you found yesterday," Betty confirmed, running her fingers along the glossy images.

"Yeah. I told you. Young girl. Early-twenties at most."

Picking up some of the photos, Tommy said, "She looks so peaceful in these pictures."

"I know her." Betty looked up at the detectives, seeing the surprise on their faces.

"You do?" they asked in unison.

"But it's impossible. It can't be her," Betty replied. "It was too long ago. It doesn't make any sense. She looks just the same."

"Who is she?" Ben prompted, his pulse beating slightly faster.

The excitement in his voice was hard to control. All day long, he'd been waiting for a lead so he could begin the investigation in earnest, and suddenly, they could be about to learn everything they needed to know about the mystery girl.

"What do you mean, she looks just the same?" Tommy questioned. "The same as what?"

"She looks exactly like she did when she disappeared…*forty* years ago."

Chapter Twenty

"Excuse me?" Tommy was the first to speak.

Ben was only seconds behind. "What do you mean forty years ago?"

Betty laid the photographs back down on the desk, a close-up shot of the poor girl's face on the top of the pile. From her pocket, she pulled out a pack of cigarettes—not the ones Ben saw earlier—and looked to Tommy for a lighter, who quickly obliged. Ben wasn't even going to bring up the fact she couldn't be smoking in the office this time. Experience taught him it wouldn't do any good anyway, but this time, he was willing to overlook it. He had a sinking feeling by the end of whatever Betty was about to tell them; he might even need a smoke himself. Not that he'd ever smoked before.

As she lit up and took the first drag, Tommy sat down at his desk, waiting for the story to begin. Ben closed the door so the smoke didn't filter out into the hallway, then he picked up the photos and leaned on the edge of his desk.

After sending a couple of rings of blueish-gray smoke toward the ceiling, Betty leaned forward and said, "I know you're going to think I'm just a crazy old lady seeing things, but I know that girl. Not personally, of course. But I remember her. Her disappearing was all anyone could talk about at the time because she was the daughter of a big muckety-muck ambassador that moved to Parker City after he retired. They had a big estate heading out towards Middleboro, where Larry and I lived at the time. That was long before we moved into the city here.

"Anyway," she said, readjusting the way she was sitting at Ben's desk. "It was all over the papers and the radio. Something like this happening was big news. All anyone could talk about. If I remember correctly, there was even something about a big-time detective from the old Stride Detective Agency getting involved."

At the mention of the Stride Agency, both Ben and Tommy shared a look with one another.

"Do you remember the detective's name?" Tommy asked, the eagerness in his voice unmistakable.

"I remember the girl because her picture was all over at the time. It makes her hard to forget. Especially because of everything that happened back then. But the name of the detective...I don't know. I just remember hearing that there was a detective involved. I might not have ever even known the man."

"What's the girl's name?" Ben laid the photo down in front of her.

"Martin. That's it! It was Ambassador Conrad Martin's daughter."

"Shit! I remember this," Tommy said, jumping out of his chair, then immediately sitting back down and opening his bottom desk drawer.

Pulling out an old, ratty accordion file, he unwrapped the band, holding it closed, and began digging through the yellowed and brittle folders inside. Pulling one out, he laid it on his desk. It was labeled MARTIN, CONRAD.

"The detective's name from the Stride Agency was Fitz Mason. My uncle." A triumphant grin appeared on Tommy's face. "He was amazing. Remember how he used to tell us all those stories when we were little? He was like a real-life Dick Tracy."

"What's that?" Ben walked over, looking at the accordion folder.

"When Uncle Fitz died, I got some of his old work papers and things. Everyone thought it made the most sense that I should get them, being a cop and all. He kept personal files on some of his old cases. I look through them every once in a while for fun. Some of the things he was involved with...amazing. And, apparently, according to my aunt who gave the papers to me, these were his cases that he *was* allowed to talk about."

"And he has a file about this case?" Ben was beginning to get excited as well.

"Right here. The minute Betty said it was an ambassador's daughter, I remembered." He opened the well-worn file folder and flipped through a few pieces of paper with handwritten notes on them. "The girl's name–the ambassador's daughter who went missing–was Lillian Martin."

"So, we've got an ID," Ben said, clapping his hands and rubbing them together.

"Boys, this isn't Lillian," Betty said.

"What do you mean? It says right here. Uncle Fitz was called in when Lillian Martin went missing...on her wedding day. Of all things."

"That's awful," Ben groaned.

"Yes, I remember that. Lillian was kidnapped on her wedding day. But they found *her*." Holding up the photo, Betty pointed. "This is *Lucy* Martin. Lillian's little sister."

Chapter Twenty-One

1945 . . .

When the bride, groom, and their families failed to show up at the church at the appointed time for the ceremony, word began spreading through the city that something was amiss. News always travelled quickly through Parker. Big news circulated even faster. And when that news was bad, it spread like wildfire. Considering everyone in town had been anticipating the grand wedding of Lillian Martin and Sydney Mercer, and now the wedding party was nowhere to be seen, questions were being asked at the church by the reporters assigned to cover the event, not to mention the guests. When no answers were provided at Saint Joseph's, and the news editors were hearing rumblings about a large police contingent having descended on the Martin estate, the press guys were dispatched to get the skinny.

With the number of police at the Martins' home, there was no possible way to deny something was afoot. But how much to reveal was the sticking point between the ambassador and Chief Buchanan. It only made sense the chief didn't want the press getting wind of the fact he and his men lost the bride on her wedding day. That would look terrible on the front page of the paper. He knew once the mayor saw it in black and white, his career would be over. He'd be lucky if they gave him time to clean out his desk before throwing him out of the station on his ear.

"I'm as good as done for," Buchanan confessed to Fitz, seemingly accepting the fact his time as chief would be coming to an abrupt end because of this cockup. "I've worn a badge for this city for more than twenty years, and I'm going to get the boot because some rich guy did something to make someone else angry enough to kidnap his daughter."

Trying to sound hopeful, Fitz said, "You don't know that the mayor is going to fire you, Chief." He hoped his words didn't sound as hollow as they felt. He had no reason to doubt Buchanan's dismissal would be the eventual outcome. Someone would have to take the blame. "Plus, when we find Lillian—"

Buchanan cut him off. "That's not how things work in Parker. I'm the one who's gonna take the heat on this, Mason. And all the good I've done will be completely forgotten. And *if* we find Lillian, *you'll* be the hero. So, there's no reason to try and shine me on. I can see the way this is coming down. I'm not some rube."

For his part, Conrad Martin couldn't care any less how bad Walt Buchanan looked in the eyes of the public. He'd get his comeuppance later. Martin would see to that, but not until after they'd found his daughter. At the moment, he was thinking if whoever kidnapped Lillian heard that one of the Stride Detective Agency's best operatives was on the case, they might think twice and let her go. So, Martin agreed to speak with a few select reporters, so he could share this information.

Standing on the front steps of the beautiful home, decorated with flowers and pink bunting for what was to be a joyous occasion, Martin addressed the reporters. Standing off to the side, trying to avoid attracting any attention, were Fitz and the police chief, along with his deputy, Lieutenant Earl Peters. Fitz asked if he could be excused from being at the dog and pony show so he could track down and speak with Sonny Baker, but the ambassador insisted he be seen. Even if he didn't take any questions. Fully understanding why Martin wanted him at the impromptu press briefing, Fitz was happy knowing that in the eyes of the paparazzo, it was not he who looked like a schnook. That distinction fell to Buchanan, who visibly grimaced every time one of the newsmen looked in his direction. Peters, on the other hand, seemed to already be mentally rearranging the furniture in the chief's office.

Though, for the life of him, Fitz couldn't imagine why he didn't think he'd be tarnished by the department's current situation as well. Figuring it was all small-town politics and there was something else he didn't know about, Fitz didn't give it much concern.

"So, you have no idea who might have kidnapped your daughter? Could this have anything to do with your service overseas for the government of the United States? In some way related to the war?" one of the reporters shouted, his voice much louder than it needed to be. On the younger side, his eagerness to pepper the ambassador with questions made Fitz wonder how long he'd been a newsman. The few other reporters, seemingly older and more seasoned, were deferential to Martin. They knew it was bad form to shout questions like that at a man like Conrad Martin. Especially when talking about his missing daughter.

Watching the whole affair from a distance was Joe Grainger. The ambassador's shadow was doing what he always did. Staying out of the way while keeping an eye on everything. Like a phantom just off-stage observing from the wings. He stood on the other side of the driveway, cigarette in hand, watching the reporters. At one point, he and Fitz locked eyes.

The two men hadn't had much interaction in Rome, but Fitz knew Grainger was close to the ambassador. If Martin was in some sort of trouble and Lillian's disappearance was related in any way, there was a good chance the valet would know about it. Fitz was going to need to get him alone and convince him to talk. It was always the staff that knew what was going on. But depending on how dedicated they were, it wasn't always easy to get information out of them. Fitz'd dealt with a lot of fellows like Joe Grainger. Tough, hard-boiled, and loyal. *Viciously* loyal. He might not be the easiest nut to crack, but Fitz was going to give it a go.

Chapter Twenty-Two

Fitz had three names on his list of people with whom he needed to speak. Norma Martin, though she was now sedated upstairs. The family doctor had been called to the house and asked to give her something so she could rest comfortably. Sonny Baker. And Joe Grainger. Since Grainger was standing in front of him, Fitz thought there was no better time than the present. He just needed to find a way to get the guy talking.

As the reporters were making their way down the driveway, escorted by a pair of patrolmen, the ambassador disappeared into the house, followed by Chief Buchanan and Lieutenant Peters. Neither Fitz nor Grainger moved, standing on opposite sides of the circular drive. They could have been marble statues that Martin brought back from Europe along with the other pieces in his collection.

Stamping out his cigarette as Fitz approached, Grainger eyed the detective. When he spoke, his voice was rough around the edges. "I figure now's as good a time as any."

"What's that, Joe?" Fitz asked, a disarming smile on his face.

"You've got questions."

"I've always got questions."

"So…ask 'em."

This was going to be fun, Fitz thought to himself, hoping Grainger hadn't seen him roll his eyes. His hat was pulled low to block the sun, so maybe he'd missed it. Removing his cigarette case from his pocket, he first offered one to Grainger before taking his own. The two men stood quietly smoking for several moments.

"It would have been a beautiful day for a wedding," Fitz finally said.

"Yeah. It would have been," Joe grumbled.

"Look," Fitz began, turning to look directly at Grainger, "I'm going to cut right to it. Do you have any idea what happened to Lillian?" He didn't see any reason to waste time. Because the more time that passed, the more danger the girl could be in. So, he was going to forgo his usual charm offensive and take the direct approach.

"Are you asking if I was involved?" Grainger's dark eyes narrowed until they looked like two little pinpricks on his fleshy face.

"No. I'm asking if you know any reason someone might have kidnapped her. Is the ambassador into something he shouldn't be? Is Lillian?"

"Since the ambassador left the foreign service, he's been living a quiet life. He throws a party every now and again for some of his hoity-toity friends, but other than that, he does a lot of reading."

"Then what's he keep you around for?"

Grainger ignored the jab and didn't rise to the bait. "As for the girl, she was a free thinker but certainly no troublemaker. Lucy's the one I can see rubbing someone the wrong way one of these days. But they're both decent young ladies."

"You watched them both grow up?"

"From afar. They weren't in Italy with us on the regular. They'd visit. But they lived stateside with Mrs. Martin while the ambassador was in Rome. It wouldn't always have been safe for them to be there. Especially at the end."

"Where'd they live while Conrad was overseas?"

"They had a brownstone in Washington before they moved out here to Parker when the ambassador retired."

"I see."

So far, everyone agreed. Lillian didn't have any enemies. That pretty much jibed with Fitz's gut feeling that she was just the pawn in someone else's game targeting the ambassador. At the moment, there was no proof of that, but his gut had never gotten it wrong before. He'd worked enough cases and been on enough assignments to have learned a thing or two. In his experience, with a kidnapping, the victim was just a means to an end. A way to get at someone else. Or at least their money.

As he flicked some ash from the tip of his cigarette, Fitz absentmindedly said, "You know, some people think smoking's bad for you."

"Probably the same people who think drinking isn't good for you," Grainger snorted. "But I'll take a good bourbon and a smoke anytime."

"A bourbon man? Hmm. I would have thought you drank scotch like Conrad."

"It looks like you don't know everything then. Do you, Mason?"

"I never claimed to have all the answers," Fitz shot back. "But I know I can find them. That's my special skill. Getting to the bottom of things."

Grainger blew a ring of smoke in Fitz's direction.

"The ambassador must be good to you if you've stuck with him all these years. And now into his retirement. Especially if you don't see much action anymore. If Conrad's life is really as quiet as you say it is."

Grainger raised an eyebrow, trying to figure out where Fitz was going with this.

"You really can't think of anyone who might be trying to send the ambassador a message by taking Lillian? Maybe someone from the past? Something Conrad was involved with back in the day? You may call yourself a *valet*, but I know you don't just lay out the old man's socks for him. You've always been his muscle. You know the score." Fitz didn't want to push too hard and have the guy clam up on him, but he needed to dig into anything Conrad Martin may have done before coming to Parker. Anything that could force someone to hold a grudge.

"We both know that some of the things going on before the embassy was shut down weren't on the up-and-up. You, of all people, should understand that." Grainger held the detective's gaze unflinchingly. "The ambassador had a lot of enemies in the Italian government by the time we left. It was the nature of his position."

"What are you suggesting, Joe? In some attempt at retaliation, Mussolini sent someone over here to kidnap the ambassador's daughter? From what I understand, he's got his hands full at the moment. Our boys are knocking on his front door."

"You're no dope, Mason. You know exactly what I mean. Lots of people could have reason to come after the ambassador."

"Alright, Joe. One last question." Fitz flicked the last bit of his cigarette into the grass. "Where were you this morning when this all went down?"

"You got it wrong, Mason. I have nothing to do with the girl's disappearance. I was helping the ambassador get ready. I was all over the house working on preparations. But I didn't see a thing. Because if I did, we wouldn't be standing here right now. I would have taken care of it right then and there."

Trying to rattle Grainger didn't shake anything loose. Which made Fitz think he was telling the truth, which he already knew. There was a long list of people who could have a grudge against Martin. But if those grudges were based solely on his diplomatic work, odds were none of those individuals kidnapped Lillian. Fitz still felt Grainger was holding out on him, and there was something more he knew about. Something that might not have related to the ambassador's official business. Something he wasn't going to talk about.

Watching Grainger march off into the house, Fitz's eye was drawn to a movement in the front window. The sun made it difficult to see exactly who it was, but when the shape moved again, he recognized the dress Lucy had been wearing. He wondered if she'd been observing the press conference from the safety of the house. When he got closer to the front door, he could see Lucy wasn't alone in the window. She seemed to be having an emotional conversation with Sydney Mercer, which ended with him putting his arms around her as she sobbed into his chest. An interesting interaction, considering how awful they'd been to one another during their interview.

Even though she was still a puzzle to him, Fitz realized after his brief exchange with her, he'd become quite partial to Lucy Martin. She was a real firecracker. But he could see through her tough exterior, she was hurting. He wanted to promise her he'd bring Lillian back, but he knew never to make a promise he wasn't one hundred percent certain he could keep.

Chapter Twenty-Three

Fitz pulled the Chrysler coupe through the gates of the Martin estate onto the road and turned towards town. Needing a more convenient means of getting around than relying on Joe to chauffeur him in the family's big limousine or having to call a cab, he'd borrowed a car from the ambassador. Conrad had a few extras sitting in the garage, so it was no imposition. Leaving word that he was on his way to see Sonny Baker, the drive gave Fitz time to think through everything he'd seen and heard in the last several hours. He also figured it was time to grab a bite to eat. His stomach was letting him know in no uncertain terms that it was well past lunchtime. Not that he thought taking the time to eat was more important than continuing his inquiry and searching for Lillian. He couldn't even begin to count the number of meals he'd skipped while on the job. But he figured it would also give him a chance to make a few telephone calls, including one to the Stride Agency in Baltimore, so he could have one of the detectives there look into Mercer-Avery and Sydney's family. Even though his gut was telling him this was all about Conrad Martin in some way, he was going to make sure he ticked all the boxes and followed up on every possible lead. That also meant looking into Martin himself, which could prove to be tricky. But he had a friend he thought might be in a position to assist him.

If Fitz stopped in at the little diner he'd been frequenting, he was afraid he'd be too distracted by the kitten who'd been waiting on him all week to concentrate on the case at hand. As much as he'd like to see that smile again and her bright blue eyes, there was work to be done. So, he decided to head back to the Parker House Hotel. The staff there wasn't as distracting.

Finding an empty parking spot right in front of the hotel's main entrance was the first lucky break he'd gotten all day. Once out of the car, he dashed into the lobby, sidestepping a woman weighed down with an armful of shopping bags and made straight for the hotel's front desk. An older gentleman with a bowtie and a neatly trimmed gray mustache was seated on a stool behind the desk, flipping through a newspaper as he approached. He'd been on duty when Fitz checked in a few days ago and had introduced himself as the manager. Fitz got the impression he was an all-around stand-up fellow, but he liked to talk.

Asking if any messages arrived for him while he was out, Fitz placed an order for a roast beef sandwich to be delivered to his room with a fresh pot of coffee. He also asked if the manager had a telephone directory he might be able to borrow.

"If there's a particular telephone number you're looking for, Mr. Hampton, I'd be happy to find it for you," the fastidious little man offered, referring to him by the alias he used when signing the registration book. "We do strive to provide our guests with the very best service here at the Parker House."

"And you and your staff have been doing a wonderful job of it, Mr. Orendorff. But the directory and a roast beef sandwich are all I require at the moment. I wouldn't imagine troubling you any further. Really, I wouldn't."

Handing over the telephone directory and promising to have the sandwich and coffee delivered presently, the manager watched as Fitz darted off, bidding him a good afternoon.

Once in his room, Fitz locked the door and went to the bathroom to splash some cold water on his face. His mind was racing, and he needed to clear his head so he could think through the events of the day. The cold water didn't help much. It never did. His mind was still doing somersaults.

As he waited for his lunch to arrive, though it was now getting closer to dinner, he sat down at the little writing desk in the corner of his room with the leather portfolio he took from his suitcase. Taking some clean sheets of paper from the folder, he began scribbling notes on everything that had happened and he'd learned throughout the day. He made notes about when

Lillian disappeared, what she was supposed to have been doing at the time, where the various individuals in the house were when she went missing. He jotted down every detail.

When he'd finished with the facts of the case, he began transcribing his interviews. Lucy was correct when she said he didn't take notes. Instead of stopping in between questions to write down what had been said, interrupting the flow, he preferred to keep the conversation moving. He didn't want to break eye contact, and he didn't want to hinder the rhythm of the interview. His goal was to keep the person talking and saying as much as he could get out of them. It was then afterwards, as he was doing now, when he'd go back over what was said and note the pertinent information. It was a system that worked well for him.

Before he was able to complete his notes, a knock at the door announced the arrival of his meal. Grateful to finally have something that he could sink his teeth into and satisfy his hunger, he happily handed over a dollar to the young man with the delivery cart. The boy's eyes grew to the size of golf balls as he began thinking of all the things he was going to spend the money on. From the door, Fitz watched the boy scurry back down the hall with a dopey grin on his face.

Rolling the small cart with his sandwich and coffee back to the desk, he finished writing up his recollections. Eventually, when the case came to its conclusion, all of these notes would end up being included in his official report. With his papers in one hand and half a sandwich in the other, Fitz reread everything he'd written, making sure he hadn't overlooked anything. Finally satisfied that his personal notes were in order, he looked at his watch. There was still plenty of time to make the call.

Pouring a second cup of coffee, he crossed the room to the telephone and clicked through to the operator.

"I would like to be connected to the War Department in Washington, please. The main switchboard is fine," he said before taking a sip of coffee.

As Fitz waited for his call to be connected, he thought about the time he'd visited the new U.S. military headquarters right after construction was completed a couple years earlier. The Pentagon building was a site to behold.

The miles of corridors, the acres of office space. It was a structure worthy of the military it represented.

His thoughts snapped back to the present when a pinched voice asked, "How may I direct your call?"

Clearing his throat, he responded, "The Executive Procurement and Resources Office, please."

"Executive Procurement and Resources Office," she repeated. "One moment."

There were several clicks, then another voice came on the line. "Executive Procurement and Resources Office."

"Yes. I'd like to be connected to the director, please."

"I'm sorry. The director is unavailable. Is there something I can help you with?"

Fitz smiled. That would be the end of the conversation if the person calling didn't then say, "Bravo seven smokescreen. This is Francis Mason calling for the director."

"One moment, please."

Another series of clicks followed, then, "Fitz! How the hell are ya? Where the hell are you? Where have you been keeping yourself?"

"I've been busy. There's a lot of nefarious doings going on out here. But I don't need to tell you that, Jerry. How are you settling into your new office?"

"It's hardly new anymore. It's been almost two years. Not that I've spent that much time here. You're lucky you caught me. I just got back from St. Petersburg and I'm getting ready to head out again. Can't tell you where, though. All hush-hush, you know."

"I understand."

"Fitz, I know you got out after what happened in London. But now that we have an operation set up here in the states, if you ever want back in, I will always have a place for you."

Lieutenant Colonel Jerold Hopkins was the head of an intelligence unit buried deep inside the War Department, separate from the other military intelligence divisions. It dealt with extremely high-level assignments, and if it had not been for the "accident" in London that ended Fitz's military service, many believed he'd be the one in charge of the Executive Procurement and Resources Office right now. But if it wasn't him, he was glad that it was Jerry. They were good friends and had worked closely together in Europe at the beginning of the war.

"Thanks, Jerry, but Uncle Sam can't afford me anymore."

"You're still buying those expensive suits, aren't you?" Jerry laughed.

"I think it's important to help safeguard the U.S. economy here at home while you're keeping an eye on our secrets abroad. Someone's got to do it."

"Fair enough. I'm guessing this isn't a social call. What can I do for you, Fitz?"

"This one's a little delicate, Jerry. I need to know if you can do me a favor and take a look at the files on former Ambassador Conrad Martin."

"Do you mean look at the files or look at *the files?*" Jerry's tone was much more serious now. Like Fitz, he knew when it was time to get down to business and be serious.

"I need to know if there was ever anything he was involved with that might not have been on the up-and-up, but that was kept under wraps because of his position."

"What's this about, Fitz? You don't normally call in favors like this."

Fitz ran through the recent events so that Hopkins could have some context for the request. If there'd been something the ambassador did while in service that pissed someone off enough to come after him all these years later, the Executive Procurement and Resources Office would know about it.

After promising to look into Martin's files and get back to him, Jerry rang off, saying he needed to get to a meeting with individuals he was not at liberty to identify. Fitz laughed, told him to pass along his regards to Admiral Leahy, and promised the two would get together soon.

Emptying the coffee urn before making his next telephone call, this time Fitz asked the operator to "Connect me with the Stride Detective Agency in Baltimore, please."

When the call went through, the voice on the other end of the line was exactly who he'd been hoping to speak with.

CHAPTER TWENTY-THREE

"Hi, doll. How's tricks?" he said into the receiver.

"Fitz! When ya comin' home? We've missed you this week."

Eleanor Straitt was Archibald Stride's Girl Friday. She kept the agency running like a well-oiled machine. If she'd been in the Army with Fitz back in the day, there was no doubt in his mind she would have been a five-star general with Eisenhower himself reporting directly to her.

"It turns out I have to stick around Parker for a little longer. Something's come up."

"The Conrad Martin thing?"

"That's the one. But if you miss me so much, you could always jump on the next train and come see me."

"Francis Mason, you devil. You know I would but I don't think Philip would know what to do alone with the kids."

"Why are all the good ones married?" Fitz asked.

It was the type of conversation the two had on a regular basis. They were good friends, as were Fitz and Philip, so there was no talk that Fitz was seriously trying to get Eleanor to run away with him. They all knew the score. It was just some harmless fun. If anything, Eleanor was always asking if she could set him up with one of her single friends. She was praying for the day Fitz found himself a nice girl to settle down with.

"What can I do for you?" Fitz could hear her fingers working the keys of her typewriter as she spoke.

"I need some background. Can you have O'Brien do some digging on Mercer-Avery and the Mercer family? Make sure they're on the up-and-up. Send him to City Hall and make sure they aren't in any trouble with any of their buildings. Make sure no one's trying to squeeze them."

"Or the other way around?" Eleanor offered.

"Exactly. If anyone might be trying to hurt Sydney Mercer from out there, I want to know about it."

"No problem, Fitz. O'Brien will definitely be able to find out if there's any dirt to be dug up. I have a friend in the mayor's office I can call, too. If there's anything hinky with the Mercers, he'll know."

"Thanks, doll. You're aces," Fitz said as he hung up the telephone.

Chapter Twenty-Four

The next call Fitz placed was to the residence of Wilson Baker. Using the directory borrowed from Mr. Orendorff at the front desk, he wasn't surprised to see Senator Baker's address and telephone number listed. It was no secret where the Baker family lived. They were one of the city's five founding families. All of whom were extremely wealthy and extremely powerful. And all of whom lived next door to one another in magnificent old mansions along Grandview Avenue with beautiful views of Jefferson Park.

Fitz remembered playing ball with his friends in the expansive park when he was a child and seeing the houses across the road. They all looked like castles to him when he was little. Come to think of it, they still did, even though he was much older now. Sometimes, one's perspective changes as they grow, literally and figuratively. But not in this case. All five of the estates loomed over the park and the rest of the city beyond.

The older gentleman who answered the telephone at the Baker residence informed Fitz that Sonny was not at home and did not know when he would be returning. When asked where he might be found, the man—who identified himself as the Baker's butler-said he could not provide that information.

"Are you saying you can't say where he is? Or you don't know?" Fitz inquired.

"I am saying that even if I did know where he was at the present moment, young Master Baker's privacy is of the utmost importance, and I would not share it with a stranger. Now, if you will excuse me, I must be—"

Fitz didn't want him to hang up. "This is regarding a serious matter. I am calling on behalf of the Parker City Police Department, and I need to speak with *young Master Baker*." It was just a little white lie, Fitz thought.

There was a moment of hesitation on the other end of the line. Then, "The police? Well. I… I guess that would change the circumstances. Unfortunately, I don't know where he is at the moment. He just said that he made dinner plans and would be out this evening. Master Baker does come and go quite a bit."

Fitz was glad the butler wasn't able to see him roll his eyes. "When was the last time you saw him?"

"Not very long ago. Just before he went out."

"Has he been home all day?"

"I'm not sure I should be–"

"Listen, Mack. I'm calling about a crime that took place earlier today. You're going to read about it in the paper tomorrow morning. Mr. Baker might be able to help us out here. That means I need some answers. Now, was he there all day before he went out for dinner?"

Again, there was a pause. "No. He went out first thing this morning after breakfast was served. Then he returned home several hours later."

"Did he say where he'd been?"

"No. And I didn't ask. It's none of my concern."

So, Sonny had gone out in the morning. Could he have gone to the Martins' to try and talk to Lillian? Did things get out of hand? But if kidnapping Lillian Martin was a spur-of-the-moment idea, then why did he have a handkerchief dosed with chloroform? That's not something one just carries around with them *in case* they need to use it. Lillian's kidnapping was planned. Even if the descriptions of Sonny Baker he'd been given didn't add up to the type of person capable of committing a kidnapping, Fitz still needed to speak with him.

Lightening his tone somewhat, Fitz asked, "When Sonny goes out for dinner, what is his favorite restaurant?"

"I'm sure I don't know."

"You seem like the type of fella who knows a lot more than he lets on, my friend." Trying to coax information out of someone usually worked better in person. Fitz had no idea if his usual tactics would also work over the phone. But he pressed on regardless. "That's probably why you're so invaluable to the family. You know what they like and how they like it. If I had to guess, I'd say they rely on you more than anyone realizes. And you most likely pick things up. Like what food they like most and where they enjoy eating."

"I have been with the Baker family for quite some time. That is true. Mister… I'm sorry. I don't believe I got your name?"

"Fitz Mason."

"And you're a detective with the Parker City police?"

"I'm a detective. Yes. And I'm really hoping you will be able to help me."

"Well, I do know that, as of late, young Mr. Baker has been dining quite frequently at La Cucina. It's a new Italian restaurant. I believe it's on High Street."

That was going to make things easy. Fitz remembered seeing the sign for the restaurant just a few blocks away. After thanking the man for his assistance, as reluctant as it was, Fitz hung up the telephone. He thought it was a good time to take a little walk. Right down the street to see if, by some chance, Sonny Baker was dining at his new favorite ristorante.

After adjusting the holster under his arm so it fit just a little more snuggly, Fitz grabbed his jacket and hat from where he'd laid them on the bed. Casting his eyes around the room to see if there was anything else he thought he should take with him, he pushed the small room service cart into the hall and locked the door behind him.

Chapter Twenty-Five

After returning the directory to the hotel's front desk and managing to avoid being drawn into a long discussion with Mr. Orendorff about absolutely nothing of any significance, Fitz stepped outside, ready to go in search of Sonny Baker. If he was, in fact, dining at La Cucina, the restaurant was not far down the street from the hotel, so Fitz opted for an evening stroll. As the sun was eyeing the horizon, the detective found himself enjoying the fresh air and atmosphere surrounding him. It was Saturday night and young couples were starting to appear as their evenings were just beginning.

The last few days in Parker City had brought back a flood of memories. Things he hadn't thought about in years, he now found himself reliving. Passing Riggler's Menswear, the venerable clothing store that had been a part of the city for generations, Fitz was suddenly taken back to the day his mother took him into the shop to purchase his first "big boy" suit. His mother couldn't have known then that the blue Riggler's Youth Special was going to one day lead to a former Army intelligence officer turned Stride agent having a closet that rivaled the store's front showroom. Fitz smiled thinking about his mother and the fussing she did over that blue suit. If she were still alive and ever found out he now had ties that cost more than that first suit, he couldn't even imagine the grief she would give him.

As a relatively successful attorney, Fitz's father made a decent living. The Masons were by no means "rich," but they were certainly comfortable. They would have been the poster family for today's upper middle class. Even when the stock market crashed in '29, it didn't seem to affect his family in the same way it did so many others. Fitz was twenty-three at the time and already in the Army, but his younger brothers never went without. They'd all been taught by their parents to be grateful for their good fortune and that it could all disappear one day. An idea that remained with Fitz. He knew how lucky he and his family had been. Which is why whenever he'd buy himself a new bespoke suit or fancy pair of Italian leather loafers, he'd make sure to put a little something extra in the charity box on Sunday after mass.

Fitz enjoyed dinner with his youngest brother the previous evening and was happy to see John and Irene were doing so well. John followed in their father's footsteps and became a lawyer, now working at the same firm where their old man had been a partner all those years ago. He was a legacy and, according to the discussion they had over chicken and rice, was on track to become a partner in the not-too-distant future. While John was spending his days in court, Irene was making the two a beautiful home. Fitz definitely wanted to try to get back to Parker more often to see them. It would be a lot easier than trying to catch up with their middle brother, Bobby, who'd moved out to Los Angeles years earlier.

A sudden chilling breeze caught Fitz off-guard and snapped him out of his thoughts and back to the present. He was on the hunt for Sonny Baker. Pulling the collar of his jacket up around his neck, he crossed the street and saw the restaurant in front of him on the corner. It looked like the American version of an Italian restaurant. Fitz had had the luxury of being able to enjoy the real thing for years, so finding a "true" authentic Italian bistro in the States was difficult. The closer he got to the front door, though, the more he realized the smells emanating from the kitchen came very close to some of his favorite eateries in Rome.

Looking through the windows, he could see the dining room was filled with diners of all ages. La Cucina appeared to be a popular new place. As he was about to step inside, the door next to the restaurant caught his attention. A very unassuming sign read SMOKEY JOE'S. A bar, judging by the sound that burst onto the street when a man exited and made his way down the street in the direction from which Fitz had just come.

Thinking for a moment, Fitz decided to follow his gut and headed for the bar. Something was telling him he was going to find Sonny in Smokey Joe's. A young man with Sonny Baker's reputation was more likely to be drinking in a bar than dining at the same little Italian restaurant night after night.

Opening the large wooden door, Fitz found himself in a long hallway. Judging by the crown molding along the ceiling and the delicate wallpaper, this wasn't the typical gin joint. At the end of the hall, he could hear a buzz of voices and the clinking of glasses. It might look a lot nicer than many of the bars he'd seen, but it sounded the same.

Stepping out of the hallway, Fitz was in a large room with an enormous carved wooden bar, highly polished, running the length of the wall in front of him. A good thirty or forty feet long. Behind it, five barmen in tuxedos kept the drinks flowing while cute little numbers in French maid uniforms circulated among the tables. It took Fitz a moment to realize the whistle he just heard had come from him. At first blush, this was his sort of place. Big leather chairs around mahogany tables, some booths along the back wall for privacy. And at one end of the room, a small stage with a house band playing some swinging jazz number.

This joint was jumping.

There wasn't an empty seat in the place, and the bar was stacked three people deep to get drinks. The place reminded Fitz of a few spots he knew of during Prohibition. Not that he *ever* challenged the Eighteenth Amendment...that anyone could prove.

"Parker City has come a long way," he said under his breath as he scanned the room.

The crowd was a little on the younger side, making Fitz realize there was a chance he might be one of the oldest people in the room. Which gave him pause, considering he was only thirty-nine. This little gem seemed to be where all the cool cats and kittens hung out on Saturday night.

As one of the waitresses passed by, Fitz caught her attention and asked, "Any chance you've seen Sonny Baker in here tonight, doll face?"

He didn't know if the smile that followed was because of his charm or the dollar he'd laid on her tray. Wishing for the former, he knew it was the latter. If nothing else, Fitz knew the score. When she spoke, her voice was breathy and beyond seductive.

"Sonny's in the corner booth over there. His favorite spot. Can I get you something to drink, handsome?"

"Scotch and soda. Hold the ice and hold the soda." Fitz winked.

"I'll bring it over to Sonny's table for you," she said and disappeared into the crowd surrounding the bar.

Straightening his tie, Fitz wound his way to the back of the bar to where he'd been directed. Sure enough, sitting in the corner booth was an attractive young man. Blonde, trim, an attitude that said he could do nothing wrong. Fitz had never laid eyes on Sonny Baker before, but he knew this was the kid he was looking for.

Chapter Twenty-Six

Sliding into the circular booth, Sonny was taken by surprise at Fitz's sudden appearance across from him. He most certainly was not the person Sonny was waiting for. That message was written all over his face.

"Sorry, bub. But I think you've got the wrong table." There was no malice in the young man's voice, just an air of detachment.

"If you're Sonny Baker, then I'm right where I'm supposed to be." Pulling his Stride Detective Agency identification from his pocket, he flashed his private investigator badge. "I need to have a few words with you."

"I don't know who you are, Mister, but I'm not talking to some private *dick*."

"Sonny. Don't be that way. And you know who I am. Fitz Mason. It says right there on the card. Or did I just unwittingly stumble onto the deep, dark secret that you don't know how to read? You don't have to worry. I'm good at keeping secrets."

"Listen here! I know how to read, wise guy. I meant… It doesn't matter what I meant. If you're not outta here in two seconds, I'm gonna have the bouncers throw you out on your ear. I don't care who you are. I'm not gonna talk to you."

"Oh. I think you will," Fitz said as Sonny began to push himself out of the booth.

"And why's that?"

"Because I need to talk to you about Lillian Martin's disappearance." Fitz said it so calmly that Sonny was immediately caught off guard, causing him to stop and stare at the detective with wide eyes. Was that a look of genuine confusion on his face?

"Lillian's disappearance? What are you talking about?" he asked, sliding back down into his seat. "She got married this morning. The wedding's all anyone's been able to talk about for weeks."

"You haven't heard?" Fitz was playing things cool. "Lillian Martin went missing before the wedding. I thought word would have gotten back to you by now. Parker's not *that* big a city. And that kind of news tends to travel pretty fast."

"I haven't heard anything. I don't believe it. What happened?"

His reaction played as sincere, as if this really were the first he was hearing about it. But Fitz had seen that act before, so wasn't ready to let him off the hook just yet. Deciding to play along, Fitz filled him in on the events of the morning. Carefully watching him, Sonny was hanging on every word. He didn't even break eye contact when he reached into his pocket and pulled out a pack of Lucky Strikes and lit up, without even offering one to Fitz. Very rude, Fitz thought. Then, as the detective was coming to the end of his part in the play, the waitress popped up at his elbow with his scotch, just as he'd requested.

"Perfect timing." Fitz gave her his best smile. "Why don't you bring another for my friend, Sonny."

Happy to oblige, she returned Fitz's smile and darted toward the bar, hoping the classy gentleman was a good tipper.

Turning back to Sonny, Fitz asked, "So…why don't we start with you telling me where you were this morning?"

"Why? Wait! Do you think I had something to do with this?"

"Everyone always asks that question. I didn't say that, now, did I?"

"Why else would you be here looking for me?" Sonny used the end of his first cigarette to light another. Still not offering any to Fitz. "Why would you think I had something to do with this?"

"According to the people closest to Lillian, you weren't very happy when she broke up with you. There was something about you making a scene at the cinema one night…" Fitz trailed off, waiting to see how Sonny responded. While he waited, using the pause to make the kid uncomfortable, he pointedly took a slug of his drink and stared him down. Silence was the friend of a good interrogator. In Fitz's experience, it was more useful than threats and tough talk.

"Alright," Sonny said, running his hand through his thick hair. "Alright. Yeah. When Lillian started making eyes at Sid during my father's Christmas party, I thought she was just trying to make me jealous. I might have been spending too much time with Ilona Donovan that night. But we've known each other since we were kids. It wasn't anything. But then when Lillian went and broke up with me and started going with Sid…yeah, I got angry. I might have said some things when I ran into them at the pictures one night. But it was only a week or two later, so I was still pretty angry. I've moved on. Lillian was just another filly as far as I'm concerned."

"How did you feel when Lillian's engagement was announced only a couple months after you'd broken up?"

"I didn't much care because I'd already started going with someone else. It's not like I thought Lillian and I were ever going to get married."

Fitz leaned back against the soft leather cushion and took a hard look at the guy. Sonny Baker was the epitome of a spoiled rich kid. He felt entitled and acted tough until the cards were on the table, and then he broke and let you see he really was just a petulant child who had grown too accustomed to always getting his way. Classic story Fitz knew all too well.

There was an obvious difference between Sonny Baker and Sydney Mercer. If Lillian was looking for the type of guy who was going to be a good husband and father, Mercer was the odds-on favorite. Sonny, Fitz could tell just from speaking with him for a few minutes, was the kind who got bored quickly and never took anything too seriously. Why should he? There'd always been someone around to clean up his mess.

It never took Fitz long to size a man up. And after the number of assignments he'd been on, both for the military and then for the Stride Agency, he'd seen every kind there was. There really were only so many types of men and he knew each one of them, their strengths, their weaknesses. It was his ability to read people that made him such a good operator. Eleanor, back at the office, once said that if he ever got tired of being a private detective, he could hang a shingle out and become a psychoanalyst.

After the silence between them reached its peak, Fitz asked again, "So where were you this morning? And don't try giving me the line you were at home all morning. I already know you weren't. Your butler told me you went out. Don't be too hard on the fella. He may have been under the impression I was with the police when we spoke, and he was just trying to do his civic duty."

Sonny sat chewing on his lower lip until the cute waitress returned with the drink Fitz had ordered for him. He downed the entire glass, then used the back of his sleeve to wipe his mouth. Fitz wondered how big the kid's bar tab was that evening, considering there were already three empty glasses sitting on the table. All of which disappeared when the waitress scooped them up and headed back into the sea of bargoers.

Leaning forward, Sonny put his hands on the table and looked Fitz square in the eyes.

"I didn't have anything to do with Lillian going missing. I don't even remember the last time I saw her. As far as I'm concerned, she was just another bit of skirt. I moved on. But this morning…this morning I was out shopping for a birthday present for my mother."

That was the first time Fitz ever heard that one as an alibi.

Sonny fished around in his jacket pockets for a moment and pulled out several pieces of paper. Uncrumpling them, he found the one he was looking for and handed it over to Fitz. It was a bill of sale, dated that day, from a shop on Commerce Street. Fitz would need to check exactly when he'd been there, but this only enforced the feeling he already had that Sonny Baker wasn't involved. He couldn't say he liked the guy very much, but he was no kidnapper.

Chapter Twenty-Seven

The walk back to the hotel chilled Fitz to the bone. As he'd been poking and prodding Sonny Baker, trying to see if the kid was involved with his ex-girl's disappearance, the temperature outside took a nosedive. If nothing else, the cold air helped to clear Fitz's head. But by the time he ducked into the lobby of the Parker House Hotel, he could barely feel his cheeks. For the last week, the weather was exquisite. Beautiful spring temperatures and plenty of sun. Now, it felt like Parker was back in the middle of winter.

The warmth of the lobby felt good around him as he rubbed his hands together to get the circulation flowing. Several others standing near the door were doing the same. A pretty blonde smiled at Fitz when their eyes met. In turn, the detective, ever the gentleman, tipped his hat in her direction, then watched as she sauntered into the hotel bar, her hips swinging back and forth in an exaggerated fashion. Fitz knew it was for his benefit when she slowed to glance over her shoulder to make sure he was enjoying the show.

Even though his blood was now pumping thanks to the platinum doll, he still needed to stamp his feet a few times to get the feeling back in his toes. Fitz then stopped at the front desk to ask if he'd received any messages. As the young man behind the counter checked the box for his room, Fitz looked around at the other people milling about the lobby. For a moment, he thought about ducking into the bar for another drink and, maybe accidentally, on purpose, bumping into the blonde. But his better angels prevailed, and he decided he'd rather head up to his room and try to get some shut-eye. It had been a long day, and he didn't feel like he'd made enough progress on the case. It was no surprise that everyone he'd spoken with said they had nothing to do with Lillian's disappearance. His job would be a hell of a lot easier if the bad guy just automatically confessed.

The hotel clerk returned to the desk with a telegram.

Opening the envelope, Fitz saw it was from Eleanor Straitt. According to her friend in the Baltimore mayor's office and the quick work O'Brien was able to do, Mercer-Avery was a stand-up company and was not involved in anything shady that anyone knew of. There were also no outstanding grievances between them and anyone else, other than some of the usual neighborhood groups unhappy that the company tore down older buildings to make way for their new skyscrapers.

Seeing another dead end, Fitz folded the telegram and tucked it into his pocket. If Sydney Mercer and his company were clean and no one was trying to get at them, it had to be about the Martins. Fitz was certain of it now. He needed to start focusing his attention on the ambassador and his family.

Starting toward the elevators, Fitz slowed his pace as an uneasy feeling gripped him. Casting his eyes over the lobby one more time, he was looking for anyone who seemed out of place. Anyone who might be paying him too much attention. He was feeling as though someone was watching him. After years spent operating in the shadows and trying to stay invisible, he'd become skilled in the art of following targets. In turn, he knew how to tell when someone was on his tail. But no one in the lobby appeared suspicious. Which only served to make Fitz feel even more uneasy.

For the briefest of moments, he reconsidered popping into the bar for a nightcap. But again, he decided it was better to go straight to his room and start fresh in the morning. Plus, he wanted to jot down some notes on his time with Sonny Baker while they were still fresh in his mind.

Riding the elevator up to his floor, Fitz listened to an elderly couple complain about the dinner they'd just come from. A retirement do for the woman's brother-in-law. She couldn't stop talking about how bad the food was and how they'd traveled all the way from Philadelphia for some dry chicken. And she couldn't understand why her sister wore *that* dress to the retirement dinner. Fitz held the brim of his hat over his mouth to mask the smile on his face. He found the woman's dissatisfaction with every aspect of the evening extremely humorous. As for her husband, he looked as though he'd stopped listening to her years earlier.

Fitz was still smiling to himself when he opened the door to his room.

As the light from the hall cut into the open doorway, Fitz paused. A plain white envelope lay on the floor just inside his room.

Fitz tossed his hat on the bed and switched on the lamp next to the door. Turning the envelope over in his hands, he saw that it bore no writing or markings of any kind. Taking the small switch knife he carried with him from his pocket, he cut the envelope open and carefully extracted the single piece of paper folded inside. He didn't need to read the words, which looked to have all been cut from a newspaper, to know he was holding a ransom note.

Chapter Twenty-Eight

1985 . . .

The silence filling the room was suffocating as Ben and Tommy tried to fully grasp what Betty just told them. Tommy's uncle had been brought in to find a girl who'd gone missing on her wedding day, only to be found and then have her sister disappear...and remain missing for forty years. That is, if the body they'd found in the field was in fact that of Lucy Martin.

Before either of the detectives could think of what question, to begin with—so many were fighting for first position—the telephone on Ben's desk rang, jarring all of them. Ben, who would have been more than happy to let it ring so the conversation wasn't interrupted and they could all stay on track, watched as Betty casually picked up the receiver with the same hand she held her cigarette.

"Detective Sergeant Ben Winters's office. This is Betty speaking. How can I help you?" There was a pause as she listened to the voice on the other end. "He's right here. Hang on a second, hun." Handing the telephone over to Ben, she announced, "It's the medical examiner."

Ben sighed. They'd been waiting all morning for just one break so they could begin figuring out who Jane Doe was and from where she'd come, and in a matter of minutes, CSU delivered its report; Betty had, presumably, identified the body by sheer luck, and now the Medical Examiner's Office was on the line. It would have been nice if all of these things had spread themselves out so he could take in all of the information bit by bit instead of being bombarded with it all at once.

"This is Ben Winters," he said into the receiver.

"Hello, Detective. I'm Doctor Mark Chen, the state's deputy medical examiner. My boss asked me to give you a call personally about the female that came in yesterday. We've all taken an interest in this one. Never seen anything like it."

"It doesn't seem like anyone around here has," Ben agreed, rubbing his eyes with his free hand. If one more person said that to him…

"Sorry no one was able to telephone you sooner. But we wanted to make sure we did this right. After speaking with some colleagues, we've determined the best way to thaw the body so we can do a proper examination. We began the process a couple hours ago and we're expecting it to take thirty-six to forty-eight hours. It's going well so far, but we want to make sure we take the time we need, so we don't do any damage and are able to perform a thorough and complete post-mortem."

"I appreciate that, Doctor Chen."

Ben was momentarily distracted by Tommy waving his hands around in the air to get his attention. Finally, he mouthed the word 'what' to his partner. Tommy pointed to his fingertips, then pressed them against his arm and chest. From her vantage point at Ben's desk, Betty had no clue what kind of charades the two detectives were playing, but Ben knew exactly what his partner was saying. That frightened him a little.

"Doctor," he said, "by any chance, were you able to find any fingerprints on the body itself before you started the thawing process?"

Tommy sat rubbing a finger along his mustache with an eager look on his face. If it weren't for the mustache, he could have passed for a child waiting for his father to tell him they were going to Disneyland, he looked so excited.

After listening to the doctor's response, Ben turned to Tommy and shook his head. He watched as Tommy's lips puckered, and he slumped back in his chair with his arms crossed over his chest. Now he looked like a child who was just told they *weren't* going to Disneyland. To try and take Tommy's mind off his minor defeat, Ben grabbed a piece of paper and scribbled a note on it, asking his partner to go get the chief. Ben knew he was going to want to hear everything they'd learned.

Reading the note, then crumbling it up and throwing it in the trashcan, Tommy sighed and left to inform Chief Brent a lot had happened in the few minutes since they'd seen him in the break room.

"Speaking of fingerprints, Detective," Chen began, "we were able to pull a couple of usable prints to identify the girl. Sorry. I guess I should have led with that. Here's where it gets strange. Well…stranger…I guess you could say. We have identified her as one Lucille Abigail Martin. But…she went missing in 1945."

Ben sighed. Doctor Chen confirmed exactly what Betty had just told them. Ben quickly informed the doctor that they'd just come across some information that would support that identification, as odd as it may sound, and they were piecing things together.

Asking to be kept updated on the thawing process, Ben thanked the doctor again and said he would wait to hear from him further. After hanging up, Ben walked over to Tommy's desk and sat down. Leaning forward, he rested his head in his hands, rubbing his eyes to try and stave off the headache he felt gathering strength at the base of his skull.

Lucy Martin disappeared in 1945. Forty years ago. Her body, currently in Baltimore with the State's Chief Medical Examiner, had been identified because she looked exactly as she did when she went missing. According to Betty. That meant she died or was murdered–which was yet to be determined–sometime around her disappearance. What disturbed Ben the most was that regardless of the girl's cause of death, someone had kept her on ice for all those years.

Chapter Twenty-Nine

Ben felt as though he were performing a song and dance as he brought Chief Brent up to speed on the rapid developments of the case. All crammed into the Detective Squad's small office, the eyes of Tommy, Brent, and Betty were all on the PCPD's lead detective as he walked through all of the information they now possessed, even though it was only slightly more than they had a short time earlier. Unfortunately, the new information brought with it more questions than answers. Betty, never shy in the company of the department's top brass, continued to chime in with minor details as she'd remember them. While Brent, on the other hand, remained silent and stone-faced, leaning against the doorframe with his arms crossed as Ben spoke.

When Ben completed his overview of the case so far—a bead of sweat running down the back of his neck—the chief looked him square in the eyes and said, "So, just to recap...so I understand... The body that was discovered in the field yesterday...the body that was frozen solid, is now being defrosted out in Baltimore and has been identified as Lucille Martin, who went missing in 1945 following the disappearance and reappearance of her older sister Lillian Martin. But until the body thaws out, we do not have a cause of death. And, taking into account the appearance of the body—her looking like Betty remembers she looked forty years ago—we're thinking she's been in a freezer all that time but have no idea where. Did I get all of that right?

"On top of that, Detective Mason's uncle was involved with Lillian Martin's case, and you have his notes."

"In a nutshell," Tommy confirmed. Then, in his usual smart-ass style, said,

"I think it all sounds pretty straightforward if you ask me."

Both the chief and Ben responded to the quip with the same disapproving look.

"Come on!" Tommy said, throwing his arms into the air. "You've got to wonder what the hell is going on in Parker City. Or is it just us? That we attract these kinds of cases! This can't be normal. And this one takes the cake!" he said, stabbing a finger at the photos of Lucy Martin lying on Ben's desk.

He wasn't wrong. The consensus in the room was that, even taking into account their earlier cases, which had drawn a great deal of attention, this one really was beyond unusual. Sure, they'd solved a twenty-year-old murder once. But that was by accident. Someone had literally fallen on top of a skeleton that was never meant to be found. Lucy's frozen body was left in the middle of a field specifically to be found. Presumably. *After forty years*!

Where had she been for four decades?

Ben wanted some time to look through the file Fitz Mason had put together, which now lived in his partner's desk drawer. While he did that, he asked Tommy to head down to the Records Room with Betty and take an official statement from her since she was technically the person who'd IDed the body. He wanted everything she could remember written down so they could review it later. He also asked them to pull the original case file from 1945, assuming it still existed.

Left alone with Brent, the chief told Ben he'd be in his office and that they'd need to talk again before the day was out. The department was going to need to prepare a statement for the press. They may not have gotten wind of the story yet, but when they learned the body of an ambassador's daughter who'd been missing for forty years was now at the medical examiner's office being defrosted, there were going to be questions. Lots of questions.

"You're going to have to inform the family," Brent added. "That needs to happen before anything goes out to the press. Have you ever heard of Conrad Martin? I don't feel like his name has ever come up in all the years I've been in Parker. You'd think if he was someone so important, we'd have heard of him."

"Forty years is a long time. He could have died before you moved here, or Tommy and I were even born. The family could have moved away. We'll have to find out. But the name Lillian Martin is ringing a bell for some reason. Like I just saw her name recently. I'm just not sure where."

"Stop by my office before you punch out for the day. I'm going to go let the mayor know we've identified our Jane Doe and that it may cause a stir when the news breaks. I'll also put on a fresh pot of coffee," Brent said as he left the office. "I can tell you're going to need some."

Running his hands through his hair, Ben looked around the room. Not exactly sure what he was expecting to see that he didn't see every day. He just needed to collect his thoughts and make a plan for moving forward.

Picking up the stack of crime scene photos that Betty had continued to thumb through while sitting at his desk, he taped the close-up of Lucy Martin's face to the chalkboard he and Tommy used to visually organize their investigations and wrote under it: FORTY YEARS?

Then, retrieving the old file folder from Tommy's desk, he sat down at his own and began going through each of the pieces of paper. He didn't make any of his own notes. He wanted to go through the entire file once just to see what was there. Then he'd go over it all again with more focus. And have Tommy do the same.

What Ben found odd was the entire file was about Lillian Martin. According to the notes, Tommy's uncle was brought in as a favor to Conrad Martin when she was kidnapped on her wedding day. The two knew each other during the war, and Fitz Mason had a reputation for being a top-notch private investigator. He was one of the Stride Agency's best. But there was no mention of Lucy's disappearance. The case file ended with the report on Lillian's return.

Could there be missing pages? Or a second file, Ben wondered.

Walking over to Tommy's desk, he reached down to open the drawer from which his partner had produced the file, then stopped. These weren't his files to be going through, and it wasn't his desk to go poking around in. He'd wait until Tommy got back to have him look through the folders to see if there were any more references to the Martins.

As he slumped back into his own chair, he stared up at the ceiling, trying to remember why the name Lillian Martin sounded familiar. Then it came to him. He *had* just seen the name recently.

Wanting to confirm what he was thinking, he flipped through the handwritten pages in Fitz's file and saw the notes the private detective made about his conversation with Lillian's fiancé the day they were supposed to get married. His name was Sydney Mercer. His family owned Mercer-Avery, the construction company in Baltimore. Ben knew exactly where he'd seen the woman's name before. He was certain.

Pushing himself up from his desk, he jogged out of the office and down the hall to the break room. Noting that the chief was good to his word, he found there was a full pot of coffee sitting on the coffee machine. But the caffeine would have to wait for the moment. Ben went straight to the metal rack sitting by the window and started rifling through the stack of newspapers that had accumulated over the last week. Finding the one he was looking for, a copy of the *Baltimore Sun*, he spread the pages out on the small break room table.

Sydney Mercer passed away at the end of the previous week, and there was an article about him and his career in the paper. Ben had only skimmed the piece when he first saw it, but one of the bits he did read was that the construction mogul left behind a window, Lillian Martin Mercer.

Chapter Thirty

"I remember all the stories he used to tell us when we were kids," Tommy was saying as he looked through the rest of his uncle's files. "He was like a real-life James Bond. Well, at least that's what he seemed like when we were ten."

"I remember you thinking the same thing about him when we were twenty," Ben pointed out.

"You thought he was cool too! Don't try and deny it."

"I'm not. He *was* cool. To this day, I've never known anyone like him. There was just something about him. He was… I don't even know. He was like a movie star and a secret agent all rolled into one. Remember how we always got so worked up when he would start to tell us about one of his cases, then have to stop because the rest was *top secret?*"

"That would drive me crazy! And he knew it. I think that was why he did it."

"To torture two little kids?" Ben laughed.

Tommy closed another of the well-worn file folders and laid it aside, saying, "Looking through some of these papers, I don't think he was just stringing us along. These are just his personal files that he kept with copies of notes and things. There are some big name companies in here. Some vague references to government agencies and people in those government agencies. There are definitely things in here I could see leading to very confidential information."

"I don't think something can be *very* confidential. It either is, or it isn't."

Tommy leaned back in his chair with an exaggerated huff. "Now, why do you have to go and do that? We're having a nice stroll down memory lane talking about Uncle Fitz and how incredible he was and then you go and turn into the grammar police."

"We can still reminisce. But there's no reason we can't do it using correct grammar," Ben argued. "I feel Uncle Fitz would agree with me. He certainly would about wearing suits to work."

"Hey! That's a low blow." Tommy thought for a moment. "But you're probably right. I can't remember ever seeing him wearing anything but a suit."

"And those shiny shoes of his," Ben added.

"I know. He must have spent hours polishing them."

Fitz Mason was a hero to little Ben and Tommy. Whenever he'd come to Parker for a visit, in addition to taking them out for ice cream or a movie, he'd tell them stories. Some were about his days in the Army. Though most of his military assignments were classified, there were always one or two details he could share. He knew the boys would use their imaginations to fill in the rest. Frankly, some of the things he'd done would have been beyond the imagination of two young boys. Even some grown men would have a difficult time dreaming up some of the scenarios in which he'd found himself.

His stretch with the Stride Detective Agency, which had come to an end by the time the boys were old enough to understand the kind of work with which he'd been involved, was a little easier to discuss. But even some of those assignments dealt with secrets he couldn't reveal. Leaving large parts that needed to be omitted from his tales.

Even though he wasn't a police officer, there was still something about his job that made both Ben and Tommy enamored by the idea of growing up and having a life in law enforcement. They could have just followed in Fitz's footsteps and joined the military or become private detectives, but they both went to the police academy.

Fitz was so proud of both of them the day they joined the Parker City Police Department. Tommy was very vocal about being his uncle's favorite nephew, though Fitz would never confirm that. But everyone knew the two shared a special bond. They both loved adventures and had the kind of personality that made them seem larger than life. While Ben was slightly more reserved, the audacious spirit in him always flared when Fitz was around. Being that the boys were practically joined at the hip, Fitz came to look at Ben as another of his nephews.

He'd seen the two grown-up men he loved so much become police officers, but sadly, Fitz didn't make it to the day they were promoted to detectives. He died just a couple years too soon after having lived a life worthy of his own series of private detective novels. That's when Tommy's aunt asked if he wanted his uncle's old papers. She thought they should go to someone who would keep them safe but also appreciate the work he'd done.

As he closed the last file that was in the accordion folder, Tommy looked over at Ben and said, "There are no more papers talking about the Martins. Lucy, Lillian, or Conrad. None of them. The only case file he had was on *Lillian's* disappearance.

"I have another box of his things at home I can look through. But it's more like his old switchblade, one of his fedoras, a lighter, some business cards. Personal stuff like that. I actually think there might be a set of brass knuckles in there, too."

"If Fitz was working on the Lillian case and then Lucy went missing, why wasn't he a part of that too," Ben wondered. "Were the two disappearances related? It would help if we had the original case file."

Upon Tommy's return from his jaunt to the Records Room with Betty, he informed Ben that they had a problem. Not what Ben wanted to hear. While they were able to locate the PCPD's original file on the Lillian Martin kidnapping, slim as it was, Lucy's case file was empty. Ben immediately wondered if someone purposefully removed the contents of the file. The two had run into that in the past. But Tommy told him a large number of the files in that particular cabinet were missing their content. Betty confirmed that the records before the mid-fifties were spotty at best. Lots of folders with nothing inside them. Prior to Betty's arrival, record storage was not a high priority. Paperwork from the first half of the century did not fare very well. She was surprised they'd been able to find Lillian Martin's file. If something was important enough, the old PCPD bosses assumed the county's prosecutors would hold onto it. They were happy to pass the responsibility off to someone else.

"I guess we'll just have to ask Lillian Martin about what happened," Tommy thought out loud.

"Lillian Martin *Mercer*," Ben corrected. "I have the duty sergeant running down her address for us so we can let her know we've found her sister."

"She's not in Parker?"

"No. The article about Mercer said they lived outside of Baltimore. No specifics."

"Looks like we'll be taking a little road trip then. Any luck on the parents?" Doing some quick math in his head, Tommy said, "They'd be pretty old by now, though. In their eighties or nineties."

"That I do have an answer to. After I found the article about Mercer's death and knew where to start looking for Lillian, I made a call to the State Department. I took a shot that someone there might actually be helpful."

Tommy raised an eyebrow. "Were they?"

"After I explained who I was to about fifteen different people that I kept getting bounced around to," Ben continued, "I was able to learn that both Ambassador Conrad Martin and Norma Martin passed away back in the '70s."

Ben was tapping the edge of his notebook on the top of his desk. Then, looking at his watch, he said he was going to check in with Chief Brent to see if he'd been able to come up with a statement for the press. There was no way they'd release any information to the public until Lillian Martin was notified of the discovery of her sister's body, but they needed to have all the pieces in place. Judging by the time, though, he doubted they'd be making any notification that evening. Unless they wanted to head out to Baltimore and ruin a widow's dinner.

Chapter Thirty-One

1945 . . .

The sheet of paper with the mismatched words cut from a newspaper felt like a fifty-pound weight in his hand. Reading the ransom note for the third time, Fitz couldn't help but wonder why the kidnapper decided to deliver the demand to him and not directly to the ambassador. On top of that, how did the kidnapper even know who Fitz was or that he was involved in the case? That information wouldn't be widely known until the morning papers hit the street. The only people who knew of his involvement were the people who'd been at the Martins' home that day: the family, Sydney Mercer, Joe Grainger, the police, and a handful of reporters. It was possible word of a Stride Agent working the case was beginning to spread because of the reporters, even if the papers hadn't gone to print yet. People in a newsroom talk, and those people talk to more people.

Was the kidnapper inside "the circle" of those closest to the disappearance?

More troubling was the fact the kidnapper not only knew that Fitz was staying at the Parker House Hotel, but specifically in which room. How could he know that? Considering he was registered under the alias of Francis *Hampton.* That information was known by even fewer people. In fact, Fitz could count the number on one hand. Two of those people were in Baltimore. And there was no way Fitz was going to consider either Archibald Stride or Eleanor Straitt as possible suspects.

By delivering the ransom note to him, the kidnapper could have made a grave mistake; he thought as he looked at the envelope again for any markings. No matter how closely he examined it, a plain white envelope stared back at him. There was nothing remarkable about it whatsoever. Now that he knew what had been in it, he was doing his best to hold the envelope by the edges so he wouldn't add any more fingerprints than he already had. He wanted to give the police the best chance to find prints that weren't his. He just hoped the Parker City Police Department had the ability to examine an envelope for fingerprints. If not, he knew Ambassador Martin would have no trouble demanding the Stride Agency take care of it. Stride was in league with the large law enforcement agencies and had the same access, if not better, to all the latest advancements in detection methods.

It was getting late. But looking at his watch, Fitz knew it didn't matter what time it was. The hour wouldn't matter to Martin. He'd want to be informed that the kidnappers had made a demand for the return of his daughter. A pretty hefty demand. For fifty thousand dollars, Lillian would be returned unharmed.

"Fifty G's," Fitz whistled. "That's a lot of cabbage."

A person could disappear forever with that kind of payout. Fitz just questioned whether the ambassador would cough up the dough. Or if Chief Buchanan would even allow him to. No doubt he'd want to try and catch the kidnapper in the act of receiving the money. And the PCPD had already done such a bang-up job with security for the wedding to begin with, God only knew what could go wrong if they were involved with the trade off.

Rummaging in his suitcase, Fitz found the pair of leather gloves he'd brought with him to wear if the weather turned too cool. Putting them on, he was able to replace the ransom letter in the envelope and slide it into his inside jacket pocket without fear of leaving additional fingerprints all over the paper. The gloves would also help to keep his hands warm now that the temperature outside had fallen. Which is why he'd packed them in the first place. It came in handy they could serve two purposes.

Grabbing his hat from where he'd thrown it on the bed and a scarf from the compartment next to where he'd packed the gloves, Fitz turned and made for the elevator. When he'd reached the lobby, he diverted to the front desk and asked the young clerk if anyone had come by the hotel asking for him while he'd been out.

"Not that I'm aware of. Not while I've been on duty. No, sir," the fellow said with a shrug of his shoulders. "Were you expecting someone?"

"No, I wasn't. Could one of the bellhops have delivered a letter to my room if someone asked them to?"

"I suppose. We only have two bellhops here tonight. Ernie and Will. I can ask them if you'd like."

As the clerk struck the bell on the counter and waited for the bellmen to appear, Fitz carefully studied everyone in the lobby. He was trying to determine if anyone was paying particularly close attention to him without trying to look as though they were paying particularly close attention to him. If anyone was, they were doing a good job of hiding it. All of the guests were completely wrapped up in their own worlds. Not a single one even looked in Fitz's direction. Then, a moment later, Ernie and Will came skittering across the lobby. Fitz recognized one of them as the young man who'd delivered his roast beef sandwich earlier. Puzzled expressions crossed the boys' faces as they noticed that the guest at the front desk did not have any bags for them to carry.

Looking to the clerk behind the desk, he asked if anyone had spoken to either of them and given them a letter to be delivered to Fitz's room or if they'd told anyone which room he was staying in. Neither of the bellhops was able to help, saying it had been a quiet evening and they hadn't spoken to anyone who hadn't been checking in or out.

Thanking them, Fitz tossed each one a quarter and told them to let him know if anyone did come asking after him. He flipped another quarter to the front desk clerk and told him to keep up the good work. Fitz figured it was better to keep everyone happy and on his side as long as he was in town. The more eyes he had watching his back, the better.

Chapter Thirty-Two

itz wheeled the Chrysler through the darkened streets on his way to the Martins' with the ransom letter burning a hole in his pocket. He was still having a difficult time figuring why the kidnappers delivered the letter to him and not the missing girl's family. Something about that bothered him. Not that anything about the situation sat well with him. But this was an unusual move. Something he wouldn't have expected and certainly hadn't planned for. He didn't have a great deal of experience with kidnappings along this line, but he'd known and worked with individuals that did. Their stories didn't line up with a ransom demand being slipped under *his* door. Especially when there weren't that many people who knew he was looking into Lillian's abduction in the first place.

The bespoke leather gloves on his hands and scarf he wore wrapped around his neck weren't doing much to warm Fitz in the face of the chilly temperature that evening. He wished he were tucked up in the warmth of his bed back at the hotel right now. Not making an evening trip out to tell Ambassador Conrad Martin he could have his daughter back if he coughed up fifty thousand dollars in cold, hard cash.

On the road leading out of Parker City proper to the Martin farm, as the streetlights and buildings disappeared in the rearview mirror, Fitz found himself engulfed by a blackness darker than he thought he'd ever experienced. Without a single star in the sky or sliver of the moon, he drove through an abyss the likes of which one had nightmares of falling into. Always cool and collected, Fitz found himself unnerved on the isolated drive. The revolver holstered under his arm didn't even help to allay the feeling of unease. Luckily, Fitz knew enough to recognize that he was letting his mind gin up his paranoia. He simply needed to keep his wits about him.

Easing the Chrysler through the front gates, Fitz saw that a police squad car sat in the circular drive, a patrolman in the front seat keeping a watchful eye on the house.

As Fitz stepped from the Chrysler, he heard the door of the police car open and the sound of footsteps approaching from behind.

"Excuse me, sir."

"It's alright, officer," Fitz said with a broad smile as he spun on his heels to look at the patrolman stepping toward him with his hand resting on his service revolver. "I'm Fitz Mason. I'm working for the ambassador to try and locate his daughter. I need to speak with him."

"I'm going to need to see some identification."

"Of course."

Fitz produced his Stride identification, which the officer held up into the beam of light thrown across the driveway by the squad car's headlights. Squinting to read the credentials, he eyed Fitz carefully, not entirely ready to buy his story.

Seeing the apprehension on the man's face, Fitz suggested, "Why not radio back to the station? Chief Buchanan knows I'm working the case. Or, a much easier solution if I do say so, is you just go ask at the house. I have something very important to discuss with the ambassador, and the longer we stand out here in the dark, the colder we're going to get and the angrier he will be when I finally do have a chance to speak with him. And neither of us wants that. Do we?"

The look Fitz received led him to believe the officer was already well aware of Conrad Martin's temper and may have experienced it at some point in the not-too-distant past. If that was the case, he did not wish to do so again.

"So, if I may…" Without waiting for an answer, Fitz turned and started toward the front door. Not hearing an objection, he was about to ring the bell when he heard the door to the squad car close behind him.

It was several moments before Fitz heard any movement on the other side of the large wooden door. When it finally swung open, Joe Grainger stood there, a sour expression on his face. Not that the man held many other expressions in reserve. A look of mild annoyance seemed to be his face's natural state of repose.

The usually buttoned-up flunky appeared in his shirtsleeves and tie, loosened halfway down his chest. If Grainger was so disheveled, Fitz could only imagine how Conrad looked, being that it was his daughter who'd been kidnapped.

"What are you doing here, Mason? Have you found Lillian?" The man's voice was tired and strained. The butt of a smoldering cigarette was held between his fingers as his arm dangled at his side. So much for not smoking in the house.

"I need to talk to Conrad. It's urgent. Invite me in already. It's cold out here."

Stepping aside so the detective could enter, Grainger grumbled something unintelligible, then gestured for Fitz to follow him. A thin whisp of smoke from Grainger's cigarette guided Fitz along the same path to the library they'd walked that morning.

Dim light from table lamps spotted the way, creating shadows at every turn. The vibrant paintings he'd admired earlier now presented themselves as ominous figures peering through the darkness. As it looked and felt now, a far cry from its bright and luxurious appearance that morning, Fitz imagined the house as the setting for one of Agatha Christie's murder mysteries. Because that's what they would need to make things worse, he chastised himself, a murder.

The ambassador sat next to the fireplace with his legs crossed and a tumbler of scotch resting on his knee, a warm flame flickering away. The powerful, confident diplomat looked haggard, the wrinkles around his eyes more pronounced as his fleshy cheeks sagged a little lower than normal. Fitz had seen emotionally broken men before. He never expected he would add Conrad Martin to that list.

Looking up, Martin's eyes traveled from the glass in his hand to the detective standing in the doorway. Fitz took his hat off and handed it to Grainger, saying, "Could you give Conrad and I a moment alone?"

Turning to Martin for instructions, he wasn't about to be ordered about by a private dick. But the ambassador nodded, then said, "But don't go far. Judging by Fitz's expression, we may need you."

Chapter Thirty-Three

Ambassador Martin finished his drink before setting the empty glass aside and taking the ransom demand from Fitz. To keep him from adding any fingerprints to the letter, Fitz passed it over using a handkerchief.

"Am I going to get something on me?" he asked, puzzled by the handkerchief.

"I'm hoping the police will be able to test the paper for fingerprints," Fitz explained. "The less we touch the letter directly, the better."

"Fine. Just let me see it."

As Martin read the ransom, his face began to flush as his eyes narrowed, severely creasing his brow. Fitz could tell he was grinding his teeth by the way his jaw was working back and forth.

"Fifty thousand dollars? They believe I have fifty thousand dollars I can just drop into a bag and hand them?"

"Do you, Conrad?" Fitz looked around the ornately appointed library, paying particular attention to the expensive artwork hung on the walls.

"Not that I can organize in less than twenty-four hours. They want the money tomorrow! Or today. What time is it?"

"It's still Saturday," Fitz answered. "It does seem like they believe you have access to that kind of cash. Any reason why?"

"What are you saying?" Martin's eyes bore into Fitz.

Taking a seat in the chair on the opposite side of the fireplace, Fitz leaned toward the ambassador, trying to pose as non-threatening as possible. He needed to have a serious discussion with Martin but he couldn't have that conversation if the ambassador was on the defensive. And Conrad Martin was nothing if not combative. So, Fitz needed to tread lightly.

"Conrad, have you had a chance to think about who might have taken Lillian? Has anyone threatened you recently? Have you had a disagreement with a business associate or maybe someone from your State Department days?"

"Fitz, when I retired, I retired. I'm not a businessman; I have no partners to piss off or clients who would want to hurt me. And as far as my days in the diplomatic corps… I probably have just as many enemies as you do. Well, knowing your record, maybe not *as many*. But I've been out of the game since we left Rome. It's been years. Why would someone come after me now?"

"You clearly have done well for yourself. I know I'm no art expert, but I imagine just one of those paintings there," Fitz said, pointing to a pair of canvases depicting serene seaside scenes, "is worth more than most people living in Parker make in an entire year."

"Probably more," Martin said under his breath. Always trying to impress. He couldn't help it. It was part of his nature. "Those are Monets."

"And you have two of them."

"Three. There's another upstairs," Martin said absentmindedly.

Fitz raised an eyebrow. "Hard to imagine why the kidnapper would think you have fifty thousand dollars."

"Those pieces are investments!" Martin sprang to his feet and charged across the room. When he reached the other side, he stopped, shoulders drooping. He realized he couldn't walk away from the conversation. "Yes. I have a fortune in artwork. But there is no way to sell a painting like that in a few hours. Some of the paintings I wouldn't even be able to sell."

"I'm not necessarily saying you should pay the ransom," Fitz finally said, leaning back in his chair.

"But Lillian…"

"What I *am* wondering is why this person thinks you have that kind of scratch at your disposal. And why he delivered the ransom note to *me*. Only a few people even know what hotel I'm staying in or the name I'm staying under. If I wagered a guess, the kidnapper thinks you have the money because he's been in this house and sees how you live. Also…the only way for him to know I was working on this case is if he were here today."

"I don't understand what you're saying." Martin was vacillating between anger and defeat.

"The person that sent this ransom letter is very close to this investigation, I believe. May I please see the letter again."

Fitz stood and met Martin in the middle of the room. Holding the letter up to the light, Fitz saw once again the words that had been cut from what looked to be a newspaper. It was of particular note that the kidnapper was able to find the words CONRAD and LILLIAN and AMBASSADOR. Not the most common words to find in a newspaper on any given day, unless that newspaper had been running articles nearly non-stop on the upcoming wedding of *Ambassador Conrad* Martin's daughter, *Lillian.* The words must have all been cut from an edition of the *Blue Ridge Herald.*

Of note were some of the words glued to the stark white piece of paper. The newsprint was slightly discolored, the words blurry as if the ink smudged. Like ink does when it gets wet. Looking closely at these particular words, he thought he might have an idea of what could have caused the change in the paper's color. Holding the letter to his nose, the smell, though subtle, was unmistakable. It was coffee. Someone spilled coffee on the newspaper, then used it to create the ransom note.

With that realization, several moments from earlier in the day came back to Fitz. Moments, when taken individually, meant nothing. But put together, created a story of where the ransom note had come from. It was starting to make sense to Fitz. At least part of the puzzle.

Looking at Martin, Fitz announced, "This ransom letter is fake. The person who made this letter doesn't have Lillian."

"Do you know who sent it?"

Fitz sighed. "Unfortunately…I think I do."

Chapter Thirty-Four

1985 . . .

When neither the Baltimore County Sheriff's Department nor the Maryland Department of Motor Vehicles had gotten back to the duty sergeant with the home address of Lillian Martin Mercer by 8:30, Ben and Tommy decided to call it quits for the day. Even if they got the information in the next few minutes, they thought it better to make the notification in the morning. This wasn't the sort of thing to be done late in the evening.

They were both frustrated that the original case file was missing, giving them no idea what work had been done on the case forty years before when the disappearance occurred, and details were fresh. They also couldn't understand why Fitz didn't have anything in his own files on Lucy's disappearance. Why would he have only been asked to find Lillian and not her sister? He'd been successful once.

Ben was packing up the CSU report and crime scene photos to take with him so he could have another look at them at home when his telephone rang. Looking at his watch, he couldn't imagine who'd be phoning him. Unless someone finally came through with the Mercer address. From the other side of his desk, Tommy shook his head and mouthed, *don't answer it.*

"This is Detective Winters," Ben said into the phone while pointedly raising his eyebrow in disapproval at his partner. Tommy sighed.

"I'm glad I caught you. They said you were still in your office." It was

Darlene from down in Dispatch.

"We were just packing up."

"Since you're already on your way out, we just got a call from Thompson. There's a fire over on East Fifth. He says a witness saw someone running away from the building before the fire broke out. He's requesting a detective on the scene."

Neil Thompson, as far as Ben was concerned, was one of the best officers on the force. He was young, energetic, and had a good head on his shoulders. He'd shown himself to be the kind of officer the PCPD needed more of in the future. The instincts and analytical skills he exhibited put him on Ben's short list to join the Detective Squad if the chief's reorganization plan was approved and the unit was expanded. So, if Thompson thought there was a need for a detective on the scene, Ben was going to give him the benefit of the doubt.

"What's up?" Tommy asked after Ben jotted down the address of the fire and hung up with Darlene. "No. Wait. Let me guess. There's a naked man's body suspended from a tree in Jefferson Park, and no one knows how it got there. Or...the Civil War museum was just broken into by a gang dressed as Revolutionary War soldiers. You see, that's the real mystery. Why were they dressed as colonists to break into a Civil War museum?"

"Are you finished?"

"Reports of a marauder squirrel terrorizing City Hall?"

"There's a fire on Fifth."

"Didn't see that coming," Tommy said dryly before letting Ben get any more out. "Why'd they call us?"

"Well...if you would let me finish."

Tommy huffed. "Sorry."

"Thompson is on the scene. He says there's a witness who saw someone running from the building before the fire started."

Tommy's eyes lit up. "Arson! That's a new one. We've never handled an arson case before."

"You're like a kid in a candy shop. No one is saying it's arson..."

"Yet."

It was Ben's turn to huff.

"If they don't think it's arson," Tommy continued, "then why are they asking for us?"

"Calm down. There hasn't been a determination one way or the other as to the cause of the fire yet."

"Why is that?"

"Because the building is *still burning*. Thompson just requested a detective on the scene in case what this person says they saw turns out to be something."

"Like arson!"

"I hate you. I *really* hate you."

Chapter Thirty-Five

en parked his unmarked Crown Vic behind one of the two PCPD patrol cars on the street as Tommy's Bronco pulled up behind him. Both had red gumball lights affixed to their roofs. Between the police cruisers, the pumper trucks, and the ambulance, the street was bathed in bright red and blue lights. The neighborhood was an older residential area in town with buildings dating back to the 30s and 40s. This particular block was lined on one side by narrow single-family homes and on the other by several small apartment buildings. All aging structures that were a throwback to a bygone era, none taller than three stories. Though the Great Flood of '78 did not impact this part of the city as badly as others, these apartment buildings and houses were showing their age and desperate need of refurbishment.

Lights shown in the windows of all of the buildings except the one now being sprayed down by the firefighters. A group of residents who'd decided they wanted a closer look at the action than what they could see through their windows were gathered across the street from the house, which was the focus of the emergency rollout.

"Damn. When an old house like that catches fire, it can be bad." Tommy was looking around, trying to get his bearings. "I hope no one was hurt."

"As of right now, we don't think anyone was," came the voice of a silhouetted figure walking toward them. The flashing lights behind him made it difficult to see who was approaching until he was a few feet away.

"Neil," Ben said when he was able to make out the officer's features.

"Hi, Sarge." Thompson greeted Ben, then turned to Tommy. "Detective."

"We've told you before, Neil," Tommy reminded him, "you can just call us Ben and Tommy. No need to stand on ceremony and Ben doesn't like using his rank anyway."

"Noted."

Ben looked toward the assemblage of firefighters in front of the house and asked, "Did everyone get out?"

"Um…no. I mean. There was no one to get out. The place is empty. Supposedly. One of the neighbors I spoke with said the house's been vacant for as long as he's lived here. At least fifteen years."

"It's just been sitting there empty?" Tommy repeated. "Other than the fire damage, it looks like it's in better condition than some of the others on the street. Why wasn't anyone living there?"

"The neighbor didn't know. Just said no one lives there."

"What's the fire situation?" Ben was trying to see what was happening but didn't have a clear view past the fire trucks to see the façade of the old home. He was hesitant to move any closer, not wanting to get in the way of the firemen trying to do their jobs.

"The fire's been contained. They got here pretty fast. Plus, all the rain we had today soaked everything, so I think that might have helped, too. Kept the fire from spreading and all. I haven't had a chance to talk to any of the firefighters. Dunkin and I have been keeping people away over here, and Spurrier and Bronson are down on the other side of the fire trucks working that side of the street."

"We'll have to wait until we can get inside to see how much damage was done. What about this person who said they saw someone running from the building before the fire broke out?" Ben was beginning to make notes on a fresh page in his notebook.

Officer Thompson led the detectives to the apartment building directly across from the fire where a middle-aged man was standing on the front steps. He was wearing a Washington Redskins football jersey and jeans. Ben tried not to grimace. He'd always been a Colts fan. Even after the team up and moved out of Baltimore in the middle of the night last year, he still felt a semblance of loyalty. A husky guy, he gave Ben and Tommy the once over as Thompson introduced them as detectives from the PCPD.

"Mr. Burns, this is Detectives Winters and Mason with the Parker City Police Department. Detectives, this is Cliff Burns."

Tommy smiled to himself at the thought that the guy's name was Burns and he was the witness to a fire. It was the little things that entertained him. Ben could tell why his partner was smiling just by looking at him. But they were there to do a job, so Ben didn't say anything.

"Mr. Burns, can you tell us what you told Officer Thompson, please?"

"Yeah. Sure. Um…I came out to have a smoke because my wife won't let me smoke in the apartment. I used to be able to, but all of a sudden, since she's been going to this gym and working out, she says it isn't healthy to be breathing the smoke, so I have to come out here."

Hoping to keep things on track, Ben asked, "About what time was this?"

"Guess it was around eight-thirty. Yeah. Because I came out right after *The Cosby Show*. I wanted to watch *Magnum P.I.,* but my wife likes that Bill Cosby. Hey, did anyone ever tell you you look like Magnum P.I.?"

"No, never," Tommy said, rubbing his mustache. At which point Ben subtly elbowed him in the ribs with the unspoken message of *don't be an ass*. But since he just couldn't help himself, Tommy said, "Oh! You mean *Magnun* P.I. Yes, people tell me I look like him all the time."

The guy gave Tommy a confused look.

"Anyway, Mr. Burns." Ben was wishing Tommy would have just gone home and let him handle this. But little boys and fire trucks. And Tommy was nothing if not a big kid at times. "When you came out, what is it that you saw?"

"Well, I was just sittin' here on the steps smoking and all of a sudden, I see a guy come out from around the side of the house there." He pointed in the direction where a group of firefighters was now standing. "He just kind of came running out and took off down the street."

"Which direction did he go?"

Burns pointed in the opposite direction from where Ben and Tommy had arrived.

"Then what happened?"

"A few minutes later, I started to see smoke coming from between the houses. From where the guy'd come from. Then the window right there—the one next to the corner of the house—popped and I saw flickering light inside. Then smoke started coming out that window, too."

Tommy then asked, "Did you get a good look at the guy you saw running away?"

"Not really. I mean, he just looked like a guy. And it was already dark and the streetlights aren't that bright. He was a white guy. I think he might have had on a leather jacket. Does that help?"

"Every little bit helps," Ben said.

Though he, Tommy, and Officer Thompson all knew how spotty eyewitness recollections could actually be. Some people possessed photographic memories and could recall every minor detail of a person or situation. While others could barely remember anything about a person, they saw running away from a house that caught on fire a few minutes later. Frankly, unless Burns had seen the guy actually run out of the house itself, they couldn't be sure that he hadn't just been taking a shortcut through the yards and came out between the two houses.

Until there was a determination as to what caused the fire, there wasn't anything for Ben and Tommy to do. Thompson did the right thing, calling them in. That way if it was ruled arson, they'd been there and had a chance to see things firsthand and talk to the witness while everything was fresh in his mind. If it was just faulty wiring or something like that, then there was no harm done.

It was much like the Lucy Martin case they were working on. They had to wait for more information to know exactly *what* they were working on. After asking Burns a few more questions and making sure they'd taken down everything he could remember, Ben and Tommy stuck around long enough to see that the fire was extinguished and to get the name of the fire captain in case they needed to speak with him in the future. After that, they both headed home for the night.

Chapter Thirty-Six

After a restless night's sleep, Ben spent the morning with Natalie before she left for school. He filled her in on the connection their current Lucy Martin case had with Tommy's uncle's Lillian Martin case from the '40s. This, in turn, produced a string of questions that he tried to answer as best he could. After a few minutes, he felt like his history teacher fiancée was giving him an oral exam for which he hadn't studied. But it helped him to review all the facts, so the exercise wasn't all bad.

"Two sisters go missing around the same time and one is found, and the other isn't," Natalie summed it up perfectly. "And you haven't spoken to the living sister yet…whose husband just died?"

"Correct. I'm hoping to get my hands on her address today so that Tommy and I can go see her. She lives out towards Baltimore. The idea is that she might be able to explain why Uncle Fitz investigated her kidnapping but not her sister's."

"Was her sister kidnapped?" Nat asked before taking a sip of coffee.

It was at that moment Ben realized that all Betty had actually said was that Lucy Martin went missing. He'd been so surprised by the revelation that Fitz Mason was involved, that the frozen girl they'd found in the field was last seen forty years before, and that Betty could identify her that he'd never specifically asked how she went missing. He'd assumed he'd learn more from the case file. But when the files from the original investigation turned up empty, he started questioning why that was instead of what the missing reports said. He'd never circled back to the original question. Then the call about the fire came in, and he'd become completely distracted.

Ben wasn't happy with himself for taking his eye off the ball as he thought about it. Nat could tell by his expression he was having an internal argument with himself.

"What's bothering you the most?" she asked, hoping if he could get to the core of his frustration, he'd be able to start figuring out a way to deal with whatever else was bothering him.

Sighing and putting his bagel down, he thought about it for a moment, then answered, "When you look at everything, I really have very little information to work with. So, I don't have a firm grasp on what this case is really all about. I don't know if Lucy Martin was a victim of a kidnapping, if she was murdered, or where to even start looking to figure out where she's been all these years."

"I don't think you need me to tell you this, but I think the best answers you're going to get are going to come from talking to the sister. Since there's no case file to work off of and you said Fitz didn't have anything in his notes. She's the best source of information you have. However, you're forgetting one thing."

"What's that?"

"Lucy Martin was the daughter of an ambassador. *And* the sister of a woman kidnapped on her wedding day. Which happened not long before she went missing herself."

"Riiiight," Ben said, tilting his head like a little puppy trying to understand what his owner is saying to him.

Holding up the day's edition of the *Herald-Dispatch*, Nat pointed and said, "You don't think the newspapers around here wouldn't have plastered the story all over the front page?"

"The newspapers. Of course!" Ben shook his head, even more upset with himself now that he hadn't thought about looking at old editions of the paper. Especially when doing just that helped crack a case only the year before.

"Don't worry. I won't tell Tommy it wasn't your idea," Natalie offered with a wink.

Chapter Thirty-Seven

Even though connecting with Lillian Martin was top of Ben's mind, as well as learning the details of hers and her sister's disappearance back in the '40s while they were at it, he wasn't able to completely forget about the previous evening's fire. He just wanted to keep ahead of it in case it turned into something big that required a formal investigation. Even though he wasn't expecting anything sinister to be discovered–no matter how badly Tommy would like to jump into an arson investigation. The fire was surely caused by nothing more than faulty wiring in an old house. It happened all the time. But just to cover the bases, on his way into the PCPD, Ben decided to swing down Fifth Street past the site of the fire. Before leaving the scene, the firefighters had successfully doused the blaze. He and Tommy stuck around long enough to see them gain full control of the situation. Once the drained and soot-covered emergency workers began rolling the hoses up and storing the equipment, the detectives rolled out themselves so they wouldn't be in the way of the cleanup.

Now, coming down the street, Ben saw an official county government car parked in front of the burnt-out house. An older man wearing a windbreaker with PARKER COUNTY FIRE MARSHAL stenciled on the back and carrying a clipboard was examining the damage to the front of the building. He was paying particular attention to the charring around the windows. The inspector was making some notes as Ben walked up behind him, trying to avoid the large swaths of mud and soaked grass left over from yesterday's storm and the gallons of water used to fight the flames. The two events combined left the house's front yard looking like a swamp. It didn't smell much better, either.

"Excuse me," Ben said, presenting his badge and introducing himself. "I'm Detective Ben Winters."

"Paul Dorsey," the man responded, extending his free hand. "Good to meet you, Detective. Sorry if I'm a little surprised to see you, but I haven't made the call yet. It was gonna be the first thing I did when I got back to the office."

"The call?"

"Yeah. Captain Charles, the fire commander on the scene last night, he's my brother-in-law. He said he noticed some things that bothered him while they were puttin' the fire out. Said I should come take a look first thing. From what I've seen this morning, it looks like he was right. I've seen enough to file a report saying this wasn't an accidental fire. Which is why I was gonna call you guys."

"Arson then?"

"Yep. It's pretty clear-cut if you ask me. I've been investigating fires for some thirty years now and have seen it all in one form or another. The burn pattern in that textbook. And there's a lingering smell of gasoline. Not everyone would be able to smell it, but I can. I've got a good nose."

Ben sighed. "My partner and I were here last night because one of the neighbors reported seeing a man run out from between these two houses. According to the neighbor, this house has been empty for years."

"Yeah. The fire only affected the first floor. But I didn't see any furniture inside. Well, just one of those freezer chests in the back room. The outside's pretty messed up, but it survived the fire. For the most part. Interesting, though," Dorsey said, rubbing the back of his neck as he thought about it. "The fire was started in the room with the freezer."

Ben's stomach clenched as a natural shot of adrenaline coursed through him. He knew immediately. Even though he hadn't fully thought it through yet, subconsciously, he'd already made the connection.

"Would it be possible for me to have a look inside? To see the room where the fire started? Is it safe?"

The fire inspector smiled. "Oh, yeah. It's safe. There was a good bit of damage, but the houses along this here road were built when things were made to last. They may be old, but they're sturdy sons-of-guns. I'll show you around inside, but for the moment, don't touch anything."

"Don't worry. I won't. I want CSU to have a chance to go through and see if they can find anything usable. I have a feeling this could be related to another case I'm working on."

"Really?"

"Just call it a hunch."

"That's why you get paid the big bucks, Detective. Follow me. Be careful. There's still a lot of water. And even though the structure is still relatively sound, you never know."

Following Dorsey through the front door, which the firefighters had broken down to get inside, Ben was surprised to see the extent of the damage. From the outside, it didn't look terribly bad. Black soot was caked around the windows on the first floor from where the smoke billowed, but other than that, the brick façade remained mostly intact. Only the house's age was visible from the outside. Inside, however, the fire and water damage was significant.

Ben was immediately struck by the overwhelming smell of smoke and burnt wood, and who knew what else had been in the walls and used to build the house in the '30s. Some construction materials used back in the day weren't used any longer for one reason or another. He also knew that some old wallpapers were made with arsenic. He couldn't remember exactly when the practice had ended, but the thought of a poison floating around in the air didn't sit well with him. At which point he also remembered that it was only a few years ago that Asbestos was banned in residential construction. Houses in the 1920s and '30s were filled with it.

"Mr. Dorsey," Ben said, reaching into his pocket for his handkerchief, "is there any concern about toxins in the air? Like Asbestos, arsenic, things like that that could have been… I don't know, stirred up by the fire?"

The fire marshal chuckled. "I wouldn't suggest spending too much time walking around in here. But if you just want to take a quick look, you'll be fine. The owners are definitely gonna have to do some serious cleanup to bring the place up to current standards though. There are a lot of new building codes in place since this baby was built."

Ben's shoulders loosened a bit, knowing he was in no imminent danger. But he still didn't like the idea of what the fire could have kicked into the air.

"And they stopped putting arsenic in wallpaper at the end of the 1800s," Dorsey added as he led Ben through what was once the kitchen into the small back room where he'd determined the fire originated.

Looking around the space, there would have been no way for Ben to guess the color of the walls. Whatever color they'd been was replaced by black, charcoal, and more black. As badly burned as they appeared, Ben was surprised they were still standing at all. There were several spots where the fire—or the men fighting it—punched through, creating a hole open to the next room, but for the most part, the walls were intact. If not all in one piece any longer.

Pools of filthy, debris-filled water languished on the floor where the wooden planks were beginning to sag. Ben tried stepping around the muck as best he could but was finding it difficult to navigate a clear path. As long as he could keep his foot from landing in the middle of one of the murky puddles, he'd be satisfied.

As the inspector said, the only thing in the room was an old freezer. It reminded him of the one his parents used to keep in their basement. Where his mother would put all of the meat they were saving for future dinners. Looking at the once cream-colored rectangular chest sitting up against the back wall of the room, Ben sighed. He didn't need to measure it. He could tell just by looking at the size it would have easily been able to hold a body. And if this chest was where Lucy Martin had been kept, then it made sense someone would want to try and destroy it. What better way than with a fire?

Ben felt sick to his stomach. He couldn't be sure if it was because of the noxious smell left behind by the blaze or the fact he might have just discovered the disturbing answer as to how Lucy Martin's body was frozen. It was all supposition. Even a leap to draw that conclusion, some would say. Ben understood that. But his gut was telling him this fire, and Lucy Martin's case were connected. He just needed the forensic team to find the physical evidence to actually support that theory.

Chapter Thirty-Eight

1945 . . .

Accompanied by a captain, two plain-clothed detectives, and a pair of uniform troopers from the Maryland State Police, Fitz anxiously waited on the front porch for the door to be answered. Well after two o'clock in the morning, the residents of the street having long since retired for the evening, the neighborhood was perfectly still and quiet. Serene, in fact. A part of town Fitz was not familiar with; only the light from a set of streetlamps at either end of the block allowed him to find the address for which he was searching, having arrived a couple of minutes before the police cruisers silently rolled up behind him.

Brightly colored flowers in the window box next to the front door of the two-story brick duplex were in full bloom. A comforting floral scent floated through the air as a wooden swing hung from the rafters facing the street so the homeowners could sit and talk to neighbors strolling by in the evenings. Fitz hated to think such a pretty little picture was about to be irrevocably destroyed.

"I believe this should be done as discretely as possible, Captain Crandel," Fitz suggested without taking his eyes off the front door. He was feverishly rubbing his hands together to keep them warm.

After knocking for a second time, this time louder, it took a moment before a lamp was switched on inside the house. A dim glow shown through the front window, then a light hanging over the door lit up. Finally, after hearing a string of swearing from behind the front door, it swung open.

"Mason?! What in hell are you doin' here at this hour? What happened? What's going on," Chief Walt Buchanan grumbled, standing in the doorway dressed in his robe and striped pajamas. A restless sleeper, judging by the state of his hair, Buchanan's expression wordlessly let the detective know this intrusion would not go unpunished. It was only then that his eyes seemed to focus, and he saw the other members of Fitz's cadre.

The anger in his eyes was instantly replaced with something much different. His flushed cheeks, now as pale as a ghost. Slowly taking a step back, Fitz wondered how Buchanan was going to play this.

Clearing his throat, Buchanan croaked, "Mort? What are you–"

"Walt, may we come in?" Captain Crandell cut him off.

In a small community like Parker, all the members of law enforcement knew one another. It didn't matter if they were with the city police, the sheriff's department, or the Maryland State Police, their paths all crossed at one time or another. And the top brass of each were all friends. But under the circumstances, Fitz had had no choice but to turn to the state police. After speaking with the ambassador, and then the mayor, it was agreed that the PCPD should be kept out of it.

"I don't think this is appropriate," Buchanan half-heartedly protested.

"Chief," Fitz began in a calm, even tone, "we know."

As Buchanan stuck his hands into the pockets of his robe, the group of men standing on the porch all reached for their revolvers, including Fitz.

"Hold on, now!" Buchanan said, quickly pulling his hands out of the pockets and holding them harmlessly in front of himself. "I'm unarmed. I was just putting my hands in my pockets. It's cold."

"Then you should invite us in," Crandell tried again.

With a show of defiance, Buchanan quickly responded, "I don't think I will until I know what this is all about. Showing up to my house in the middle of the night. Estelle is asleep upstairs."

Fitz leveled his gaze. "We're here because we know you slid a ransom letter under the door to my hotel room this evening. A ransom letter asking for fifty thousand dollars for the return of Lillian."

"Don't be a sap, Mason," the chief sputtered. "I didn't kidnap the girl. I don't know what this is all about. How dare you accuse me of kidnapping her."

At that, Fitz smiled. "Oh, no. I'm sorry. I didn't mean to give you the impression I thought you were the kidnapper. I know there's no way you could be. Your entire morning was accounted for. No. You didn't kidnap Lillian. But you did send me that fake ransom demand."

The two men stood glaring at one another for what felt like an eternity. Neither man's ego would allow him to blink first. But someone was going to need to give, and Fitz had the evidence on his side. He also had five armed police officers behind him.

The standoff was finally broken when Buchanan stepped out onto the front porch, closed the front door, and walked over to the swing, sitting down with a deep sigh.

Crandell motioned for his men to step back as he and Fitz walked over to the chief. "What were you thinking, Walter?"

With an air of resignation, he answered, "My career was over the minute Martin's daughter disappeared. Even if we do find her, it won't matter. A guy like Martin will make sure I take the heat. It doesn't matter that I've given my life to the department or the city. Guys like him make the rules."

"So, you thought you'd take a chance and try and cash in." Fitz shook his head.

"Yeah. I thought if Martin paid up, I'd have something to *retire* on. It's not like he can't afford it. Just look at how he lives. He won't miss that money. But that's life-changing money for me."

Fitz wouldn't even entertain his argument. "And when Lillian wasn't returned after he paid the ransom? What then?"

Buchanan shrugged. "Everyone would think the kidnapper welshed."

"You didn't think a fake ransom demand might hamper our efforts to find Lillian?" Fitz was trying to remain calm, but Buchanan's betrayal of his duty was infuriating. He wore a badge, promising to protect the people of Parker City from criminals. From the sort of lowlifes looking to cause harm. And here he was, trying to make money off the kidnapping of a young girl.

"The rich sonsofbitches in this town think they can do whatever they want. I was gonna lose my job because of him! For somethin' that wasn't my fault."

"His daughter was kidnapped!" Fitz snapped. "And you tried taking advantage of that. I know Conrad Martin isn't always a stand-up guy, but he doesn't deserve this. Lillian certainly doesn't deserve to have one of the men who should be out there trying to find her muddying the waters. As far as we know, her life is in danger!"

"I get it, Mason!" Buchanan shouted, shooting to his feet, coming nose-to-nose with him. Crandell's hand reflexively grabbed the chief's arm in a vice grip. "I didn't have a choice," he haplessly suggested.

"Detectives," Captain Crandell summoned. "Place Chief Buchanan under arrest."

"Wait," he protested. "How did you do it, Mason? How did you figure it out so quickly?"

Fitz shook his head in disbelief. "You made the mistake of delivering the ransom note to *me* at my hotel. Only a few people even know I'm on this case. Not to forget, I'm registered under one of my aliases. The *real* kidnapper couldn't have known where to find me. And I knew you didn't *actually* kidnap Lillian. No matter what you've done, I don't think you would go that far.

"Setting all of that aside," Fitz continued, "there was something that bothered me about the ransom letter itself. Some of the words you cut out and used were smeared, and the newsprint was a funny color. It's because you'd spilled coffee on the paper. I saw it in your office yesterday morning."

The corner of Buchanan's lip curled up into a tight sneer. "But I threw that paper away."

"Because the county prosecutor likes to have hard evidence," Fitz pointed out, "I stopped by the station on my way to the State Police barracks. I found the paper with the missing words in your waste basket. No one emptied it today. It was right there."

"You didn't even get rid of the evidence," scoffed one of Crandell's detectives as he placed his handcuffs around Buchanan's thick wrists. "That shoulda been the first thing you did."

Incensed as he was by what Buchanan had done, Fitz still thought everybody deserved a modicum of dignity. As the state boys began to lead the disgraced police chief off the porch and down toward the awaiting patrol cars, he suggested to Crandell that they allow Buchanan to at least change out of his night clothes and let his wife know what was happening. After a brief discussion, Fitz prevailed, though one of the troopers was sent upstairs to keep an eye on him.

As he stood on the sidewalk and watched the taillights of the police cars disappear down the deserted street, Fitz was filled with a mixed sense of accomplishment and sorrow. He was pleased that he'd been able to solve this bit of the puzzle, but it seemed like a hollow victory, considering Lillian was still missing. It was difficult to believe it hadn't even been twenty-four hours since she'd been taken. That morning seemed like a lifetime ago. The worst part was, Fitz felt as though he were back at square one.

An unseasonable, bone-chilling breeze forced a shiver to run down his spine. The gloves and scarf were of no help. Walking toward the borrowed Chrysler he was using, Fitz wondered why they hadn't received a ransom demand from the real kidnapper yet.

Chapter Thirty-Nine

Fitz spent what little of the night was left tossing and turning in his bed at the hotel. He'd sleep for half an hour, then be jolted awake just to do it all over again. His mind wouldn't allow him to relax even though his body was desperately begging for rest. The battle waged on until sometime before seven, when the sunlight began to trickle through the curtains. Even then, Fitz lay on the bed motionless, staring up at the ceiling, hoping a brilliant idea would come to him. Or, at the very least, a somewhat useful idea of the best way to proceed.

It was possible that the story being in the papers that morning might shake something loose. Maybe someone somewhere saw something yesterday but didn't think much of it at the time. When they read the paper, they may put two and two together and contact the police. Fitz wasn't holding out much hope for that scenario. Even if a witness did come forward, how helpful would the Parker City Police Department be now that their chief was behind bars. And Fitz was the one who put him there.

Far from the highest-ranking official he'd ever helped bring to justice, he was wondering what the fallout was going to be like from the arrest of Walt Buchanan when there was a knock at the door. Looking at his watch, he saw it was only ten minutes after seven. He hadn't left an order for breakfast, nor was he expecting a visitor. There were still very few people who knew where he was staying, and they would all telephone if they needed to reach him. Registering under a false name was supposed to keep people from showing up at his door. It wasn't working out like that on this assignment.

Grabbing his robe and quickly pulling it on over his silk pajamas, he retrieved his revolver from the holster draped over the chair and stuck it in his pocket. Padding across the room, he smoothed his hair down as he asked, "Who is it?"

"Major Mason, sir, I'm Lieutenant James Tanner from the Executive Procurement and Resources Office. I have a delivery for you from Lieutenant Colonel Hopkins." The voice on the other side of the door was crisp and commanding.

Feeling more at ease, Fitz opened the door, now less concerned that he was about to come face-to-face with a threat. Standing in the hallway was a sharp-looking United States Army officer, his uniform perfectly pressed, the polished silver bar on his collar glinting in the hallway light. Fitz also noted the very noticeable sidearm on his hip. If his friend in the Pentagon opted to send an armed courier–an officer, no less–with information instead of simply briefing him over the telephone on what he'd discovered about Conrad Martin, Fitz realized it must be serious.

"Sorry to disturb you so early, Major. But I was instructed to deliver this to you in person first thing this morning. Lieutenant Colonel Hopkins hopes it assists you with your current assignment."

From a thin, somewhat battered briefcase, Tanner retrieved a large, brown folder with the seal of the United States Army in one corner and handed it to Fitz. The word CONFIDENTIAL was stenciled across the cover. Easily a half-inch thick, it looked to contain a number of documents.

"These files are just duplicates," Tanner informed him, very matter-of-factly. "Lieutenant Colonel Hopkins says he trusts that you will properly dispose of them when you have finished with them. He suggested doing what you did in Warsaw."

The lieutenant shrugged, obviously not knowing what that meant. Fitz certainly knew and had to laugh thinking back to that night in Poland. But there was no time to blow up a water tower when there was a missing young woman to find.

Giving the officer a quick salute and thanking him for delivering the documents personally, Fitz closed the door as the lieutenant turned on his heels and marched down the hall. Fitz wondered if Hopkins had told the guy he was a *retired* major and not necessarily entitled to the confidential information or if that minor detail had been left out. But, knowing Hopkins, he probably listed Fitz as an active asset for the Executive Procurement and Resources Office, so he'd found a way to cover his ass. However he'd managed it, Fitz was grateful for the assistance in tracking down information on the ambassador and promised himself he'd make a trip to Washington to take his friend out for a nice dinner sometime soon.

Eager as he was, before diving into the file, Fitz rang down to the front desk and asked for them to send a breakfast tray up to his room with a large pot of the strongest coffee the hotel had to offer. He was going to need the caffeine after his lackluster night of sleep. He also thought a cold shower might help to wake him up and get him moving, so to pass the time until his breakfast arrived, he went into the bathroom to shower and dress for the day.

Twenty minutes later, he was sitting at the little desk in his room, eating scrambled eggs as he thumbed through the classified pages.

Officials who held sensitive positions in the government all had files on them somewhere. Whether it was a background check performed at some time by the Federal Bureau of Investigations or a particular agency's personnel office, those who reached a certain level in government knew there was a record of them and their activities locked away in a file cabinet. Most of these files were simply biographical in nature, outlining one's family background, education, career history, the details of one's life. If someone had run afoul of the law, legal and criminal records would also be included. Certain individuals, if this information was discovered, would sometimes try and use it as leverage over another. But anyone who committed a serious crime—the type that *could be* used against them—usually never made it very far in the first place.

There were, however, occasions when criminal indiscretions were known, but that information was kept highly guarded because the offending individual was a greater asset to the nation in their official position rather than behind bars. At the end of the day, there were still people in the government who knew of these illicit activities so they could not only keep an eye on the offender but be prepared for any type of reprisal in the event the information was made public. Fitz's old unit had dozens and dozens of such files on people they were keeping their eyes on. They were an intelligence group, after all.

Conrad Martin's record looked very much like the others Fitz had seen before. Pages on his early life and education. There was some background on his wife and her family. Summaries of his career path that led him to the diplomatic corps. And quite a few reports of his work overseas negotiating deals with countries who'd never been friendly with the United States. His success in the face of anti-American sentiment and difficult adversaries seemed to be what garnered him the post in Italy. As events were heating up and the State Department was watching the moves Adolph Hitler was making in Europe, they wanted someone in Rome who would be able to take on the Nazi leader's influence.

Fitz was impressed with what he was reading. There were some personal notes describing Martin as arrogant, egotistical, brash, and domineering, but when he thought about the Italian officials with whom Martin dealt on a regular basis, Fitz realized those were probably good qualities to have at the time. While Conrad Martin would never have made the list of Fitz's ten favorite people, he respected the difficult work he'd done.

It wasn't until the final page of the file that Fitz pushed aside his breakfast plate and focused solely on the typed report in front of him. Reading over the document once, he found it difficult to remain in his seat. This was something he hadn't expected but thinking about it, he wondered why the thought had never crossed his mind before. Standing, he began pacing back and forth across the room as he reread the last page a second time.

From the start of the war, there'd been reports that priceless works of art were disappearing as the Nazis marched across Europe. Fitz had heard the stories as he'd been conducting his own missions, but art was not a part of his portfolio and what he was in Europe working to safeguard. While many were accusing the Nazis, and Hitler, for ransacking museums and absconding with these paintings and precious artifacts, there were others, it seemed, using the war as a cover to steal expensive artwork.

There were those that the U.S. government knew of who were moving the art to safety, afraid of what would happen if it fell into the hands of the Nazis. But there were other groups working for themselves to enrich their own lives when they returned to the States. In Rome, where Conrad Martin was stationed, there was a ring of thieves made up of United States military members who'd managed to pinch several million dollars in paintings.

Fitz was feeling his face begin to flush with anger. Not just over the fact that American servicemen were stealing these works of art but that members of the government knew about it and did nothing to stop them. The most troubling part of all of this with regard to Conrad Martin was the final portion, which stated that there was a belief that the stolen paintings were being transported out of Italy through diplomatic channels. In other words, official, diplomatically sealed shipments. The final paragraph summarized:

IT IS HIGHLY LIKELY AMBASSADOR CONRAD MARTIN WAS AT THE CENTER OF THIS NETWORK, USING OFFICIAL DIPLOMATIC POUCHES TO SEND THE STOLEN PIECES TO LOCATIONS OUTSIDE OF ITALY. AS 1.) THERE IS NO SOLID EVIDENCE OF HIS INVOLVEMENT, 2.) HE DEVELOPED A STERLING REPUTATION WHILE REPRESENTING THE COUNTRY AT OUR EMBASSY IN ROME, AND 3.) HE IS NOW RETIRED, NO ONE IN THE STATE OR WAR DEPARTMENTS BELIEVES IT WOULD BE BENEFICIAL TO OPEN AN OFFICIAL INVESTIGATION INTO THE MATTER.

Chapter Forty

In a fit of fury, Fitz threw the file across the room sending pages cascading through the air. While friends of his—honorable, brave, good men—ave their lives in the defense of democracy, there were soldiers looting the country they were supposed to be aiding. It was unthinkable. The Americans were supposed to be the good guys!

Fitz had the urge to telephone Hopkins that minute and demand to know if he'd known anything about this band of thieves. Or if this was all as new and horrifying to him as it was to Fitz. And if he intended to do anything about it. But as he stormed over to the telephone, he had a moment of clarity. As angry as he was, catching art thieves wasn't his responsibility. It wasn't his assignment. If he was forced to admit it, it wasn't the responsibility of military intelligence either. Hopkins's office was in the business of dealing in secrets that could alter the very shape of the world. When one took into account the lives being lost on a daily basis in Europe and everywhere else, the damnable war was being fought, were paintings really that important?

In a perfect world, yes, the theft of these works of art would be important. If he were in charge, Fitz would handle it differently and personally see to the prosecution of those who'd been involved with the crimes. But Fitz reminded himself it wasn't a perfect world. And he wasn't in charge. He had a case and a job to do. A young woman's life may very well depend on him. No matter how angry he was at what he'd just learned, he needed to stay focused on his assignment and bring Lillian Martin home safe and sound.

Collecting the papers from where they'd landed around the bed, Fitz stuffed all of the pages back into the folder and started thinking about this new information in regard to how it could shed light on Lillian's kidnapping. Could one of the men the ambassador worked with in Italy to get the paintings out of the country have come calling? Or someone who knew Martin was involved? Did they try to blackmail him and when they realized he was not that easy to threaten, they decided to up the ante? It was certainly more plausible in his mind than someone being angry with the Mercer family over a building they didn't like or Sonny Baker being so distraught over the loss of a lover.

He needed to find out what the ambassador had to say about all of this. Fitz fully expected the man to deny the accusation. But then again, if he was concerned enough for his daughter's safety, maybe he would admit to his part in the scheme and name his cohorts. All of whom would instantly become suspects in Lillian's kidnapping.

Shrugging into his shoulder holster and making sure it was snug under his arm, he then slid into his suit jacket and adjusted his tie. Looking at the folder lying on the bed, he didn't want to leave that sort of damning information lying about. But he also didn't want to have it on him either.

Walking into the bathroom, Fitz took the gold lighter from his pocket and held it under the corner of the folder until the flames were creeping their way towards his fingers. As the folder and papers inside began to burn away into smoldering ash, he dropped them into the claw-foot tube and watched until there was nothing left but twisted, charred fragments of what used to be a highly sensitive and potentially incriminating government report.

Chapter Forty-One

Sunday mornings in Parker City were usually quiet and serene. On a beautiful, sunny spring day, they were simply magical. With flowers and trees in full bloom, the colors that spread through the town only highlighted the dignified historic buildings that sat on practically every corner. Parker became a living canvas worthy of a George Seurat painting. The typical hustle and bustle of the workweek would subside as Parkertons spent the day with family, tending to chores around the house and preparing for the week to come. As they did, the steeples that dotted the city's skyline performed a weekly symphony as their bells rang out, welcoming everyone to church services.

Fitz remembered how every Sunday morning, his mother would wake him and his brothers, dress them in their Sunday best, then herd them out the door to the car where their father was waiting, most mornings talking to their next-door neighbor. They'd all pile into the shiny black Model T–they were the first family on the block to own one–and head off to Saint Michael's for mass. After church, they'd go to Ginny's Café for brunch, where they'd be allowed to order whatever they wanted from the menu. It was the one time each week his mother would not insist the boys needed to eat vegetables or something to help them grow up big and strong. Then, after they ate, they would walk to the bakery next door and each pick out a donut to take home as a special treat for an afternoon snack.

It was funny, the things one thought of; Fitz smiled to himself as he walked past the coffee shop next to the hotel. For that brief moment, being transported back to his childhood, remembering his family all being together and laughing while crammed into the booth at Ginny's, the stress of his current situation, and frustration over the lack of action by U.S. authorities to deal with the art thieves, all disappeared.

The momentary feeling of peace quickly vanished when he saw the crowd gathered around the newsstand at the end of the block. Before heading to the Martins' estate, Fitz wanted to see a copy of the morning paper. To see how the press was covering Lillian's kidnapping.

Judging by the expressions on the faces of those standing around reading the paper right there on the street, it was the front page story. Sure enough, both the *Blue Ridge Herald* and *Chronicle Dispatch* ran headlines announcing the kidnapping of Ambassador Conrad Martin's daughter. Even the *Washington Post* ran a front-page story. Albeit smaller and below the fold. Other than the facts that Lillian Martin was abducted from her home on the morning of her wedding, that her father was a former diplomat who'd been stationed in Europe as the war broke out, and that she was supposed to marry the wealthy heir to a construction company, there weren't too many additional details to report. The *Dispatch* did briefly mention the employment of a private investigator from the Stride Detective Agency to help with the investigation but did not name Fitz specifically. All three newspapers quoted the ambassador as saying how displeased he was with the protection provided by the Parker City Police Department.

Of course, the papers had gone to print too early to include anything about Walter Buchanan's arrest. That would no doubt be tomorrow morning's headline. Word of the chief's arrest for the fake ransom demand would begin to spread once the mayor made the announcement. Fitz wondered if that would end up overshadowing Lillian's kidnapping. At the very least, he could see it interfering with the department's ability to give its full attention to finding the missing girl. If the PCPD was anything like other police departments Fitz had dealt with in the past, and there was no reason to think it wasn't, then there was a lot of internal politicking and grandstanding that went on. He could only assume Lieutenant Peters would take over as acting chief for the time being. Even though he'd only met him at the Martins' the day before, he hadn't been impressed with the deputy chief. Fitz came away with the distinct impression Peters was more interested in *getting* the top job than actually doing the top job.

As far as he was concerned, going forward, he was handling this investigation on his own. If the Parker City Police could be of help in some way, all the better. But he wasn't going to count on them.

Right now, he needed to speak with Conrad Martin and confront him about his role in the art trafficking ring. If he'd played a part and he would give Fitz the names of the other men involved, he might have a solid lead. If any of those men were in Parker, he definitely planned on paying each one a visit.

Chapter Forty-Two

The drive from his hotel to the Martins' home gave Fitz time to stew over everything he'd just learned. By the time he spun the wheel, turning the big Chrysler through the gates and up the driveway toward the house, he was fit to be tied. As much as it pained him, he knew there was nothing he could actually do about the stolen artwork at the moment. If individuals in the government already knew that Martin might be part of an art trafficking ring and they weren't willing to stir up any trouble by looking into it, what could he realistically do? Even if Archibald Stride gave his blessing–no doubt only through divine intervention–to use the firm's resources to launch their own investigation, though the Stride Agency was a powerful organization, it was no match for the United States government. If there were people in the Pentagon and State Department willing to look the other way on this, it was going to stay buried. But the fact it could be the motive for Lillian's kidnapping infuriated Fitz.

Stepping from the car and adjusting his tie and jacket, Fitz saw the same police officer from the previous evening asleep in his patrol car. Shaking his head, he wondered what the guy'd missed while he was dozing. Or if the family had been in any danger while their appointed security detail was catching some shut eye. In the end, it didn't matter that much, Fitz realized, because if anyone did try returning to the house to cause any more trouble, Joe Grainger would be a lot scarier to deal with than the schnook with the badge out front.

It was only a little before eight thirty when Fitz rang the bell. He imagined everyone in the house would be awake. No one could have gotten any sleep last night. Other than Norma, if she'd remained sedated.

Waiting for the door to be answered, Fitz took a deep breath and let the fresh spring air fill his lungs. He could have used another cigarette. He'd only had two so far that morning and he was fighting the urge to try and light up a third before he spoke to the ambassador. He decided if Grainger answered the door and was smoking as he'd been before, then he'd join him. When the large door finally swung open, and Lucy Martin was standing there, a slight feeling of disappointment washed over him.

Lucy looked him up and down with her dark brown eyes. "You look tired."

"So do you," Fitz snapped back, uncharacteristically. "Sorry. It was a long night. May I come in? I need to speak with your father."

"Have you found Lillian?"

The tone in her voice sounded neither excited nor concerned. If he'd only been able to hear her ask the question, he'd have thought she simply inquired out of a sense of formality. But something in her expression told Fitz she was genuinely worried about her sister.

"Not yet, Lucy," he said, softening his tone. "But I'm working on it. Some things have happened, and I have some new information. That's why I need to talk to your father."

Stepping aside to let him in, Lucy said, "Well, ever since he got a phone call earlier this morning, he's been in the library with Joe. He says he can't be disturbed. Mother's having breakfast."

"I'd like to speak with her too. If I could. But right now, it really is important that I see your father. I'm sure he'll want to talk to me."

"I can let him know you're here."

"Actually…that's alright. You said he was in the library? I think I know my way around by now. You should stay with your mother." Fitz gave her the broadest smile he could muster.

He still couldn't figure out why he was so perplexed by this young lady. He could charm a company president or a politician without breaking a sweat, but he felt like she was able to look straight through his rakishness and bravado. Lucy Martin was not a girl easily swayed.

Fitz wondered what she was thinking. And still, if there was a chance she was hiding something from him. But he reminded himself again, there was no way he could know what a teenage girl was thinking with any certainty.

"Mother and I are in the dining room. Hilda's floating around somewhere cleaning something, I'm sure. If you get lost on your way to the library, just holler," she said over her shoulder, having turned and walked off into one of the rooms off the entry hall.

Alone, encircled by paintings on every wall, they all took on a new meaning for Fitz. How many of them were stolen? How many of them were thought to be destroyed in the war? He could no longer see the brush strokes of the masters represented on those canvases, just greed and deceit. The vibrant colors could not overcome the shadows surrounding them.

Chapter Forty-Three

The door to the library was not fully shut, opened just enough so that Fitz could hear the ambassador's deep voice rumbling through the opening as he walked down the hallway. The other voice he could hear was Joe Grainger's. No surprise there. But the two men, whose voices always seemed to thunder off the walls around them, were speaking much quieter. Though still with great urgency.

Quietly, Fitz stepped to the door and listened, not wanting to announce himself yet. He was curious as to what the men were discussing in such hushed tones. Did it have something to do with the telephone call Lucy mentioned?

Standing with his hat in his hand, his ear to the door, Fitz wondered if it was right for him to eavesdrop on his own client. If he could trust Martin without question, he'd have no reason to listen to his conversation. But since he no longer trusted the man to tell him the whole truth, he felt the *only* person he owed anything to was Lillian. Her father might be footing the bill, but her father might also be the very reason she was taken.

"Hardly anyone even knew about the Caravaggio," Martin hissed. "It was one of the last pieces shipped out."

"Then that narrows it down, sir," Grainger responded in the same harsh whisper. "We know exactly who we should be looking for. Just give me the word, and I'll hunt the sonofabitch down."

"But he said not to come looking for him. He said he'd call again with instructions on where to leave the painting."

"Of course, he told you not to come looking for him. That means we *know* who he is. Who took Lillian? It could only be one of the crew."

"Or someone they told," Martin shot back. "At the end, there was only Eaves, Milford, Golding, and what's-his-name…that little one. Ratford. No! Ratner."

"Golding's dead," Grainger said, ice dripping from his words. "He was transferred right after we left. I heard his entire squad was wiped out."

"What do you know about the other three?"

Fitz listened at the door with his fists clenched. Everything he'd read in the report was true. Conrad Martin was a crook. And the odds were he was the guy behind the whole thing, using military men to do his dirty work. To steal what he coveted most. Artwork. It shouldn't have been any surprise then that Joe Grainger was in on it, too. He was Martin's right-hand man, after all. It also sounded as though he'd been keeping up with their cohorts.

"Ratner's still over there," Grainger continued. "He just made staff sergeant. I think he musta had something on his CO. I never thought he'd make it any farther than corporal. But he always did know the right people."

"And Eaves and Milford?" Martin demanded in a quiet growl, the sounds of his shoes clicking on the hardwood as he paced the floor.

There was a slight pause before Grainger answered. "Them, I lost track of. I know they came home in '43. But we sorta lost touch."

"I can't believe one of them would have the nerve to do something like this! They got rich because of me. Why would one of them come after me now?"

"Soldiers coming back from the war? Could be pretty easy for them to blow through the dough they made."

Taking a few steps back down the hallway, Fitz pretended to sneeze, then walked right up to the door and knocked as loud as he could. Without waiting for an invitation, he swung the door open and strolled into the library with a grin on his face.

"Excuse me, gentlemen."

"God bless you," the ambassador said, his eyes no more than two narrow slits behind a pair of thick glasses staring at the private investigator.

"Thank you. Spring flowers tend to tickle my nose." It was a good enough excuse. He didn't want them to think he'd heard anything they were saying. "I have some news."

"Have you found Lillian?" Martin sounded almost genuine.

"No. This news is on another count." Taking off his hat and laying it on the armrest of a chair near the door, Fitz went on to inform them that his theory about the false ransom letter was correct. "Walter Buchanan admitted to it. He's the one who delivered it to my hotel room. But he says he had nothing to do with Lillian's kidnapping."

"You believe him?" Grainger asked.

"There's no reason to doubt him. His movements yesterday are well known. He would have never been able to pull it off."

"What if he had an accomplice," Martin suggested.

"Conrad," Fitz lowered his voice, "You called me in because you trust me and know I'm good at what I do. In fact, I'm the best at what I do. If I do say so myself. I can tell you there is no way Buchanan kidnapped Lillian. I honestly don't think he's smart enough."

"Then why'd he send the letter trying to get money out of the ambassador?" Grainger demanded.

Fitz shook his head and sighed. "Because he knew his ticket'd been punched the minute Lillian was taken. He was going to be disgraced and out of a job, so he tried to make something out of it."

Silence fell over the room. Fitz was going to take his time and let the quiet linger. He wanted to see if Martin would willingly tell him about the kidnapper's telephone call. But as the ambassador looked to his toady of a valet and Grainger turned to look out the window, he knew the information would not be forthcoming.

So, he continued. "The mayor told me he would be phoning you to personally apologize on behalf of the city. Have you received a telephone call from him this morning?"

"Um, no," Martin stammered. "It's been quiet all morning."

"I see." Taking a deep breath, Fitz picked up his hat and locked eyes with Martin. "Conrad, now that you've had some time, can you think of *anything* you might not have thought about yesterday in the heat of the moment?"

Fitz observed carefully as the former ambassador stood before him stone-faced. For his part in the melodrama, Grainger even turned as if he were eager to hear if Martin had thought of anything. When not a word was spoken, Fitz placed his hat on his head, turned, and left the library.

Chapter Forty-Four

1985...

Sitting in the car in front of the house on Fifth, Ben couldn't get the acrid smell of smoke out of his nose. He'd even opened the windows in the hopes the cool air that swept in following the rain the day before would help dissipate the odor of charred plaster lingering on his clothing. The fire marshal explained to him that the fact the walls were covered in a plaster finish had been helpful in containing the fire–as much as it had–to the first floor. Ben's grandparents' house had plaster walls, he remembered. It was sort of ironic that houses built back then were filled with hazardous materials by modern standards, but the thick walls that were common kept all the dangers encapsulated. Until a fire broke out and allowed the toxic fumes to spread, Ben thought as a sudden coughing fit hit.

Taking several deep breaths, his chest felt congested from the thick air he'd been breathing in the house. It was just another reason that made him wonder why Tommy smoked. His friend was *knowingly* filling his lungs with those fumes. He'd been in the house for less than ten minutes and felt as though he couldn't get a full breath of fresh air.

Tommy's addiction to cigarettes wasn't his concern at the moment. Though it was something he was definitely going to address.

For the time being, he needed to decide how to proceed. Technically, as the supervising officer, Ben could split the team and assign Tommy to work on the fire investigation while he continued with the Lucy Martin case.

But he knew having Tommy with him would be valuable when he spoke to the sister. The two tended to observe interviews through different frames of reference, each picking up on different nonverbal cues. They worked better as a pair. And even without any proof that the frozen girl's body had been kept in that deep freezer, in the back of his mind, he knew the two investigations were both part of a single case. Which is why he didn't want him and Tommy to split up. He just hoped the Crime Scene Unit would be able to find some connection.

He'd looked in the freezer when Dorsey was showing him the room where the fire began, but to the naked eye, there was nothing of note. The State's CSU guys had equipment that would be able to find something if there was anything there to find. If they didn't, then Ben was going to have to start questioning why his instincts were so off. He just wasn't feeling like himself the last couple of days.

After radioing Dispatch and requesting they contact CSU, Ben looked over at the newspaper laying on the passenger seat, the headline shouted that the police found the body of a young woman and were working to identify her. The chief had been adamant about not releasing Lucy Martin's name until after her sister was notified. They'd also not gone into detail about the state of the body. The discovery itself was sensational enough. But to tell the press the body was frozen would be asking for a media circus.

Ben had read the article twice over breakfast to make sure it didn't say anything that could hurt the investigation, but they'd only released the bare amount of information they felt necessary. Because of the sparse details, Ben knew there'd be a stack of telephone messages waiting for him at the office from reporters wanting a comment. All of those little message slips would be tossed directly into the trashcan when he got in. They'd managed to keep control of the story for two news cycles already. It would probably be the first and last time that ever happened, so Ben was going to see how long they could go without having to show too much of their hand to the press. At some point, they'd have to make Lucy's identity known. But he was hoping it would be after they'd determined what had happened to her so they could present the press with the full story.

Ben knew that was wishful thinking, but he was going to hold on to the dream for as long as he could.

The fire marshal told Ben there were still a few things he needed to take care of at the scene of the fire before he could head back to his office to file the official report so he would be there when CSU arrived. He'd make sure to give them the same tour he'd given Ben.

The second call Ben made to Dispatch asked for a patrol unit to be stationed in front of the house. If someone had wanted to burn the place to the ground, they'd failed. Ben didn't want to take the chance they'd come back and try again. If someone was trying to destroy evidence, he wanted eyes on the house until everyone felt confident there was nothing left to find. Ben trusted Lieutenant Clover and his men to go through the house with a fine-tooth comb. If there was something–anything–to find, they'd find it. Even if it turned out the fire wasn't related to the Lucy Martin case, they still needed to figure out who started it. Arson was a crime.

This was what Ben was thinking about as he pulled into the parking lot behind the station a few minutes later. He was also trying to figure out how to be in two places at once. He and Tommy needed to drive out to speak with Lillian Martin in Baltimore. That was his first priority. But he also needed someone to go through the old newspapers at the *Herald-Dispatch* building to learn what was reported at the time of the girls' disappearances back in '45. On top of that, he needed to have someone go to the Courthouse and pull the land records to find out who owned the house on Fifth Street. He needed another detective on the team, which he could very well have if the chief's plan went through. But that wouldn't happen for some time. He needed an extra pair of hands *today*.

Chapter Forty-Five

en poked his head into the watch commander's office as he was passing by. Lieutenant Kevin Bowers, head of the entire Patrol Division, was sitting behind the desk shuffling through some papers. He wasn't who Ben expected to see that morning.

"Morning, Lieutenant. You filling in for Lucas?"

Looking up over his reading glasses, Bowers tossed his pen on the desk and stretched his arms out to his sides. The sound of his shoulders popping so loudly surprised Ben. In his late fifties, Bowers was the only man Ben knew with a *pre*-ceding hairline. Every time he saw the man, it looked like his hairline was moving closer and closer to his eyebrows.

"Winters," he said with a sharp nod. "Yeah. He's out sick. I said I'd take the shift. Hey, I hear you have a *cold* case you're working on." It was Bowers's attempt at humor. Honestly, Ben was surprised more people around the station hadn't made the joke already.

"Yeah. We think we're going to be able to make some progress on it today," Ben said, leaning against the door frame. "I could really use an extra set of hands, though. Tommy and I have to head out to Baltimore, and I need someone to run down some information for me here in town. You have anyone you might be able to spare? I'll take anyone you've got...except LuCoco. Don't suppose Thompson's available?"

Bowers reached over the stack of papers in front of him and picked up a clipboard. Running his finger down the list of names, he said, "Sorry. He has forty-eight off. He clocked out after the fire call last night. You can have O'Connor. He's in the bullpen. I'll send him up to you."

"Thanks, Lieutenant."

Ben turned and headed for the second floor.

When he walked into the Detective Squad's office, Tommy was already at his desk. Ben looked at his watch. It was rare that Tommy beat him to the office in the morning. Even if he hadn't stopped by the scene of the fire, he would still have only been twenty minutes behind his usual schedule. Obviously, the case was getting the better of his partner.

Tommy looked up for his notepad when Ben walked in. "Hey, Shepherd was looking for you."

"Oh. Why?"

"I'm guessing because he couldn't find you," Tommy answered, leaning back in his chair and clasping his hands behind his head.

"You know what I mean," Ben said, raising an eyebrow at him while reaching for the telephone.

"He had Lillian Martin's address for you. The DMV coughed it up. Here. . .I wrote it down," Tommy said tossing his notebook over onto Ben's desk.

Ben hung up the receiver and looked at the address.

"Thistle Road in Catonsville," Tommy said. "Any idea where the hell that is?"

"I think it's just west of Baltimore," Ben said, opening the bottom drawer of his desk and pulling out a road map of the state.

Spreading it out, he ran his finger along US 70 which would take them east toward Baltimore, then started following one local road after another until he found the address.

"It shouldn't even take us an hour to get there," Ben told Tommy.

"Should we call first? Make sure Lillian's there."

Ben thought for a moment. He would hate to waste the time driving out to her house for them to find she wasn't home. But if a police detective from Parker City called her and asked if she'd be home for him to come speak with her, she was going to ask what it was all about, and he didn't want to tell her they'd discovered her sister's body over the telephone. He thought it better they take their chances.

As he was about to explain that to Tommy, there was a knock on the door.

The detectives turned to find a patrolman standing there. Without saying a word, his bright red hair and pale, freckled complexion betrayed his Irish heritage.

"I was told to report to you, Sarge. The Lieu said you needed me to track down some information for you."

"Hi, Patrick. Yeah. We've got a few things going on at the moment and need some extra hands. And you can call me Ben."

"He's just one of the guys," Tommy added with a roll of his eyes.

Ben gently lobbed Tommy's notebook back to him, making sure it hit him square in the forehead.

"You hear about the fire last night on Fifth Street?" Ben asked O'Connor.

He nodded, starting to jot something down in his own pocket notebook.

"I need you to go over to the Courthouse and search the land records for the property's owner. The house has supposedly been vacant for years according to one of the neighbors."

"You just need the current owners?"

"No reason to go back any farther," Ben told him. "We just need to know who's house caught on fire last night. After that, head over to the *Herald-Dispatch*. You'll need to go through the old newspapers. There were two cases where a pair of sisters went missing back in 1945. Lillian Martin and Lucy Martin. Lillian was found, Lucy wasn't."

O'Connor was scribbling notes as Ben spoke.

"We need to know everything the paper reported at the time. The department's case files are rather lacking."

After asking a couple of questions to make sure he understood exactly what types of details the detectives were looking to learn, Officer O'Connor set out on his assignment, leaving Ben and Tommy to gather their things and begin the drive east to meet Lillian Martin and inform her that the body of her missing sister had turned up in a field two days earlier. They just needed to figure out exactly how they were going to break the news.

Chapter Forty-Six

1945...

Before leaving to begin his own search for information about the two men who'd been in cahoots with Martin and Grainger back in Italy, Fitz went looking for the dining room and Lucy and her mother. Having no idea where exactly he was going, he began opening doors randomly, only to be confronted by painting after painting, statue after statue. There wasn't a single room in the house that couldn't have come straight out of an art gallery or museum in one of the world's capital cities. Magnificent as the pieces were–some positively breathtaking– Fitz could only wonder how many of the valuable works were obtained legally.

It now appeared as though Conrad Martin's illicit behavior was coming back to haunt him. From what he overheard, it sounded like whoever kidnapped Lillian was offering to let her go in exchange for a painting by Caravaggio. Fitz knew nothing about the artist other than he was a famous Italian painter. For all he knew, he'd seen the very painting in one of the rooms he'd just been in.

Turning a corner, Fitz stepped into a room lined on either side by intricately carved mahogany columns, a chandelier that rivaled the one hanging in the Paris Opera House, and a dining table that could easily seat twenty guests with room to spare. He'd obviously found the dining room. At the far end sat Lucy and Norma Martin. Both women were sipping coffee from china cups as he made his way toward them, keeping an eye on their reaction to seeing him.

Lucy shot him a concerned look, then quickly averted her gaze, opting to stare out the large window behind her mother and into the garden beyond. Norma Martin, sitting at the head of the table, looked like a queen who'd been delivered the devastating news that her kingdom was being invaded and falling to pieces without much resistance. The matronly woman's face was pale and drawn. Though Fitz could only remember interacting with the woman on one or two occasions, he remembered her to always be chatty and full of life. A hostess with a warm smile and motherly personality. The Norma Martin he saw before him now he would have hardly recognized to pass her on the street.

Standing a few steps from the ladies, Fitz began to introduce himself. "Mrs. Martin, I don't know if you'll remember me. I was stationed in Rome during your husband's time at the embassy. My name's Fitz Mason."

Setting her cup down on its saucer, the tiny clink made by the two pieces of porcelain coming together echoed around the room. It was such a simple, everyday sound yet it was oddly unnerving at the present moment. Wordlessly, Norma Martin cast her eyes over the private detective. Fitz couldn't be sure if she was trying to remember him from their paths crossing in Italy, or if she was sizing him up to determine if he would be able to bring her daughter home. Either way, he felt the scrutiny like a weight hefted upon his shoulders.

"Of course, I remember you, Mr. Mason. But you were an officer at the time, were you not?"

"Yes, ma'am. I was a major in the Army."

"Now you work with the Stride Detective Agency? My husband says you are Mr. Stride's best man. Is that true?" Her voice was weak and tired. He wondered if she was still under the effects of the sedatives she'd been given.

"I don't know if I would say I am the best, but—"

"Would others?" she interrupted.

With a sly smile, Fitz said softly, "They would."

"Do you know who has my Lillian?"

Taking a deep breath before answering and doing some quick calculations in his head as to the best way to respond, Fitz said, "I have some leads I am leaving to follow up on now. I'm hoping to have some answers soon. But I believe I'm on the right trail."

The woman's eyes slowly began to fill with tears. Before Fitz was able to offer his handkerchief, she stood and started for a door off to her right. Stopping halfway there, without turning around to face him, she said, "Please, Mr. Mason. Do whatever you need to do to bring Lillian home to me."

Regaining her strength in dramatic form, Fitz watched as Norma's shoulders straightened as she strode through the door out of the dining room, leaving him alone with Lucy. The younger girl, he'd noticed, hadn't once taken her eyes off the flowers in the garden during his exchange with her mother. He knew there was something she wasn't telling him. But in Lucy Martin, he'd found a surprisingly formidable foe. She wasn't susceptible to the tactics that served him so well over the years. There was a wall she'd put up that he could not scale.

"How is your mother doing?" Fitz asked.

"As well as can be expected." Lucy slowly turned from the window and looked at him through a pair of tired, sad eyes. "She keeps asking why someone would do this to Lillian."

"I might be getting closer to an answer," Fitz offered. "Some new information has come to my attention that I'm going to check on right now."

"Does it have to do with the phone call from earlier?"

Fitz paused before responding, "I would like to ask you for a favor, Lucy." For a moment, she appeared puzzled. "Don't mention to anyone that you told me about the telephone call. Not even your father."

"So many secrets," she whispered.

Fitz couldn't argue with her. He'd built his life off of secrets. Learning them. Keeping them. In some cases, trading them. They weighed on a person. The darker the secret, the heavier the burden. Fitz couldn't help but wonder what secrets Lucy was harboring. She was too young for her to have the types of secrets that would carry with them such strain. But then again, he had no idea what she'd seen in her short eighteen years living with a man like her father. Though much of his work as an ambassador was public—frequently designed for mass consumption—there was also a large part that was required to be conducted behind closed doors. Negotiations where it was necessary to use...*leverage* to achieve a goal. How much of that world had crept into Lucy's?

"If you'll excuse me. I should be going."

Lucy suddenly shot to her feet, her movement catching Fitz off guard. So much so that he began to instinctively reach for his revolver. But he caught himself, hoping she hadn't noticed his reaction.

"Fitz. Did you find Sonny? Did you talk to him? Does he have anything to do with Lillian's kidnapping?"

"I did have a chance to speak with him. He was as surprised as anyone about what's happened. And I don't think he's good enough an actor to fool me."

Something between a sigh and a huff exited her lips. In that instant, Fitz thought he might have figured it out—what Lucy wasn't saying. How could he have missed it? Was he getting so old that he missed the cues? Sometimes, it was simply human nature. Lucy might have eyes for her sister's ex-beau. Unrequited, Fitz imagined. But it wouldn't change the fact she was worried about him and his involvement. Part of the detective in him wanted to ask Lucy what she thought of the young Mr. Baker. To see if his theory would hold water. But, considering he believed wholeheartedly that Sonny Baker had nothing to do with Lillian's disappearance, there was no reason to delve into the younger Martin daughter's personal feelings. It would have been too much of an intrusion upon her, and Fitz wouldn't cross that line.

Chapter Forty-Seven

After making another wrong turn that landed Fitz in the middle of the Martins' kitchen, he found his way back to the front hallway with a sense of urgency. He needed to find out where former military men spent their free time in Parker City. In Baltimore, he knew of a few watering holes frequented specifically by veterans. In Parker, he'd need to ask around. To do that, he needed to head back into town.

Fitz opened the front door just in time to see Lieutenant Peters ring the bell.

"Mason! What are you doing here?" the officer demanded, standing on the steps of the house flanked on either side by patrolmen.

"Sorry, Lieutenant. I'd love to ask you in, but I'm just leaving." Fitz closed the door behind him as he stepped out into the pleasant morning sunshine.

"What? I'm not here to see you. I'm here to see Ambassador Martin," Peters snapped, scratching the top of his head. The few pieces of hair covering his scalp now going in several different directions.

Physically, Peters, who Fitz could only guess would be assuming Walt Buchanan's duties as police chief under the current circumstances, was the opposite of his predecessor. He was short and compact and looked at the world through horn-rimmed glasses. While Buchanan was grouchy and set in his ways, Fitz was able to excuse that and explain it away as a symptom of years of apathy as the head of a small-town police department. Peters was too young to be as brusque and pompous as he behaved. That was Fitz's analysis after having only just met the man the day before and having virtually no interaction with him since then. But Fitz was a brilliant judge of character.

"If you're here to talk to Conrad, I'm sure if you ring again, someone will be right along to let you in. Everyone is terribly busy this morning," Fitz said, pushing past the trio of policemen, much to their astonishment and indignation.

Spinning on the heels of his freshly polished shoes, Peters caught Fitz's left arm. "Where are you off to in such a rush? Maybe there's something you'd like to share with the police? We are the ones running this investigation. And now that Walt is…out of the picture, I'm the acting chief. I need to know what's going on."

"Lieutenant Peters," Fitz said with his broadest grin, "I assure you. There is nothing at all I would like to share with you."

"That's *Acting Chief*, Mason," Peters corrected.

"My apologies," Fitz said, maneuvering his right hand in a way to remove the *acting* chief's grip on his arm. In doing so, he was able to shake the man's hand, appearing to congratulate him on the promotion–which he owed entirely to Fitz's actions the night before. It was a slick little trick Fitz'd found to be useful on a number of occasions.

"Congratulations on your new post. But as I said, I really must be off. I promise, if I learn anything I believe will help the Parker City Police Department find Lillian Martin, you will be the first to know."

"I don't care who you work for, Mason. You need to let the police handle this," Peters called out to him as he double-timed it across the driveway to where he'd parked the Chrysler.

Fitz noticed that the dozing officer from earlier was now fully awake and leaning against the hood of his patrol car. Tipping his hat to him, Fitz slid into the driver's seat of the car and started it up. The sound of the engine drowned out whatever it was Peters was shouting at him from the other side of the driveway.

Pulling away from the Martin estate, Fitz recognized that police departments, in general, did not care much for having a private detective come in and work one of their cases. It was understandable. Which also meant it was not surprising to him how much resentment he'd garnered being asked by the Worthington Trust Company to handle the Wendell Kittman case and now by Conrad Martin to find his kidnapped daughter. Police departments didn't like to be shown up by outsiders. Especially those who didn't wear a badge.

But over the years, Fitz had also had very positive experiences working with police agencies around the country on a variety of assignments. If Fitz was asked what all of the police outfits had in common that put up the biggest fuss when he came to town, he'd have to say their size. The bigger the department or the smaller the department, they hated having someone like him come in and make them look bad. It was the medium-sized police forces that seemed to be most cooperative. It was like they had nothing to prove to anyone. Not like a police commissioner in New York City or a single sheriff in a rural community.

It was never Fitz's intention to come into any town and step on anyone's toes. He was there to do a job. If he happened to do the job better than someone else, well, he couldn't help that very much. So, if they were unhappy with him because of their own inabilities, he wasn't going to lose too much sleep over it.

Chapter Forty-Eight

After speaking with all of the Martins and then the brief run-in with Lieutenant–*Acting Chief*–Peters, Fitz was desperate for a cigarette. He'd already smoked one on his drive back to the hotel. Now, with the car parked in the lot next to the Parker House, he leaned against it, finishing a second. The wisps of gray smoke circling his head helped to ease the tension he was feeling. He thought he'd feel even better after a cup of coffee.

With the sun shining down on him and only the hint of a spring breeze rustling the bright green leaves on the trees, Fitz made his way to the little diner where he'd spent most of his mornings since arriving in Parker City. He knew there he'd find a good cup of strong coffee, a pretty waitress, and possibly some useful information.

A little bell above the door jingled as he opened it, holding it for a pair of ladies who were just leaving. A tip of his hat and a friendly wink made the women blush. His mother would never approve of his cavalier behavior even though she always told him it was important to enjoy life, no matter how difficult things appeared or what pressures surrounded him. Plus, his actions were harmless.

A good deal of the time, Fitz took his meals in restaurants with expensive linens, imported flatware, and snooty waiters. His years of service in Europe had vastly broadened his pallet to truly appreciate what a talented chef could do with a piece of meat and vegetables most people had never heard of. At the same time, though, he felt just as satisfied sitting in a tiny greasy spoon ordering fried eggs and hashbrowns or a pastrami sandwich with extra mustard.

Sideling up to the counter, Fitz laid his fedora on the stool next to him and waited for his new favorite waitress to take his order. She had flowing brown hair, sparkling green eyes, and dimples that appeared when she smiled. Which she did frequently while talking to him. And as a red-blooded American man, he couldn't help but notice her teal uniform clung to her in all the right places.

When she'd finished with another customer at the other end of the counter, the waitress sauntered toward Fitz with a mischievous grin spreading across her ruby-red lips as she recognized him. While Fitz would have liked to believe it was simply his personality and devilish good looks that appealed to her, he knew it probably had more to do with the overly generous tips he'd been leaving. But that was just another part of his charm.

"Back so soon?" she said, leaning her elbows on the counter in front of Fitz and making herself comfortable. "I thought you said you were going back to Baltimore."

"Well, Miriam, dear, my plans changed rather unexpectedly as I was heading to the train station yesterday morning. It looks like I'll be in town for a little while longer. At least until my current job is concluded."

"Lucky for me," Miriam said with a wink. "What can I get you?"

"A cup of coffee would be much appreciated."

"Coming right up, sugar," she said, hurrying off into the kitchen.

Fitz tapped his fingers on the laminate countertop as he looked around the eatery. The breakfast rush must have just ended because there weren't many diners at the moment. A group of elderly men sat at a table toward the back, smoking and laughing as they talked about their week. A young couple tried their best to wrangle their young and energetic little boy in a booth by the front window. And a single, middle-aged gentleman in a suit was seated at the opposite end of the counter, working on a stack of pancakes.

A moment later, Miriam, the waitress, returned with a steaming cup of coffee and a slice of apple pie. Laying them down in front of Fitz, she said, "I thought you looked like you could use something sweet to go with that coffee. It's on the house."

Fanny Fern, the novelist and newspaper columnist, did say, "The way to a man's heart is through his stomach," Fitz thought as he graciously accepted the treat.

"You know, Miriam, maybe you could help me out with something."

"Oh. And what would that be?" Her interest was obviously piqued, a twinkle in her eye.

"Is there somewhere in town former military men go to drink, tell war stories? A particular bar, maybe?"

The waitress screwed her face up at the question. Clearly, she was expecting something different.

"I know a couple of the regulars who come in here used to be in the Army. They fought in the last war. Other than that, I can't say that I know many servicemen. You know who would know? Let me go get him."

Leaving Fitz alone with his pie and coffee, she scurried back into the kitchen. A moment later, she returned, followed by a guy in a dirty white t-shirt and greasy apron. He was big and square. Not the kind of fella Fitz wanted to run into in a dark alley. The detective noticed the naval anchor tattoo on his forearm as he stepped up to the counter.

"Miriam said you wanted to ask me a question." Surprisingly, his voice was higher than Fitz was expecting. But somehow, Fitz thought his massive, beefy arms kept people from pointing out the tenor of his voice.

"This is Hal," Miriam introduced him. "He's our cook. He used to be in the Navy."

"Nice to know you, Hal," Fitz said, extending his hand. "Major Fitz Mason. Retired United States Army. I was hoping you might be able to tell me where you and your fellow servicemen get together to bend the elbow. I have a couple of acquaintances I'm trying to track down. Haven't seen them since I was stationed in Rome, and I hear they may be in town."

"You were in Rome?" Hal asked.

"All over Europe, really. But based out of Rome, yes."

Looking him up and down with a particularly stern expression, Hal said, "I'm not gonna bother to ask what you did during your time because I get the feeling you wouldn't be able to say."

"Very astute." Fitz smiled.

"You remind me of one of the guys I knew back in the day. He was never able to talk about his assignments. You're looking for old friends, you say?"

"Acquaintances. Friends of friends, really. Just thought I'd look them up since I'm in town longer than I was expecting."

"Fitz here has been working in Parker this week," Miriam offered.

"Sure. Well, there's a little bar next door to the American Legion office over on Braddock. A lot of guys hang out there."

"Thank you so much for the information," Fitz said. "*And* my compliments on the food here. I've enjoyed all my breakfasts."

"Yeah, well, I hope you find your buddies."

The bell over the door jangled, drawing all of their attention, as a pair of new customers entered. Miriam motioned for the men to pick any table as Hal retreated back into the kitchen. As Fitz ate his pie, he overheard the guys discussing the rumor one of them heard in church that morning that the police chief had been arrested during the night.

"First, that ambassador's girl gets kidnapped, and then the chief of police gets arrested…" the second man said from behind a copy of the morning newspaper. "What's this town coming to?"

If only you knew, Fitz thought to himself. *If only you knew.*

Chapter Forty-Nine

The Blue Ridge Saloon was the complete antithesis of Smokey Joe's. It wasn't much like a saloon either, for that matter. While Smokey Joe's was a happening, elegant watering hole for the young and affluent members of the community, the Blue Ridge's style could best be described as neo-Spartan. Some wooden tables and chairs were scattered around the large, square room. An oak bar with a handful of stools in front of it sat in the far corner. A single window next to the front door provided the only natural light, which wasn't very much. The rest emanated from old brass lamps hanging around the room. Not even noon, with only a couple of guys sitting at the bar, a heavy layer of cigarette smoke already hung overhead.

Fitz noticed that the few items decorating walls around the place were photographs of various military units. Young guys all standing around in their uniforms, smiling. A few of the men in the field in their battle gear with their rifles looking much less cheerful.

As Fitz approached the bar through the veil of smoke, the round bartender with terribly unruly eyebrows looked him over. "Sorry, mister. It's Sunday. We're closed."

Fitz looked to the two men sitting at the bar, each with a beer in front of them, then back at the bartender.

The guy shrugged and said, "It's a private meeting."

"Uh-huh."

Fitz began reaching into his jacket when the bartender said, "I'm not looking for any trouble, mister. I don't need you coming in here shutting me down."

He must have thought Fitz was getting ready to pull out his official government credentials. Credentials that would cause a problem. Fitz paused, his hand still inside his jacket, holding his cigarette case.

Thinking quickly, Fitz slowly pulled his hand from inside his jacket and leaned on the bar.

"What's your name, fella?"

"Roger. Roger Tipton."

"This your place?"

"It is."

Fitz smiled and took a seat on the empty stool next to him. "I'm not here to hassle you, Mr. Tipton. I hate the way the little guys like you get pushed around all the time."

The bartender's shoulders lowered ever so slightly. He was still leery of what Fitz was peddling, but it looked like he was at least going to hear him out.

"Maybe if you can help me, I can forget that I was ever even here." Now Fitz took out his cigarettes and lit up. He was trying to present a cool, casual attitude.

"What is it I can do for you?" Tipton asked as he absentmindedly started wiping down the bar in front of Fitz with the rag he'd been fidgeting with.

"You get a lot of military folks in here? Being neighbors with the American Legion next door?"

"You could say that. All the guys here like to shoot the shit and talk about their time. Sometimes, it's easier to talk to other guys who went through the same thing."

"I understand. I'm retired Army myself. I served in Europe."

"You look like you're doing alright," Tipton said, raising an eyebrow.

"I landed alright. Been out for a few years now."

"Officer?"

"Major."

"Figured. So, what is it I can help you with?"

"I'm looking for a couple of guys I served with in Italy. Eaves and Milford.

I heard they might be in Parker. Thought I'd see if I could try and find them. Catch up."

The bartender chewed on his lower lip, not taking his eyes off Fitz.

"Any chance either of them is a regular here?" Fitz nudged.

"What were their names again?" Tipton asked, though Fitz knew he'd heard him full well the first time. He was just trying to buy himself time to think.

Fitz watched the bartender's reaction carefully when he answered, "Eaves and Milford." And there it was. The slightest twitch of his eyes.

Tipton shook his head. "I don't know Eaves. But if you're talking about George Milford, yeah. He comes in every so often. Not really a regular but I know him. He gets real loud when he gets drunk."

"Does he get drunk often?"

"Like I said, he only comes in now and then."

"When was the last time you saw him?"

"A couple weeks ago. Maybe."

"Can you remember anything he said when he was here?"

"I usually didn't listen to him unless he was ordering a drink."

"Was there anything different about the last time he was here? Anything you can think of." Fitz was pushing harder now. This could be a big break for the case.

The bartender sighed and tossed the rag on the bar. "George was going on about how he was a captain in the Army, and now he can't catch a break. Said he'd done things while serving that people owed him for now."

"George said that, did he?" Fitz asked. *George* Milford. Now he had a first name. "Any idea what he meant by it?"

"Nah. He was just lookin' for some attention. He probably didn't even know what he was sayin.'"

"Does he live around here?"

"I don't know, Mack. I told you what I know. Alright? Are we good here?"

Fitz stubbed out his cigarette and stood up.

"We're good, Mr. Tipton. Thank you."

As Fitz was walking toward the door, Tipton hollered after him, "You're not actually from around here, are you? You're not an inspector."

Fitz turned and smiled. "I told you I wasn't here to cause you any trouble."

He tipped his hat and opened the door, allowing a plume of smoke to escape.

Chapter Fifty

A Texaco filling station down the street from the Blue Ridge Saloon had a pay phone on the side of the building. Fitz pulled up and jumped out of the Chrysler. Flipping through the telephone directory attached to the phone booth, Fitz ran his finger down the list of M's, stopping when he came to a MILFORD, G. It was the only one in the book. He was starting to feel like the odds were turning in his favor. But what were the chances Milford—if he was the guy Fitz was after—would be holding Lillian at his place? It all depended on how stupid he was, Fitz thought as he noted the address.

Climbing back into the car, he made a quick turn out of the parking lot and drove in the direction of G. Milford's residence. There was still the possibility G. Milford wasn't *George* Milford. Just because he lived in town and drank at the Blue Ridge didn't mean he was listed in the telephone directory. For all Fitz knew, he might not even have a phone and the G. Milford whose door he was about to knock on was a Gladys or Gertrude Milford.

Regardless of who answered the door, the pieces of the puzzle were starting to fall into place. The Milford lead was the best one Fitz had gotten so far. If this mug was a part of Conrad Martin's gang in Rome, helping him to plunder the nation of its priceless artwork, then he'd have no qualms turning around, stabbing the ambassador in the back, and kidnapping his daughter to make some dough. Especially if he was really down on his luck like he told Roger Tipton during his last drunken visit to the bar.

Fitz turned the Chrysler from Braddock Street onto Fourth, then a few blocks later onto Antietam Way. Once on the quiet residential street, he started watching the house numbers pass by as he slowly inched along, looking for G. Milford's place. At the end of the block, he pulled up in front of a small, single-story brick home that matched all the others around it. The yard was decently tended, but the house itself must have been built somewhere around the turn of the century because it was beginning to show its age. Some of the bricks on the front porch were chipped, and the roof looked like it needed to be replaced.

Driving past the house, Fitz parked on the next block. Before exiting the car, he double-checked that his revolver was loaded and ready in case he found himself in a jam and the only way out was to burn some powder. Fitz just hoped the guy wouldn't put up too much of a fight once he knew he was cornered.

Walking back toward the house, Fitz saw no car sitting in the driveway and the curtains drawn in all the windows. There was no way to tell if anyone was home. He needed to think about how he wanted to play this.

Ducking around to the back of the house, the backyard was small and empty except for a rusty trashcan. At the far corner of the yard, a crusty wooden lawn shed sat with its door slightly ajar, allowing Fitz to see nothing more than a reel mower and muddy shovel. But still no sign of Milford.

Making his way back to the front of the house, the next-door neighbor—an elderly gentleman—was stepping out of his front door. A small, grey Scottish Terrier followed behind on a long leash. The man saw Fitz walking up to Milford's front door and waved.

"If yer lookin' fer George, he ain't home. Said he was visitin' his sister fer a few days," the terrier's owner hollered. Fitz couldn't place the man's accent. It was a hodge-podge of vowels and consonants.

"That so?" Fitz answered back.

"You a friend of his? Or is George in some kinda trouble?"

"Why would you say that?"

"Cause you sorta look like a copper. But yer dressed too nice. You a shylock or a shyster?"

Fitz turned on his most charming smile. "Not a loan shark or a lawyer.

Just a friend. George and I served in Italy together. I was in town, so I thought I'd look him up. But you say he went to visit his sister?"

"That's what he tol' me when I saw him packin' his car the ot'er day."

"It's a shame I missed him. Maybe I'll catch up with him the next time I swing through Parker," Fitz said, turning and making a show of starting to walk away.

He waited for Milford's neighbor to patter off down the street in the opposite direction with his little dog leading the way before he turned and hurried to the front door. Fitz moved swiftly so there was no chance any of the other neighbors could see him. Using his fist to hammer on the door, the small, inset window rattled in its rusty casing. When there was no answer–which he hadn't been expecting–he tried the door handle. To his surprise and consternation, the door was unlocked and swung open with ease. Fitz knew right away he wasn't about to find Lillian in the house. If this was where she was being kept, there was no way Milford would leave the front door unlocked so anyone could happen to walk in and find her tied up and gagged. Milford would be one unlucky Schmoe if that happened.

Stepping into the front room, Fitz immediately took a defensive posture. Someone had obviously beaten him there. The room was tossed. The cushions of a threadbare sofa were ripped apart, leaving their stuffing everywhere, a rather uncomfortable-looking wooden armchair was flipped upside down, and the bookcase had been emptied. The few books and mementos strewn across the floor. A small desk in the corner hadn't fared much better. Papers, envelopes, and a week's worth of old newspapers found themselves dumped wherever was convenient for whoever ransacked the place.

Fitz wondered if they'd found whatever it was they were looking for.

Easing his revolver from its holster, Fitz stood in the center of the room, listening for sounds coming from any corner of the house. From his vantage point, he could see a small kitchen off the back of the living room. Just looking through the doorway, he could see chairs overturned and a shattered coffee mug on the ground. The only other way out of the living room was down a short hall that Fitz assumed led to a bathroom and a couple bedrooms.

Keeping his back to the wall, he worked his way down the hallway to the first open door. A bathroom. Other than a towel lying on the toilet and a razor in the sink, it looked untouched.

Next was what appeared to be Milford's bedroom. Like the other rooms in the house, it was a shambles. Whoever tossed the place was extremely thorough, Fitz thought as he eyed the mattress on its side next to the bedframe and all of the drawers pulled out of the small bureau and emptied.

As he slowly stepped into the bedroom, Fitz thought he heard the faint sound of a floorboard creaking somewhere behind him. He was beginning to turn when the hint of a familiar scent filled the air. Then, he heard a crack just as a bolt of searing pain surged through his skull. And everything went black.

Chapter Fifty-One

When he finally came to, Fitz wondered if someone had actually hit him over the head with a sledgehammer. The pain was radiating like electric tendrils from the back of his skull. Through the haze of trying to get his eyes to focus, he could see stars and flashes of color all around him. It didn't help that his eyes felt as though they were going to burst from the throbbing. Gently, he felt the back of his head to see how large a hole was left by his assailant, only to find a small amount of blood on his fingers and the shape of his skull intact.

Maybe he was as hardheaded as his boss always accused him of being. In this instance, it paid off.

Lying on the floor in George Milford's bedroom, Fitz took several deep breaths to help stop the world from spinning. If it wasn't for the unpleasant smell of the stained rug, he'd have considered staying right where he was for a little while longer as he let his senses come back to him.

He was obviously getting too close to something, so he needed to get himself up and moving again.

Even though his eyes were still working their damnedest to focus, he could make out his revolver lying next to him on the floor. Whoever attacked him wasn't looking to take his piece or to do any more harm to him than knocking him out for a little while. Interesting. Who had he walked in on?

Slowly pulling his arm from under him, he squinted to read the hands on his watch. It was just after one. He'd been out cold for... Doing the simple math was hurting his head.

Taking another deep breath, he counted to three, then carefully began to push himself up onto his hands and knees. As he was doing so, he noticed an envelope under Milford's bed. It was stuck to the bottom side of the bedframe. And if one wasn't lying flat on the floor like he was, it wouldn't be visible. Getting whacked on the back of the head might not be an entirely bad thing. Reaching under the bed, Fitz pulled the weathered envelope from between the wooden slats.

Struggling to get himself into a seated position, he leaned against the bed to steady himself.

From inside the envelope, Fitz removed a piece of paper and laid it in his lap. The handwriting was not the most legible, but he could read it. It was a list of items followed by notations indicating dates and locations. It only took him a moment to recognize some of the names he was reading. Names like Bernini, van Gogh, and…*Caravaggio*. Fitz had the feeling he was holding a list of all the pieces of art that Milford and his crew had helped Conrad Martin steal and smuggle out of the country. *He'd kept an inventory*. Incredible. There were close to two dozen items. The pieces would have added up to several fortunes.

Looking around at the meager furnishings and condition of the house, Fitz understood why George Milford might have turned on Martin. It didn't look like he'd gotten a fair share of the ill-gotten gains. Certainly, nowhere near as much as the ambassador must have made from the scheme.

He didn't know what he was going to do with the list yet, but Fitz was taking it with him. As he went to return it to the envelope, he noticed a folded photograph he'd missed. In it, four men, dressed in Army fatigues stood next to a jeep. One of them was holding an expensive-looking frame with a painting of a woman and child—quite possibly the Virgin Mary and baby Jesus. Squinting to read the soldier's name tag on his chest, Fitz thought he could read RATNER.

Flipping the image over, he found the men's names handwritten on the back in what looked to be the order they were standing. JOE RATNER, GEORGE MILFORD, JIMMY GOLDING, and ROGER EAVES.

Turning the photo back over, Fitz examined the men closely. Now he had an idea what Milford looked like, at least. He was a tough-looking fella.

Clean-shaven, with a firm jaw and black piercing eyes. Definitely could have passed for a boxer. As Fitz looked at the line of men, he noticed Eaves's wild eyebrows. The same eyebrows he'd seen just a couple hours earlier. The date on the back of the photo read 1940. Five years later, Roger Eaves had a little less hair, was wider in the gut, and went by the name Roger *Tipton*.

"Dammit!" Fitz swore as he jumped to his feet, only to feel a sudden wave of nausea and dizziness come over him, forcing him back down to his knees.

Tipton…or Eaves…lied about who he was and knowing Milford. It was entirely possible he was in on the kidnapping. Or, he'd just been covering for himself and his friend because of what they'd done during the war. Either way, Fitz had a lot of questions for the bartender.

Using the bed as support, he struggled to get to his feet and keep his balance. After a few more deep breaths, he thought he'd try taking a step or two. When he didn't find himself crashing back to the floor, he thought things were going in the right direction. His only regret at the moment was having naturally put his hat back on his head without thinking. The fedora weighed less than a pound but the way it rested on the sore spot on the back of his head, it might as well have been a boulder sitting on the goose egg.

As much as he would have liked to charge out of the house, jump in the car, and speed back to the bar to confront Eaves, he knew enough to know until he was feeling steadier, he probably shouldn't be rushing anywhere. Especially behind the wheel of a car as big and heavy as that Chrysler. The idea of hoofing it back to the Blue Ridge Saloon didn't really appeal to Fitz either. His shoes certainly weren't made for that. And calling Joe Grainger for a lift was out of the question because he didn't know how much he could trust him or Martin at this point.

Stepping outside, the fresh air filled his lungs, providing a glorious moment of relief. The light breeze felt comforting against his face. Doing something he never did, Fitz loosened his tie. For a moment, he even thought about removing it altogether but couldn't actually bring himself to do the deed.

Walking back to where he'd parked the car on the next block, Fitz felt the fog in his head beginning to lift. The headache was still pounding away like a construction crew hard at work on one of Mercer-Avery's skyscrapers, but he was feeling much steadier on his feet.

Climbing into the Chrysler, Fitz revved the engine and slowly eased away from the curb. He wasn't planning on driving like a maniac. If he was forced to admit it, he'd felt worse behind the wheel of a car before. He was going to be fine. But he couldn't say the same for Roger Eaves when he got his hands on him.

Chapter Fifty-Two

1985 . . .

The drive east from Parker to the address they'd been given for Lillian Martin Mercer would have taken less than an hour, as Ben predicted, if it hadn't been for a couple of wrong turns they made as they reached Catonsville. Even though it wasn't that far from Parker, neither Ben nor Tommy had ever visited the Baltimore suburb. Once there, they ended up needing to stop at a gas station and ask for directions to Thistle Road. In their defense, it was not one of the town's main thoroughfares, instead jutting off into an area of dense woodland.

"It must be beautiful out here in the fall when all these leaves are changing colors," Ben thought aloud as he eased the car down the tree-lined road.

"Yeah. But a bitch in the winter with the snow," Tommy countered. "I bet it takes forever for this road to get plowed."

"I don't know. It could be like a winter wonderland out here."

Tommy blew a line of smoke out the window, then flicked the butt of his cigarette after it.

On the drive, Ben filled Tommy in on what he'd seen when he stopped at the sight of the previous evening's fire. To his credit, Tommy did not dwell too much on the fact he'd been correct about the cause of the fire being arson. He was more intrigued by the theory that it somehow fit into their Lucy Martin investigation. He loved a good conspiracy theory. He couldn't deny it.

"So, the odds are, when we find out who owns the house, we'll know who killed Lucy," he said, deciding if he was going to be able to have another smoke before they reached their destination.

"First of all," Ben corrected, "we don't know she was murdered. Not until the ME makes the official call."

"Are you kidding me?" Tommy turned in his seat so he was staring straight at his partner. "Lucy Martin was put in a freezer for *forty years*. We don't know if it was the one that someone tried to torch last night, but *a* freezer somewhere. You don't do something like that if you aren't trying to cover up a murder. I mean, come on, man."

"I'm not saying that doesn't make sense, but we can't jump to conclusions."

"Oh, I'm jumping to a conclusion on this one. Because it is just bat-shit crazy enough to go along with all the other crazy crap we've dealt with over the last few years. I'm going off of precedent." Tommy crossed his arms, punctuating the pride in his argument.

"*Precedent*? Really? Now you decide to use legal jargon?"

"If it helps support my case. And I know how much you *love* precedent. Almost as much as you love filling out forms."

"I think there could be something seriously wrong with you," Ben said as he slowed the car so he could read the bronze address plate on the stone pillars sitting on either side of the entrance to a drive leading even further off into the trees. "This is it."

Turning the car through the stately entry, they followed the driveway until they emerged from the trees onto a sprawling estate. In the center of the lawn rose a three-story mansion. The house, a prime example of a Colonial Revival with hints of the eclectic Queen Ann style, practically glowed in the morning sun with its bright white stone and siding façade.

"This looks peaceful," Tommy said as he and Ben stared up at the house through the front windshield. "Maybe you and Natalie could find something like this for after you're married."

"I don't know. It looks a little small. I only count four chimneys. We were really hoping for a place with at least half a dozen fireplaces."

"Do you ever think we're in the wrong business?" Tommy asked, pushing the door open with his foot and starting to get out of the car.

"To live in a house like this?" Ben asked, following his partner out of the car. "Absolutely."

A wrap-around porch ran the length of at least three of the house's sides. Flower pots filled with colorful blooms decorated the outdoor space, along with a number of rocking chairs. It must have been the perfect place to sit and listen to the sounds of nature in the evening, Ben thought as he rang the bell next to the front door.

As they waited for someone to answer, he looked over to Tommy, who was adjusting his tie. Ben smiled to himself. Clearly, someone wanted to look their best.

Ben was about to ring the bell a second time when he saw a shadow emerge behind the colorfully frosted glass in the door. A moment later, it swung open, a man not much older than themselves standing there.

Wearing a light blue button-down shirt under a cream-colored cardigan, Ben knew the man must be Sydney Mercer's son. He was the spitting image of the late developer whose photograph he'd seen in the newspaper, only thirty years younger.

"Can I help you?" he asked, eyeing the men standing before him. It was obvious by his expression, not many people dropped by without an appointment.

"Good morning," Ben began. "We're sorry to disturb you, but I'm Detective Winters; this is my partner, Detective Mason. We're with the Parker City Police. We were hoping to speak with Mrs. Mercer. Is she available?"

In an instant, a number of emotions flashed across the man's face. Annoyed, confused, afraid. He finally settled on curious.

"What is this about? If I may ask. I'm her son. Richard." His tone was guarded. Understandably. Very few people expected to open the door to a pair of police detectives.

"We have some information that we need to share with your mother," Tommy said with a warm smile. "You're more than welcome to sit in."

"Has something happened?"

"Mr. Mercer, this is a rather delicate matter," Ben said, trying to set the man's mind at ease. At least enough to invite them in.

After a moment's thought, he stood aside and gestured for the detectives to enter.

"I'm sorry," he said. "It's just that my father recently passed away, and my mother hasn't really been up to seeing anyone since the funeral."

"Yes, we're sorry for your loss. We saw that your father passed away last week. Had he been ill?"

"He was a workaholic. And an alcoholic. The two things didn't do so well for his heart."

Richard Mercer's explanation of his father's death felt cold to Ben. But he could understand. A man who worked too much or drank too much might not have had the best relationship with his children. Still, there was something about the way he said it that bothered Ben. As if there existed an additional level of resentment and anger. He wondered if Tommy picked up on it as well.

"Let me show you into the living room. I'll get my mother. She was just finishing breakfast. She got a bit of a late start this morning. Would either of you like some coffee? I know I can't get going if I don't have at least three cups before ten."

"Coffee would actually be very nice. Thank you," Ben answered for both of them.

The minute Richard Mercer walked out of the room, under his breath, Tommy said, "He's hiding something."

Chapter Fifty-Three

A mint green wallpaper with yellow and white flowers covered the walls of the Mercers' living room. Several paintings hung on display in various spots, each with a little lamp above it to illuminate the piece. In no way an art aficionado, Ben thought he might have recognized one or two of the pieces. Or at least the styles. He was trying to read the signature in the bottom corner of a landscape when he heard a voice behind him.

"That's an original Monet. My father was an art collector."

The voice was cool and melodic.

Ben turned to find a striking woman standing in the doorway. Lillian Martin Mercer's eyes sparkled like emeralds as she appraised the visitors to her home. An air of confidence hung on her like a well-tailored gown. Tall and noticeably fashionable, her otherwise dark hair was highlighted by wisps of pure white. Though he knew she was in her sixties, Ben would have believed she was at least ten years younger if that's what he was told.

"I'm Lillian," she said, extending her hand and walking over to Ben. "My son said you wanted to speak to me. I can't imagine what about. I haven't been to Parker for quite some time."

"Mrs. Mercer," Ben said, shaking her hand, somewhat surprised at the firm grip. "I'm Detective Ben Winters. This is my partner, Tommy Mason."

"We're from the Parker City Police Department," Tommy added.

"Please, have a seat," she said, gesturing to a pair of expensive-looking armchairs that matched the equally expensive-looking cream sofa opposite them. "Richard will be right in with coffee."

"First," Ben began, "let me say how sorry we are for the loss of your husband."

A sad smile appeared on Lillian's lips. "Sydney was my rock. Forty years together wasn't enough. But thank you."

Before Ben was able to respond, Richard Mercer stepped into the room carrying a large tray with a silver coffee service. Placing the set up on the coffee table, he poured everyone a cup, then took a seat next to his mother on the sofa.

"Now, what is this all about, Detectives?" he asked, trying to sound as indifferent as possible. Though his words sounded rather apathetic, there was a recognizable eagerness in his eyes.

Ben didn't want to simply blurt out the news that Lucy Martin's body had been discovered lying in the middle of an open field in Parker City. The girl had disappeared forty years ago. Enough time had passed for the family to assume the worst—that they would never see her again—but there was always that glimmer of hope. That she could still be alive and well somewhere. He didn't want to callously extinguish that flicker of hope. Even though that would be the final outcome.

At the same time, he needed to learn as much about Lucy's disappearance as he could. And Lillian was the best source of information. He needed to extract that information while not seeming heartless and uncaring of the news she was about to receive.

"Mrs. Mercer, in 1945, you were abducted," he began.

Her brow knit slightly, unsure why this long past event was being revisited. "That's common knowledge."

"What exactly were the circumstances surrounding your abduction?"

"It was the day Sydney and I were to be married. A pair of former servicemen who were down on their luck and knew my family had money broke into our house and kidnapped me. It was so…" Lillian's voice trailed off as she looked toward the Monet over Ben's shoulder.

When she didn't continue, Ben said, "I'm sorry to have to bring this up after all this time. We need to understand what happened because there is a possibility that it may be related to a case we're currently working."

Both Ben and Tommy knew there was more to the story than Lillian had shared, having read Fitz's personal notes. But Lillian was only telling them the story the public was given and believed for four decades. Ben wasn't going to press the detail about the stolen artwork that never seemed to be made public. He'd hold that card in reserve for the time being.

"After the former servicemen took you, you were then found by a private investigator?"

"Yes. A detective with the Stride Agency. A man my father knew from his time in Italy. A Fitz…Mason." Her eyes cut to Tommy, and her face went pale. "My God. You look so much like him. You're name's Mason?"

Tommy nodded. "He was my uncle."

"He saved me."

"Which is indirectly why we're here," Ben continued. "Shortly after you were found, your sister went missing."

The muscles around Lillian's eyes tensed ever so slightly at the mention of her sister. Putting her coffee cup down, she clasped her hands together and laid them in her lap.

"It was a few weeks later," she said. "We woke up one morning, and she was gone."

"Did anyone think she'd been kidnapped by the men who took you?"

"No. Your uncle," she said to Tommy, "and my father's man took care of them."

"Were there other men involved with those two who could have taken your sister after my uncle rescued you?"

"Not that I'm aware of."

"Shouldn't you know all of this?" Richard Mercer interrupted.

"It's always good to hear things like this firsthand," Tommy offered.

"You're here about my sister," Lillian said, now understanding where the questions were leading.

"At the time, what did you think happened to Lucy?" Ben asked, answering her question with his own.

"My sister was a bit of a troublemaker at times. A freethinker. Outspoken. A girl ahead of her time, perhaps. She liked to push the boundaries. She was terribly intelligent. Loved her books and reading. But she had a slight rebellious streak. We used to hide it from my parents, but she would often come home from a night out…I believe the kids nowadays call it *trashed*." She paused, letting her mind drift back to the days when she and her sister were young and didn't have a care in the world. Before she was kidnapped. Before she learned of her father's activities during the war. Ben picked up on the sadness in her voice. "She told me once, when she'd had too much to drink, that there was someone she'd fallen in love with. I just assumed she ran off with him."

It was an unexpected piece of information. Ben looked to Tommy to gauge his reaction. He knew exactly what he was thinking. Lucy Martin ran off with a lover. Probably someone her parents wouldn't have approved of. The affair lost its luster, and somehow Lucy ended up dead. The boyfriend then hid her body…for forty years. It was a solid theory. One that was not uncommon either. Well, except for holding on to the body for four decades.

"If the assumption was that Lucy ran away, didn't you ever wonder why she never got in touch with you?" Ben asked, trying not to sound accusatory. That was the last impression he wanted to give. But for the life of him, he couldn't understand how so many people could simply accept the story that Lucy ran away with some guy never to be heard from again.

Lillian thought for a moment. Ben saw her lower lip begin to tremble. "It was the easiest thing to believe, Detective. I didn't *want* to think what might have happened to her."

"Do you know who it was your sister was seeing at the time she disappeared, Mrs. Mercer?" Ben was leaning forward in his chair, his pen poised over his notebook. This was the first solid theory they had to work with, so he was anxious to follow the path for as long as he could to see where it led.

Taking a deep breath, Lillian crossed her arms over her chest and finally said, "I believe it was Sonny Baker."

Chapter Fifty-Four

Ben and Tommy were well acquainted with the Baker family. They were one of the most prominent and powerful families in Parker. One of the city's five founding families. Sonny Baker was not only the son of the late state Senator Wilson Lee Baker, but the brother of Beverly Baker. The first victim of the Spring Strangler, the first case Ben and Tommy worked as detectives.

Both men did their best not to react to hearing the name tumble from Lillian's lips. Parker was a small city. There were bound to be times when individuals involved with one case overlapped with another. But when his sister was murdered four years ago, Sonny Baker was the one demanding the killer be brought to justice, or he would use his extensive financial resources to go after the mayor and police department. Ben and Tommy were now faced with him being a possible suspect in the disappearance of Lucy Martin. The investigation was already complicated. This detail made it exponentially so.

"Your sister was dating Sonny Baker? Why would she need to run away with him?" Tommy asked.

"Lucy didn't know I knew she was seeing him. She tried to keep her affair secret, but I was her sister. I *knew* what was going on. I knew she was sneaking around."

"But why would she keep the relationship a secret?" Tommy asked. "I assume, your families both being so…influential, you would have associated with each other. It would have been a good match."

"I believe what you're trying to say, Detective, is that rich families only mingle with other rich families." Lillian raised a knowing eyebrow.

Tommy smiled.

"I do understand what you're saying, though. It was, regrettably, true back in the day," she said, letting Tommy off the hook. "That wouldn't have been the problem. The Bakers were…are…a fine family. But…Sonny was older than Lucy by several years. And a terrible playboy. He was a cad in many ways. I figured it was just a fling. And… at one time, Sonny and I were an item. Before I met Sydney."

"That still doesn't really explain why she would have felt the need to run away," Tommy pressed.

"Detective, why do teenage girls do anything they do?" Lillian asked in turn. "She wasn't thinking straight. She had love in her eyes."

"Did Sonny Baker leave Parker after your sister disappeared?" Ben asked, trying to follow this line of thinking.

"Not that I recall. But it was a long time ago."

"After she went missing, did you ever confront Sonny Baker about his relationship with your sister?" Tommy's tone was beginning to sound accusatory…frustrated, at the least.

"No. I did not," Lillian answered. "It wasn't my place. And when I told Sydney that I thought Sonny and Lucy might have been seeing one another secretly, he told me he'd have a word with him to see if he knew anything about where Lucy was."

Tommy was about to follow up when Richard cleared his throat and put his coffee cup down. "I'm sorry. I still don't understand why you're here. Is this about my mother's kidnapping or my aunt going missing? Are you looking into her disappearance again? Like a cold case?"

Tommy stifled a cough brought on by the choice of phrase.

Ben looked at Lillian and wondered if she'd already worked out why they were there.

"Mrs. Mercer, I'm sorry to inform you, but your sister, Lucy Martin, is dead. Her body was discovered in Parker City two days ago."

"Two days?!" Richard shouted. "And you're just informing my mother now?"

"Mr. Mercer, we didn't know who she was when she was discovered. She had no identification, and we weren't able to officially ID her until yesterday. There were also some extenuating circumstances that prevented us from speaking with you until this morning."

Before Richard was able to assault Ben with another question, Lillian–her voice barely over a whisper–asked, "How did she die?"

"That has not been determined yet. As I said, there are some extenuating circumstances. The Medical Examiner's Office is currently working on determining the cause of death."

Ben then placed his notepad on the coffee table and began to explain to Lillian and her son how and where Lucy had been discovered and the state in which she was found. He then told them how the medical examiner was in the process of preparing the body for an autopsy. Neither Mercer spoke, both sitting, staring directly at Ben. He couldn't tell if they understood what he was telling them or if they were in disbelief at what they were hearing. Which he would also understand.

When Ben was finished, he waited for a reaction. The only sound that could be heard was the ticking of the mantle clock, which, in the awkward silence, sounded like a cannon firing every second. Lillian sat silently on the sofa; her long, manicured fingers trembled as they covered her mouth. A tear ran down her cheek.

When she was able to speak, she asked, "Detective Winters, will you be able to find who did this to my sister?"

"Mrs. Mercer, we're going to do everything we can. We may have some additional questions in the coming days."

"I will try to help however I can, but if you will excuse me for a minute, I need some fresh air."

When she was gone, Tommy asked Richard, "Did your mother ever talk about her sister?"

"What? Sorry. Um…" He shook his head as if he were trying to clear away the cloud of thoughts swirling around his mind. "No. Not really. Once, when I was little, I saw a picture of them together. I asked my mother about her, but she said that Aunt Lucy had gone away."

"Do you have any brothers or sisters, Mr. Mercer?" Ben asked.

"A brother and a sister. But they don't live around here. Jonathan lives with his family in Chicago, and Melissa has moved to New York. They went home after my father's funeral."

"And where do you live?"

"My family and I live in Ellicott City. Only about ten minutes down the road."

"What is it you do, Mr. Mercer?"

"I'm in real estate. Like my father. I'm a broker. Commercial. My father sold the company about ten years ago or I'm sure I'd be working there now."

When Lillian returned, she had a shawl wrapped around her shoulders. "Detectives, if you don't mind, I need to lay down. This isn't how I was expecting my morning to go. If you need any other information, please let me know."

"Of course, Mrs. Mercer. I really am very sorry for everything you've gone through. If I could just ask one last question. When you were kidnapped, your father brought in Fitz Mason to find you. When your sister disappeared, why didn't he bring in the Stride Agency again?"

Both Ben and Tommy already knew the answer to the question. Fitz had written in his files that immediately after the Lillian Martin kidnapping case, he was sent off on another assignment. But even if he hadn't been, the odds of Conrad Martin turning to the man who'd threatened to hand him over to the authorities for stealing priceless artwork while serving as an ambassador in Europe were pretty slim. Ben was just curious as to how Lillian would answer the question and if she knew about her father's dirty dealings.

"If I recall correctly, my father and Mr. Mason had a falling out after he found me. At least that's what my father told me. I knew not to ask any questions. My father did hire other investigators to find my sister, though. They just had no luck. I guess they weren't as good as your uncle."

Chapter Fifty-Five

1945 . . .

By the time Fitz returned to the Blue Ridge Saloon, the door was locked and he could see no light on inside the bar. Fitz was furious with himself for tipping off Eaves, who most certainly ran right to Milford. The question still remained: was Eaves a part of the kidnapping or just a loyal friend? Using his fist to pound on the door on the off-chance someone was inside and willing to answer, Fitz wasn't surprised when there was no response. He decided to see if there was a back entrance to the bar, so he followed the sidewalk around the block to a narrow alley stretching behind the row of squat buildings.

A line of trashcans filled most of the space, leaving just enough room for a person to pass by. Counting the doors, Fitz stopped in front of the one that should have belonged to the Blue Ridge. The garbage next to the door was filled with empty liquor bottles, so he knew he was in the right place. As he expected, the door was locked when he gave the handle a twist. The lock was old and could have easily been picked, but Fitz was tired of playing games and knew he was running out of time. Bracing himself for the impact, he stepped back as far as the alleyway would allow and charged the door. Slamming his shoulder into it with as much force as he could muster, there was a loud crack as the doorframe snapped. A second hit forced the door to swing wide open, leaving the handle dangling in place.

Using the now broken frame to steady himself, Fitz realized the jolt from smashing into the door did nothing to help the pounding in his head.

The only light in the room was spilling in through the open doorway, casting shadows in all directions. Fitz assumed it was a storeroom. Searching the wall for a light switch, Fitz finally found one behind a stack of crates. When the single exposed light bulb hanging from the ceiling came to life, he saw he was, in fact, standing in a small storage area. Cases of different liquor bottles filled most of the room.

Through the only other door, Fitz found himself back in the bar area where he'd spoken with Eaves earlier. It was dark and empty now. The smell of stale beer and cigarette smoke hung in the air.

Returning to the storeroom, Fitz made for the table in the corner that functioned as a makeshift desk. Bills of sale littered the top of the badly scarred wooden surface. A few letters addressed to Roger Tipton lay unopened, along with the front page of a newspaper from several days earlier with a headline article about Lillian Martin's wedding.

Pulling a rickety chair over to the table, Fitz took a seat and looked over everything lying there again. All of the bills and mail were addressed to Tipton at the Blue Ridge Saloon, so no home address. He'd need to look in a telephone directory. Leaning back and exhaling in frustration, Fitz watched as his breath caused the pages of a small calendar tacked to the wall over the table to flutter in front of him. Eaves had circled yesterday's date.

Circumstantial as it was, Fitz was getting the feeling Eaves was involved in the kidnapping. Which meant he knew that Fitz was on to him and Milford. Assuming Milford was even in the picture for any of this. Sure, someone tossed Milford's place, but he told his neighbor he was going to visit his sister. Maybe that was the truth, and he really was out of town. The only reason Fitz had zeroed in on Milford in the first place was because he lived in Parker, and when he spoke with the bartender, *Tipton* said he'd been complaining about how down on his luck he was. Putting those two bits of information together led him to assume Milford was the guy he was looking for.

"Dammit," Fitz said to the empty room.

Just when Fitz thought he was finally able to answer some of the questions he'd been dealing with for the last day, he was now faced with new ones.

Fitz slammed his hand down on the table in exasperation. Then he heard something metal hit the cement floor. Looking down, lying next to his shoe, was a key. Reaching under the table, he found a tiny hook where the key must have been hung to keep it out of sight.

Picking the key up, Fitz walked to the center of the room, where he could hold it up to the light and have a better look at it. It didn't look like anything special. Just a regular key to a door lock. But what door? And where?

Fitz looked around the room, something tugging at the back of his mind. He was missing something. No, he thought, the *building* was missing something. It was two stories. But there weren't any stairs in this room or out in the bar.

How do you get upstairs, he wondered.

He stepped back out into the larger room to see there was a set of steps obstructed from view. Somehow, he'd missed it at first because of how dark the bar was, but there was a door at the end of the bar.

Taking his revolver from under his jacket, he crept over and looked for a keyhole but didn't find one. Carefully opening the door, he found a toilet and sink in a space barely larger than a broom closet.

Fitz slowly turned, taking in the entire place. There was a front door, the door to the bathroom, and the door to the storage. No way to get to the second floor from inside the bar itself. So, he walked back into the storeroom. Two stacks of wooden crates sat against the side wall. At their base, in front of them, he thought he saw scratches along the floor.

"If this were London in an old manor house in one of Agatha Christie's novels, this would be a bookshelf covering a secret room," he said, walking over and taking a firm grip on one of the crates. "What are the chances?" he asked, pulling the crates toward him.

Chapter Fifty-Six

"Thank you, Agatha," Fitz said as the two stacks of crates, which had been nailed together, swung toward him, revealing…a hidden door. A hidden door with a lock, he noted.

The key he'd found slipped easily into the keyhole, and with a quick turn, he heard a click and was able to open the door. Behind it, he found a wall of darkness. Pulling his lighter from his pocket, he used the orange glow from the flame to peak into the opening. The hidden door and masking crates had been covering a staircase leading up to the second floor. At the top of the stairs, he could see the faintest outline of another door. Light was trickling in around it through the frame.

There didn't appear to be a light switch at the base of the steps, so Fitz started up the stairs with the lighter in one hand and his revolver in the other. The stairs moaned and creaked as he took them as quickly as possible. He wasn't concerned with the sounds because if either Eaves or Milford were upstairs, the door downstairs wouldn't have been locked and covered up. If there was any chance of anyone being upstairs right now, it was going to be Lillian Martin, Fitz thought as his pulse began to quicken.

Snapping his lighter closed and tucking it back in his pocket, Fitz tightened his grip on the gun and reached for the door handle. It turned effortlessly. Inching the door open, Fitz peered through the crack into a large room that sat above the bar. Sunlight from two windows in the front of the building lit up the entire room, making it infinitely easier to take in the space than it had been in the dark storage room.

Listening, Fitz thought he heard the sound of someone breathing. But, with his head still throbbing and his senses still not fully returned to him, he couldn't be certain. There was only one way to find out. Pushing through the door, he instantly crouched down in a defensive position in case anyone tried taking a shot at him. Once his eyes fully adjusted from the quick transition from the darkness of the stairwell to the bright sunlight in the room, he saw that he wasn't alone. But he was in no danger.

There were only two pieces of furniture in the room. A wooden chair was leaning against the wall that matched the one down in the storage room and in the corner, an old metal bed. Upon which lay Lillian Martin in her wedding dress, bound, gagged, and blindfolded.

Chapter Fifty-Seven

1985 . . .

"Well, that was something," Tommy said as he climbed into the car. "*It wasn't her place* to tell the people looking for her sister that she was secretly seeing some rich playboy, giving them a solid suspect to look at. What the hell, dude? She seemed perfectly happy to think her sister just picked up and left. Didn't seem to question it at all. I mean, if I was the child of a wealthy father and had been kidnapped myself, then my sister goes missing…I don't know… maybe, just *maybe,* I would think there was some sort of foul play involved. There you go. Possibility number two."

"I understand your frustration. But hindsight is twenty-twenty. We don't know what the actual circumstances were at the time. It was forty years ago. And, as far as it *not being her place*…she was a child. I have a feeling she grew up in a house where she and her sister were meant to be seen and not heard," Ben argued, trying to play devil's advocate.

Ben sat behind the steering wheel, staring out the window, thinking for a moment. "There's no benefit in litigating what she should or shouldn't have done back in 1945. We just need to focus on the here and now and the information *we* have available to us. And *we* just learned that Lucy was secretly seeing Sonny Baker. So, *we* need to talk to Sonny."

"That's going to go over real well. *We,*" Tommy said, mocking Ben, "have to question one of *the* Bakers about another murder that happened in Parker

City. How are the same people always involved in our cases?"

"First of all...*we*..."

"Can we please stop saying 'we' that way?" Tommy erupted.

Ben smiled, then continued by once again pointing out, "We don't know Lucy was murdered."

"Still! You know what I mean." Tommy shook out a cigarette, then offered one to Ben.

"Thank you. But no matter how many times you offer, I'm not going to accept."

"One of these days, you will."

It was a scene that played out in a similar fashion at least once a day. Ben had never smoked a day in his life and didn't intend to start. Tommy partially did it to annoy his friend, and...no, that was the only reason he did it.

"And second," Ben continued, "since when do you care about ruffling feathers?"

"Admittedly, it isn't like when old Stanley was around. He nearly had a heart attack the time he found out we questioned the mayor's sons." Tommy smiled, thinking back to the late chief's reaction.

One of the victims of the Spring Strangler had been the ex-girlfriend of one of the mayor's twin boys. Naturally, they needed to speak with him to cover their bases. If it had been up to Edgar Stanley, there would have been a list of people in Parker City who would never be questioned under any circumstance. The mayor and his family would be on the list. Luckily, Chief Stanley wasn't around any longer. Tommy had used a poor choice of words, though, because Stanley had, in fact, suffered a massive heart attack and died at his desk. Not that it was a surprise. He was overweight, easily agitated, and was never seen without a cigar in his mouth.

Just to be on the safe side, Ben decided to let Chief Brent know they were going to want to talk with Sonny Baker. On their way back to Parker, Ben radioed the station and asked to be put through to the chief. After explaining what they'd learned from talking to Lillian and Richard Mercer, he said they'd like to have a chance to speak with Sonny Baker. He was in no way a suspect, considering they didn't know how Lucy died, but he was someone who might be able to shed some light on the events of forty years ago.

Brent offered to set up a meeting with Sonny. He'd ask him to come in for an informal conversation as a way for him to help fill in some blanks for the detectives in their investigation.

"We just need to keep it as non-confrontational as possible," Brent said. "I'm talking to you, Detective Mason."

Tommy took the radio mic from Ben and said, "I promise to be on my best behavior. But if he starts anything…"

Ben snatched the mic back before he could finish.

They let the chief know when they expected to arrive back at the station, and he said he'd try to get Sonny in as soon as he could.

"Thanks, Chief," Ben said, signing off.

After a few minutes of silence, as Tommy watched the other cars on the road around them, he turned to Ben and said, "I have an important question. What are we going to do for lunch?"

Chapter Fifty-Eight

Sonny Baker was seated at the small conference table across from Chief Brent when Ben and Tommy walked into the chief's office. Older now, in many ways, he still gave off the impression of being a bit of a rake. He had a long line of ex-wives who were happy to attest to his wandering eye. But for his personal flaws, he'd proven to be a savvy businessman. Sharing the reins of the Baker family's extensive holdings with his sister Beverly, they'd parlayed the family's enterprises into a multi-million dollar empire before her death. One he continued to oversee and expand.

"Detectives," the chief said as he gestured for them to have a seat at the table, "I believe you both know Sampson Baker."

"Good afternoon, Mr. Baker," Ben said as he sat down and laid his notebook on the table in front of him.

"Please, it's just Sonny," he said with a cheeky smile that rivaled Tommy's. Then, to clear up any confusion, added, "I've never been a fan of the name Sampson. Makes me sound like a character in the Bible. It was my mother's father's name."

Ben was glad Sonny Baker was looking directly at him, and wasn't able to see Tommy roll his eyes.

"Thank you for coming in on such short notice. We really appreciate you taking the time," Ben said.

Leaning back so the chair was balancing on its back legs, Sonny clasped his hands behind his head, making himself more comfortable. "Chief Brent says you're working on a case I might be able to help with. I can't imagine how, but I'm intrigued."

Ben took a deep breath before diving in.

"Mr. Baker…Sonny, in the last couple of days, we've begun looking into the disappearance of Lucy Mercer."

The smile on the man's face suddenly disappeared. "Lucy Mercer? As in the same Lucy Mercer that went missing what, thirty-forty years ago?"

"Yes. There have been some new developments."

Sonny slowly sat forward, leaning his elbows on the table. "New developments? What does that mean? And what could *I* possibly have to do with this? I barely even knew her."

"We understand that at one time, you and her sister, Lillian, were dating."

"Sure. But I dated a lot of girls back then."

"Did you ever have a relationship with Lucy?" Tommy pointedly asked.

Sonny's face showed signs of confusion. "We…well, we may have run into each other out at bars from time to time. We ran in the same social set. There was this one place the gang used to hang out. What was the name of it? Smokey Joe's! I'd see her there a lot. But we didn't have a *romantic* relationship."

"Would Lucy have called it a romantic relationship?" Tommy pressed.

"I have no idea. She was a smart girl. I certainly didn't lead her on if that's what I think you're implying. If I remember correctly, Lucy wasn't as innocent as people would have assumed. I'm sure she had her share of flings. Hell, I remember the first time she met Sid and the way she threw herself at him." Running his hand through his hair, he looked to Brent and asked, "Chief, what exactly are you looking for here? Am I being accused of something?"

"That depends," Tommy said.

"Hold on, everyone," Brent said, raising his hands. Looking at Ben, he raised his eyebrows, wordlessly asking how much they should tell Baker.

Ben bit his lower lip as he mentally ran through the benefits and the possible downfalls of sharing too much information with a potential suspect. Telling him the truth could earn some goodwill and cooperation. But if he was the cause of Lucy's death, he'd know what cards they were holding and how to play his own.

"Mr. Baker," Ben began slowly, "we were recently told that you were secretly seeing Lucy around the time of her disappearance."

"*Secretly* seeing her? Who told you that?"

"It was her sister."

"I have no idea why Lillian would think that. Lucy and I were friendly. That's all. There was nothing romantic between us. Lucy was too headstrong."

"Didn't like women with opinions back in the '40s, did you," is what Tommy would have liked to have said. But to his credit, he kept his mouth closed.

"Why would Lillian think you two were seeing each other?" Ben asked.

"I told you. I have no idea. I know I had…have a reputation. I accept that. It's just who I am. But Lucy was nothing more than a friendly acquaintance. I swear to you."

"What did you think when you found out Lucy had disappeared?"

"I didn't think much of it really. I guess, like a lot of other people, I assumed she ran off. Decided to leave Parker and start a new life somewhere. I honestly can't even think of the last time I spoke to her."

"So, for the record, you are saying you have no idea where she could have gone or if she ran away with someone?"

"Not at all, Detective. I don't know anything about her disappearance."

"After she went missing, at any time, did Sydney Mercer speak to you about her?"

The bewildered look reappeared on Sonny's face. "Why would he? Sid and I rarely spoke after he and Lillian got together. But, no. He never talked to me about Lucy."

Chapter Fifty-Nine

"I hate to admit it," Tommy said when he and Ben were back in their office, "but I don't think he had anything to do with it. I don't like him very much. But he seemed pretty genuine to me."

"I think I agree with you. And when I asked about Mercer talking to him, that really confused him."

"Do you think Mercer just told Lillian he'd talk to him and never did? After all, it wasn't a woman's place to have thoughts back then."

Ben raised an eyebrow. "Social commentary aside, I'm not sure what I think yet. Something he said about Lucy having a lot of flings is bothering me. My mind is still percolating."

"Speaking of percolating. I'm gonna run down the hall and grab some coffee. Want a cup?"

"Always," Ben said, handing his old Baltimore Colts mug to his partner.

Letting out a long sigh, Ben opened the folder with the photos of Lucy Martin and spread them out on his desk. There was still something tugging at the back of his mind from the conversation they'd just had with Sonny Baker. Something he'd said was now bothering Ben. Unfortunately, he couldn't remember exactly what it was. He wished they'd been able to tape-record the interview, but that would have come off too much like an interrogation. But at least he'd have something to refer to.

Picking up one of the photos to examine for the dozenth time, Ben was interrupted by the sharp ring of his telephone.

"This is Ben Winters."

"Detective, Dr. Chen from the Medical Examiner's Office in Baltimore."

A surge of adrenaline brought Ben to his feet. "Hello, Doctor. What can I do for you?"

"It's actually what I can do for you. We were successfully able to thaw the body in a manner that allowed us to conduct a full postmortem. The report is being typed up as we speak, but I thought you'd want to hear the broad strokes of our findings as soon as possible."

"That I do, Doctor," Ben said, sitting down and grabbing his notebook so he could take notes.

"First off, I can confirm that Lucille Martin died due to blunt force trauma to the back of the skull."

"The contusion on the back of her head?" Ben asked.

"Correct. The bruising was visible when she was brought in. We found that the blow caused a hematoma, which caused her death."

Ben scribbled some notes as he asked, "Is there any way this could have been an accident? That she fell backwards and hit her head?"

There was a pause before Chen answered, "Anything is possible, Detective, but it is our conclusion someone inflicted the wound. We were able to see some type of pattern in the bruising when we were able to examine it more closely. I've seen enough over the years to know this doesn't look like a trip and fall. Plus, there was a good deal of force behind the blow."

"Did you take photographs of the pattern?"

"Of course, Detective. They'll accompany my report tomorrow."

"This is very helpful. Thank you, Doctor Chen. Was there anything else significant?"

"I'd say so," Chen said to the sound of flipping papers. "Miss Martin was about four months pregnant when she died."

Tommy walked back into the office with their coffee in just enough time to see Ben catch the phone as it fell from his ear.

Chapter Sixty

The case had taken an abrupt and completely unexpected turn; Ben thought as he tried to make sense of the puzzle they had before them. It didn't seem to anyone involved that Lucy Martin's disappearance was in any way related to her sister's abduction. Ben couldn't even guess the odds of two such tragic events befalling a single family. It seemed, by all accounts, at the time, everyone went along with the story that Lucy just picked up and skipped town one night. And it didn't sound like anyone looked too hard to find her. Lillian said their father hired private detectives but to no avail. When Lucy never got in touch with anyone, they all moved on with their lives.

It was something Ben was having difficulty understanding. He and his older brother were not nearly as close as he and Tommy were. But if Brian disappeared, he wouldn't stop until he found out what happened to him. At the same time, Ben couldn't see his brother running off and never getting in touch with him if for no other reason than to say that he was alright.

All of that was moot though, because they now understood why Lucy Martin never got in touch with anyone after she supposedly ran away back in 1945. She didn't run away at all. Someone killed her with a blow to the back of the head. And then stuck her body in a freezer. Presumably, so she'd never be found. Why, then, had her body just turned up in the middle of a field?

The theory that it was her secret lover who'd committed the crime was the best they had to work with. The problem was, Lillian Martin said, her sister was involved with Sonny Baker. Sonny Baker abjectly denied it but said that

Lucy wasn't an angel to begin with, leading them to believe she might have had a string of flings. One of which could have led to her pregnancy.

Four months pregnant, according to the ME, there was no way she didn't know about the child. Did she tell the father, and that's what got her killed? He wasn't interested in having a child? Or he *couldn't* be found out to be the father because he was having an affair with someone he shouldn't have been?

Every answer led to more questions.

Shortly after receiving the call from Doctor Chen, Officer O'Connor appeared in the doorway of the Detective Squad holding two file folders. Ben nearly forgot he'd sent the patrolman on fact-finding errands that morning so he and Tommy could drive out to speak with Lillian Martin. It seemed like their little road trip had been days earlier when, in fact, it was only hours before.

"Hey, Pat. What did you find for us?" Ben asked, hoping against hope something the uniformed officer found would shed some light on the situation.

"I started at the *Herald-Dispatch*. The girl at the front desk was a little leery of a policeman showing up, but the editor was helpful. He showed me where the really old copies of the paper were kept. I would've never found them on my own. His secretary made me copies of these articles from the time Lucy Martin went missing," he said, handing over the first folder to Ben.

"There was a lot of talk about how her sister had just been kidnapped, so people wondered if there was a conspiracy against Ambassador Martin and his family. But when police searched Lucy's bedroom, they found some of her clothing was gone, so everyone assumed she ran away.

"Articles ran for a couple weeks straight, but then started to peter out when there weren't any new developments. The police chief at the time, well, acting police chief, was the first one to say he believed she ran away. With missing clothes from her room and no ransom demand, his comments read like he was happy to say she'd run off of her own accord."

"Even though her sister had been kidnapped a few weeks earlier," Tommy sighed.

"There was some bruhaha with the police chief and the kidnapping. Not the acting police chief, Earl Peters. The *actual* chief, Walter Buchanan. So the department was already smarting from one black eye."

Both of the detectives had read Fitz's notes about Buchanan and his false ransom demand. Neither of them could believe a police officer, let alone the chief himself, would pull a stunt like that. Using a young girl's kidnapping just to line one's own pockets. It was despicable. Fitz's personal notes used much stronger language.

Ben flipped through the copied articles, reading the headlines as O'Connor gave them the overview. In some instances, Ben wondered if the officer memorized what he'd read, he was so thorough with his briefing. Unfortunately, nothing he said triggered any new thoughts about the case or pointed them in any clear direction. There was one public story, and everyone stuck to it.

"Were you able to find out who owned the house on Fifth?" Ben asked after laying the folder with the newspaper articles aside.

"You didn't tell me the house fire was related to the Lucy Martin case," O'Connor said, opening the second folder.

Ben felt his pulse begin to quicken. O'Connor was correct. He hadn't told him the fire was in any way related to Lucy Martin's case because he had no evidence to back up that theory. It was just a feeling he got when he saw the giant deep freezer.

"What did you find?" he asked.

"Here's the crazy thing," O'Connor said, Ben's interest making him a little more excited to deliver the news, "the reason I've been gone so long is because it took some time at the Courthouse to find out who owned the house. It was owned by a small real estate company that was incorporated decades ago. So, a couple different clerks needed to help me do some more digging. It turns out the company that owns the house was started by one of the guys mentioned in one of those articles." O'Connor pointed triumphantly at the folder on Ben's desk.

Leaning forward in his chair, Tommy eagerly asked, "And who would that be?"

"Oh, right. Sorry. The house was owned by Sydney Mercer."

"Sonofa…" Ben began.

"…bitch," Tommy finished.

Chapter Sixty-One

1945 . . .

Forcing his gun back into its holster, Fitz crossed the room in only a couple of strides. Kneeling down next to the bed, Fitz carefully removed the man's dress tie that had been used to blindfold the young girl. A look of sheer terror stared back at him.

"Lillian, it's alright. My name is Fitz Mason. Your father hired me to find you. Everything's going to be okay. I'm going to untie you. Then we're going to scram."

Tears began to flow down the girl's pink cheeks as Fitz removed the gag from her mouth. "Help me. Please help me," she pleaded.

"I'm going to get you out of here," Fitz promised as he flipped open his switch knife and began working on the ropes binding her wrists to the bedframe. "Your family and fiancé have been worried about you. I'm going to get you home to them."

Fitz continued to comfort Lillian until he was finished cutting the ropes, constraining her.

Helping her to her feet, Fitz said, "I have a car right outside. Let's get you out of here."

In response, a voice from the doorway said, "Not so fast, Mack. You're not going anywhere with her."

Fitz and Lillian turned to see Roger Eaves and George Milford walking into the room, each carrying what looked to Fitz like their old military sidearms.

"George Milford and Roger Eaves, come to join the party, I see," Fitz said with a wry smile.

"It's Tipton now," Eaves corrected. "Changed my name not long after gettin' back. Thought it might be safer for Roger Eaves to disappear."

"Because you knew the ambassador would be keeping tabs on the gang that helped him rip off all those works of art?"

"Not the ambassador as much as his boy Grainger," Eaves offered. "He's the scary one."

"You know about the paintings?" Milford asked, his eyes narrowing.

"Afraid so, Georgie. So does the U.S. Army. Though I don't think they knew the extent of the jobs your little ring pulled. But they will when I hand over the list you made. Fitz Mason, by the way. We haven't been formally introduced. My apologies."

"What list?" Eaves barked, ignoring Fitz's show of manners.

"The one George there hid under his bed. It lists all the art you boys stole when you stole it, and from where. I bet it will be the first piece of evidence in your trial."

Fitz was hoping to keep them occupied talking about the art thefts long enough for him to figure out a plan that would get him and Lillian out of there without any bullet holes in them. Making things more complicated was the fact the arm he had wrapped around Lillian for support was the one he needed to reach for his gun.

"I forgot all about that," George said, suddenly remembering he had made a list. "You were in my house?"

"I wasn't the only one. Someone got there before me. Searched the whole place. It's a real mess. You're probably going to want to get someone in to help get things back in order. Well, you would if you weren't going to jail." Fitz winked.

"That's enough," Eaves hollered. "Nobody's goin' nowhere. First, you're gonna give me that list. Second, I'm gonna put a bullet in your head, and we're gonna dump you in the Tasker River. Then we're gonna go get the painting from Conrad."

Fitz could feel Lillian's body starting to shake.

"Gentleman," Fitz began, lacing his tone with as much charm as he could. "Maybe we can work something out here. We are all former soldiers. I'm just going to help Lillian sit down. Then we can talk. So, don't shoot."

As he helped guide Lillian back down to the bed, with the eye turned away from the two men, he gave her a wink to let her know it was all going to be alright. Taking a deep breath, Fitz paused. Then, in one sweeping motion, spun back toward Eaves and Milford while pulling his revolver. Now, the three men stood pointing their guns at one another as Lillian backed up against the wall, trying to make herself as small as possible.

"It's two against one, Mason," Milford pointed out. "Even if you got a shot off at one of us, the other would pump metal into you."

"It's actually two against two, I'm afraid," Fitz said with a disarming smile. "While you're both aiming at me, Joe Grainger is out there in the dark stairway, no doubt pointing a rather large gun at you."

"You expect us to buy that hokum?" Milford said, his gun twitching ever so slightly.

"See for yourself," Fitz said, gesturing with the barrel of his gun toward the darkness.

As Milford turned, what sounded like an explosion erupted, and a flash lit up the darkened stairs. The ex-Army man's chest exploded, sending him staggering backwards before falling to the floor. Simultaneously, Eaves raised his gun and was about to fire on Fitz, but he'd been distracted and caught off guard just long enough for Fitz to take advantage of those precious few seconds. In doing so, Fitz was able to get two shots off. Both striking Eaves just above his stomach. Before the man's body crumbled to the floor, Fitz was already turning to Lillian to make sure she was alright.

Chapter Sixty-Two

"I can't tell you how grateful I am, Fitz," Conrad Martin said, clasping the private investigator's shoulder with a firm grip. A half-drunk tumbler of scotch in the other.

The ambassador's confidence was once again on full display now that his daughter was returned to the safety—relatively speaking—of the family's home, Fitz thought. When the man felt in control, he put on a good show. But Fitz saw the façade crumble the previous evening. Now, Conrad Martin was back to his old, egotistical self.

Knowing what he did, Fitz was torn between the relief of knowing Lillian was unharmed and back with her family and the truth behind *why* she'd been taken. She was a pawn in a game she didn't even know she was playing. Because of her father's actions, she'd been put in danger. Sure, Eaves and Milford were out of the way for good. The other members of their crew were gone as well. But what else was Martin involved in? What other illegal activities was he a part of back in Europe using the cover of an American diplomat as his protection? And what dirty deeds was he doing now that he was back stateside? If Fitz started digging into it, what would he find?

"Fitz. Fitz? Are you listening to me?" the ambassador asked, giving him a shake to get his attention.

"Sorry, Conrad. I was just thinking about something."

"I have a question," Joe Grainger said after clearing his throat.

Until now, he'd been sitting quietly and quite comfortably in one of the big chairs by the fireplace. The three men had convened in the library shortly after he and Fitz returned from the Blue Ridge Saloon with Lillian and a police escort. They'd needed to answer some questions from Acting Chief Peters first, tell the tale of why they were there and what had transpired, but the minute they were able to get away, they bolted. The reason behind the kidnapping was still vague. At least as far as Peters knew. What he'd been told was that Eaves and Milford had held a grudge against the ambassador from the time they were stationed in Rome. No more was offered by either Fitz or Grainger. That was where the story ended.

"What's on your mind, Joe?" Fitz asked, leveling his gaze at him.

Leaning forward in his seat and resting his elbows on his knees, he asked, "How'd you know I was outside on the stairs?"

Fitz shook his head and let out a half chuckle.

"It was your aftershave, Joe. It's very distinct. I smelled you."

"Huh. You're good, Mason," he said, wagging his finger at the detective, then leaning back again, satisfied with the explanation.

"I smelled you…," Fitz continued, lowering his voice, "just like I did at George Milford's house. Right before you put my lights out."

The look that passed between Martin and his henchman was unmistakable. At this point, they didn't even try to hide it. And it told Fitz everything he needed to know.

"The way I figure it," Fitz went on, taking a cigarette out and lighting up, ignoring the rule about not smoking in the house, "you broke into Milford's place to see if you could figure out where he was keeping Lillian. Knowing he was one of the only people still alive who knew about the art thefts…and he was living in Parker City…you'd probably been keeping tabs on the poor slob. You were surprised when I showed up because, as far as you knew, I had no idea about George Milford and your crew of merry thieves. You had no choice but to knock me out so you could make an escape. Empty handed because you still didn't know where Lillian was. Or if Milford was even involved in the kidnapping. But you waited outside Milford's until I came to and followed me back to the Blue Ridge.

"How am I doing so far?" Fitz asked, taking a moment to let his words hang in the air. Neither man responded. Fitz would hate to play poker with these guys, the way their faces remained frozen and unflinching.

"What *you* didn't know was that Roger Eaves had changed his name to Roger Tipton and was now running a bar for former military men right here in Parker. You'd lost track of him in the last few years. But he was right here under your noses the whole time.

"The rest, you know." Fitz punctuated the end of his story by blowing a long stream of gray smoke in Grainger's direction.

Conrad Martin finished what remained in his glass then walked to the bar and poured himself another drink. With his back still to Fitz, he said, "I don't know what you think you know, Fitz, but—"

"Don't even try to blow smoke, Conrad. I wasn't born yesterday. Lillian was kidnapped because of your dirty little secret. The fact you were running a ring of art thieves while serving as ambassador in Rome. It all makes perfect sense. All the art in this house. Obviously, there's something to it because that's what Milford and Eaves were after, and you went looking for them. Well, you didn't. You sent your gorilla to do your dirty work."

The comment elicited a low animal—like growl from Grainger, who began to shift uncomfortably in his seat.

"Down, boy," Fitz snapped back.

When the ambassador turned, his fleshy face was a deep shade of crimson, his eyes boring into Fitz.

"Before you start denying it, Conrad, I heard you and Joe talking after you received the *real* ransom demand. And," pausing as he removed the envelope from his inside jacket pocket, "Milford kept a record of all the art you stole."

"What good's that going to do, Fitz? Who's going to believe a dead man?" Martin took a long slug from his glass. Fitz could tell the presentation of an actual piece of evidence surprised him. But he couldn't let on to the fact his mind was trying to quickly calculate all the scenarios of how this could play out and the trouble in which he could find himself.

"You know, Conrad, normally I would agree with you. But here's the rub. There's already a file on you. The government already suspects you of being involved in the theft of art while you were stationed in Rome. They just didn't have enough on you. But with this list, and what they'll no doubt find when they come in here and look around, they'll have enough for a prosecution. And I'll be happy to testify to what I know in court.

"Who knows, they might even send you back to Italy to stand trial. With the way things are going over there… I'd be willing to bet the Italian government would just love to put an American diplomat on trial for pillaging their country."

"Who's gonna take the word of a retired spook over a U.S. ambassador?" Grainger asked, pushing himself to his feet.

"You're forgetting, Joe, most people don't like him," Fitz answered, hitching his thumb toward Martin. "There are people in Washington who would be all too willing to hang him out to dry."

"The United States government would never admit that one of their ambassadors committed a crime like you're alleging," Martin pointed out. An air of overconfidence in his tone. "It would make the whole country look bad."

Fitz nodded in agreement. "You're probably right. No one's accusing you of not knowing how to play the international politics game. But that doesn't mean you won't be tried here in the States and held accountable. You broke enough laws in both countries. Once I turn this list over, it will be up to people smarter than me to decide what to do with you."

"You wouldn't dare," Martin snarled.

"Because of what you did, you put your daughter's life in danger. If you end up in prison, you should consider yourself lucky. I'm very happy I was able to bring Lillian back to her family. But I'll be damned if I turn my back on what you did."

Fitz dropped the smoldering end of his cigarette into the ambassador's glass, the ashes quickly disbursing through the expensive liquid. Fitz hated to ruin a good glass of scotch like that, but under the circumstances, it was better than decking Martin. Satisfied that he was leaving the two men unnerved about what their futures held, Fitz turned, leaving both Martin and Grainger standing flatfooted in the library, their jaws clenched, anger flaring in their eyes, and walked out the door.

Chapter Sixty-Three

1985 . . .

The revelation that Sydney Mercer owned the house that someone set fire to only the night before was all Ben needed to hear. The oddly shaped pieces of the puzzle with which they were dealing began fitting together. At least, he thought he was beginning to get an idea of the full picture. It also helped to jog loose from the overloaded recesses of his memory what Sonny Baker had said about Lucy. What he'd said that was tugging at the back of his mind. But he was going to need to speak with Sonny again for some clarification. Considering they concluded their initial sit down on cordial terms, Ben saw no reason for Baker to shut him out now and not be willing to answer a few additional questions. Especially when they in no way reflected badly on himself.

With the adrenaline pumping and his heart picking up the pace to match the speed his mind was now racing, Ben reminded himself everything he was thinking was all supposition. A guess. Maybe, at best, a theory. He needed proof to support his idea. Which was why he also needed to call Lieutenant Clover and find out what CSU discovered at the scene of the fire. He hadn't heard anything from the team yet.

He didn't know if that was a good thing or not.

If they were still working the scene, hours after they'd been called out, it meant they'd found a treasure trove of potentially usable forensics. On the other hand, if they'd found nothing, how important would it have been for Clover to call and let him know? It wasn't as though the State's CSU team only worked on cases for Parker City. Clover's unit dealt with cases throughout the western part of the state. The task of sharing the bad news that they'd come up empty could easily have been relegated to the bottom of his list of things to do. Even though Ben had made sure the call-out information included the possibility the fire may be related to the open Lucy Martin case.

Ben needed to get all of his ducks in a row before speaking with Lillian again. To do that, he needed to make some phone calls. More importantly, he needed to fill Tommy in on what he was thinking because his partner had been staring at him since O'Connor dropped the Sydney Mercer bomb.

Chapter Sixty-Four

"Mrs. Mercer, I just want to thank you and your son for coming out this morning to speak with us again. Since we last spoke, there have been some developments in the case that we thought we should share with you."

Ben was seated next to the chief at the same small conference table they'd sat at to speak with Sonny Baker the afternoon before. Lillian Mercer and her son Richard sat on the other side of the table while Tommy perched on the window ledge near the door. After discussing the matter with Brent, it was decided to invite the Mercers to the station rather than the detectives going back out to Catonsville. The conversation that needed to be had was not going to be an easy one. It would need to be more formal, so the setting of the PCPD was the choice.

However, no one wanted to use one of the station's two interview rooms. Ben tried to avoid using either of the "boxes," as the uniformed officers referred to them, as much as possible. It didn't matter if you put an innocent witness or an obviously criminal suspect in the harshly lit room. The reaction was the same. The individual was immediately on edge, making it more difficult to get information out of them. Whether they were there to be helpful or not. Ben wanted Lillian and Richard to feel more comfortable and not as though they were being treated as some sort of common criminals.

It had taken the remainder of the afternoon for Ben to track down Sonny Baker so he could ask him a number of follow-up questions. While he was doing that, Tommy paid a visit to the State Police Barracks on the other side of town to check in with Lieutenant Clover and his techs. After both detectives completed their tasks, they sat in their office with burgers and fries from the joint across the street from the station and worked on putting all the pieces together. Once they were finished and felt they had a solid working theory, one Chief Brent also agreed made the most sense, they called and asked the Mercers to come to the station the next morning.

Lillian, though still exuding elegance and impeccably dressed, looked tired, Ben noticed as she was shown into the chief's office. The confident woman they'd met yesterday was nowhere to be seen today. Understandable as it was. In less than two weeks, the woman had lost her husband and been confronted with the tragic reality that her missing sister had been dead for forty years. One or the other would take its toll on a person. But for both to occur so close together was devastating by anyone's standards. It was a one-two punch. Ben would have understood if Lillian had tried to avoid the meeting. There was no way for him to know how overwhelmed she was. But she'd agreed to meet again without question. She'd said she wanted to know what happened to her sister regardless. In that, Ben saw the strong woman she truly was. Which is what made Ben wonder how much she actually knew.

With trembling hands, Lillian sat playing with the wedding ring on her long, thin finger as everyone settled in around the conference table. It was the only outward sign of nerves she exhibited.

Richard Mercer, however, looked positively out of sorts. With a line of perspiration running along his hairline, his eyes continued to dart around the room as he tried to decide whether to sit with his hands on the conference table or in his lap. To the three police officers in the room, Richard was displaying the telltale signs of a man who thought he was about to be charged with the murder of his aunt. Impossible as that was, considering she died long before he was even born. But he still looked guilty of something. And that was what Ben needed to see. It went a long way in helping to prove his theory. Richard Mercer was going to be more help in getting to the truth than Ben realized.

"Have you found out what happened to my sister, Detective Winters?" Lillian asked. Her voice demonstrated the slightest tremor. Ben wondered how forcefully she was holding back her emotions.

"Mrs. Mercer, like I said, we have come across new information that we believe explains a great deal." Ben was purposefully being vague for the time being. "But there are still a few blanks he needed filled in. We're hoping you can help us with them."

When she didn't respond one way or the other, Ben continued.

"You met your late husband, Sydney, at a Christmas party at the home of Sonny Baker in 1944. Is that correct?"

"Yes. I did."

"You then started dating, became engaged, and were planning an April wedding in 1945."

"I understand that may seem rather quick, Detective. But Sydney and I fell madly in love and wanted to get married as soon as we could. There's nothing wrong with that."

"I'm not saying there is," Ben agreed. "Love at first sight; it's what many people dream of. I'm just trying to make sure I have the correct timeline of your relationship. You had never met Sydney Mercer prior to that Christmas party in 1944, correct?"

"That's correct," she said, her brow furrowing as she tried to understand where Ben was heading.

"When did your sister, Lucy, first meet your late husband?"

Lillian cocked her head for a moment before answering, "Lucy met Sydney sometime after we began dating. I believe my mother invited him over for dinner one night. Probably not long after we met. It was forty years ago. I can't remember exactly."

"Is it possible your sister actually met Mr. Mercer *before* you did?"

"I don't understand."

"Mrs. Mercer, did Lucy frequent any bars? Have a favorite one she'd go to with you or her friends? Particularly, one called Smokey Joe's?"

"I certainly remember Smokey Joe's. Yes. Lucy would…sometimes go there. It was a very popular spot with our set, you understand."

"Of course. It was also a favorite of Sonny Baker's. We spoke with him yesterday. And when he had friends in town, he'd take them to Smokey Joe's for drinks. Which is what happened one evening when your husband came to town. In fact, it was the same night Sonny Baker invited Sydney to the Christmas party where you'd meet him."

"Alright," Lillian said cautiously. "I still don't understand what that has to do with my sister."

"That same night, Lucy was at Smokey Joe's with some of her friends, and Sonny Baker specifically remembered introducing them. Your sister met Sydney Mercer before you did," Ben said, gauging her reaction.

"She couldn't have. She would have told me," Lillian protested.

"Not necessarily," Ben said. "According to Sonny, your sister took an instant liking to Syndey. And he to her. They became very friendly that evening. Sonny also said they left the bar together. He could only speculate as to what happened after that."

The color quickly drained from Lillian's face as she began to understand what Ben was suggesting. She'd stopped fidgeting with her ring, laying both hands flat on the table. Her eyes focused on Ben. No one ever said Lillian wasn't a smart woman. In the silence, Ben could see she was beginning to understand what he was saying while still not entirely grasping how the timing of her sister and late husband's meeting had anything to do with Lucy's eventual disappearance.

The silence continued to fill the room until it was Richard who spoke.

"Detective Winters, please stop. My mother doesn't need to hear this. She doesn't need to know what happened. Not like this. Please!"

All eyes quickly turned to him.

"Mr. Mercer, is there something you would like to—"

"No! I wouldn't *like* to anything. I wish none of this had happened."

"None of what?"

"Mother, I am so sorry. I'm so sorry."

"Richard, what are you talking about? What are *you* sorry for?" Lillian was the picture of confusion.

"It was Dad. Everything was his fault."

Chapter Sixty-Five

After taking a few minutes, Ben was able to explain everything they'd uncovered the previous afternoon to Lillian. Sonny had said Lucy and Syndey Mercer were obviously attracted to one another from the moment they met. During their first conversation in the chief's office, he'd said how Lucy could be very flirtatious and how he remembered the way she threw herself at *Sid*. For whatever reason, at the time, Ben hadn't realized the comment was about Syndey Mercer. Up until then, no one referred to him as "Sid," so Ben didn't make the connection right away, even though it was obvious, looking back.

Ben then had to tell Lillian that her sister was four months pregnant when she was killed. Pregnant with Sydney Mercer's child. The pain in her eyes felt like a punch to Ben's gut.

"How could you possibly know it was Sydney's child?" Lillian demanded.

From the folder lying in front of him on the table, Ben withdrew a clear plastic evidence page. In it was the charred remains of a sheet of paper. A large portion of the letter was missing, but enough remained to reveal the truth of the matter.

"Because," Ben said, sliding the evidence bag across the table, "we found a letter Lucy had written to him. Well, a fragment of a letter begging him not to marry you because they belonged together…and that she was carrying his child."

"Where…where did you find this?" Lillian managed.

"The Crime Scene Unit found it yesterday morning when they were searching through a house on Fifth Street here in Parker City that someone tried to burn down two nights ago. A house your late husband owned.

"This was where your sister's body had been kept. The person who started the fire was trying to get rid of all the evidence. This letter, along with what CSU believe were other letters–too damaged to read, as well as the deep freezer where Lucy's body was…" Ben didn't finish the sentence.

Tears began to well up in Lillian's eyes, one finally streaking down her cheek taking a line of mascara along with it.

Ben continued, saying, "Because the lid to the freezer was closed, the inside was not damaged by the fire. CSU found human tissue which they worked with the Medical Examiner's Office in Baltimore to compare last night. You see, this case has been of great interest to everyone involved, so running these tests got moved to the front of the line.

"The human tissue inside the freezer matched the sample taken from your sister."

"I don't understand. I don't understand," Lillian repeated. "Sydney was hiding Lucy's body all this time? Because… But who set fire to the house?"

Ben took a sheet of paper from the folder that had held the evidence bag. It was part of a CSU report.

"Inside the freezer, fingerprints were also discovered. We believe they belong to the person who removed Lucy's body from the freezer and who later returned to destroy the evidence."

Lillian finally understood Richard's reaction. Ben saw the realization in her tearful eyes. Turning to her son, she barely whispered, "No…"

Looking away, Richard Mercer's shoulders sagged, and he let out a deep sigh of defeat.

"The fingerprints found in the freezer," Ben said, pointing to the report, "match the ones on file with your real estate license, Mr. Mercer."

Richard turned to Ben, about to say something, but froze when Ben held up his hand.

"Before you say anything, Mr. Mercer, I need to advise you that you have the right to remain silent. Anything you say may be used against you in a court of law. You have the right to speak with an attorney before you answer any questions. If you wish to speak to an attorney but cannot afford to hire one, you will not be asked any questions at this time, and you may request the court to appoint a lawyer for you. If you do agree to answer any of my questions now, you may stop at any time and request an attorney."

Ben was not placing Richard Mercer under arrest, however still needed to Mirandize him. If and when he was charged, no one wanted anything he said going forward to be thrown out by a judge because the police hadn't followed proper procedure. But there was still one more thing Ben wanted to tell Mercer.

"Advising you of your rights is for your protection, Mr. Mercer. But I have already spoken with the Parker County State's Attorney's Office. If your lawyer contacts them, I have been assured because of the circumstances surrounding your actions, something will be able to be worked out. We just need you to answer a few questions for us now."

Neither Ben, Tommy, nor Chief Brent had any interest in seeing Richard Mercer charged with anything. The whole sordid case needed to finally be put to bed once and for all without harming any more people. But they still needed Mercer's help in closing the case.

"I understand, Detective," Mercer said. "I don't care what happens to me at this point. I just want this over."

"Well, we still care about what happens to you, Mr. Mercer," the chief said, speaking for the first time. "Before we go any further, we just need you to sign this form saying you have been advised of your rights and are currently waiving them."

Ben slid another paper from the folder. The previous afternoon, they'd planned every move that would be made. After Richard Mercer signed the form and passed it back to Ben, they continued.

"Mr. Mercer, how did you know where your aunt's body was?" Ben asked.

"I am the executor of my father's estate. After he died, our lawyers delivered a number of papers to me along with my father's will. Wishes he'd made for his funeral, certain bequests. It was all very standard. But there was also another letter. Sealed. Even the lawyers said they didn't know what it contained."

Mercer turned away, trying to hold himself together.

"What was in the letter, Mr. Mercer?" Ben gently prodded, recognizing what a difficult position the man found himself.

"It was a confession," Mercer finally said after a pained silence. "My father wrote a confession."

Chapter Sixty-Six

1945 . . .

It had been two weeks to the day since Lillian had been found and rescued from the men who'd taken her. By then, the story of her abduction had become national news. So, it was not just the local newspapers that ran the announcement of the new wedding date. Something that had taken Lucy very much by surprise. Her sister had barely left her bedroom for the first few days after she'd come home. Now, splashed across the front page was the news the wedding would be held the following week. How could it be so soon? After everything that had happened, she'd expected it to be some time before Lillian and Sydney decided to set a new date–if they ever set one at all.

Lucy was beside herself.

How could Sydney still be going ahead with all of this, she thought as she turned onto the street where the house he'd been renting in Parker City for the last several months sat.

It was one thing for him to dismiss her before. But now, there was no way he'd be able to. He'd have to call off the wedding.

Even though she'd proclaimed her love for him time and time again, he said he was marrying Lillian. Nothing was going to change his mind.

Her heart had already been aching that morning two weeks ago as she watched her sister putting on her wedding dress. But then, when Lillian was kidnapped, everything turned upside down. She didn't think she could feel any worse than she did then. But two days after her sister's return, she'd received news that had shaken her to the very core. News that she'd wanted to share with Sydney but was never able to get him alone. She'd finally resorted to posting a letter to him a couple days ago, immediately regretting it. She didn't want him to find out like that. But when she'd received no reply, she knew she needed to see him in person. To plead her case one more time.

Which is why she was on her way to see him face-to-face.

As she pulled up in front of the house, she was both relieved and terrified to see Sydney's sleek black Roadster sitting in the driveway.

She didn't even bother to knock, just turned the doorknob and marched right into the house. Sydney had a den off the entryway where he'd review plans and reports he'd brought home with him. Sitting behind his desk now, he was startled by the unexpected intrusion.

"Lucy! What are you doing here?" he demanded, pushing himself out of his chair.

"Sid, I need to speak with you. I've been trying to talk to you. I have to tell you something."

"I really don't have time for this. I'm really very busy."

"But…but…" for a moment, Lucy didn't know what to say. Then, slamming the newspaper down on his desk on top of the drawing for some building, she shouted, "How can you still be going through with this?"

Picking up the paper and reading the headline, he said, "Lucy, I told you. I love Lillian. We had fun for a few weeks, but it wasn't serious. I'm marrying your sister."

"But what I told you in the letter…?"

"What letter?"

"When I wasn't able to get you alone, I wrote you a letter this week. You didn't get it?"

"Oh. That."

She felt crushed. His response was so cold and unfeeling. Her life was about to come crashing down around her, and that was all he could say.

"I told you—"

Reaching into his bottom desk drawer, Sydney removed a stack of envelopes and tossed them on the desk. "I didn't even bother to read it, Lucy. I told you to stop sending me letters."

"But, Sydney…"

"No buts, Lucy. You have to stop this."

"I'm pregnant!" she blurted out just before she burst into tears.

Sydney's jaw dropped.

There was a long pause before he managed to stammer, "What does that have to do with me?"

"It's your child, Sydney! I'm pregnant with your child."

"How do I know it's mine?"

"Because I may like to have fun, but I'm not some cheap harlot! I haven't been with anyone but you!"

"I… I… I don't… we can't…" He slumped into his chair and put his head in his hands. Lucy slowly walked over and put her hand on his shoulder. When he looked up at her, he said, "We can take care of this. I can make a few calls. There are ways to deal with this sort of thing."

Horrified, she pulled her hand away. "This sort of thing. Take care of it."

"Yes, Lucy. You can't think you can have this child."

"We can do it together. You just need to tell Lillian and–"

"What are you saying?! After what she's been through. I can't walk away from her now and marry you! It will ruin me."

Trembling, Lucy realized she was truly seeing the man she'd fallen so much in love with for the first time. "Lillian has to know."

"Absolutely not!" he said, shooting out of his chair, scaring Lucy enough to take a step back.

As she made a move toward the door, he grabbed her wrist and spun her around, bringing them nose-to-nose. "We can't tell your sister. We can't tell anyone. I'm going to arrange to have this taken care of, and then we'll forget all about it."

"No!" she screamed, slapping him with her free hand.

Turning to run, she didn't see him grab the heavy decorative metal paperweight from his desk.

Chapter Sixty-Seven

1985 . . .

"The letter was dated years ago," Mercer said, looking to his mother. "He said how much he regretted it the moment it happened. He never meant to hurt her."

Ben was jotting down everything the younger Mercer was saying.

"So, Lucy's death was an *accident*?" Tommy just wanted to clarify that's what he was saying.

"Yes. That's what the letter said."

"But hiding the body, that part was willful?"

"I can't possibly imagine what my father was thinking at the time, Detective."

"And when you received this letter from your lawyers and read it, what did you do?" Ben asked.

"I went to the house. I couldn't believe it. But then I saw the freezer and... I wanted to get rid of everything."

"But you moved the body," Ben pointed out.

"I wanted my mother to have closure. To know her sister was actually gone."

Ben looked to Tommy to see what he was thinking. With a barely perceptible shrug, both detectives knew they were thinking the same thing. As screwed up as it was. They had a solution to the case.

"Do you still have the confession your father wrote?" Tommy asked.

Both Ben and Tommy held their breath as Mercer looked down at his hands resting in his lap. If he'd destroyed the letter confessing to the killing, then all they'd have to go on was his word. While there was no reason to doubt what he told them—it wasn't as if he could be a suspect in the death of his aunt—it still left the possibility that the state's attorney had suggested when he'd spoken with the detectives.

"You're saying Sydney Mercer was the killer. With everything you've told me, there's the chance Lillian found out Lucy was pregnant and killed her out of anger. Then Sydney hid the body to protect his soon-to-be wife," he'd argued, positing another potential theory.

Ben countered by saying, "But there is nothing that indicates Lillian knew anything about the pregnancy, the fact Lucy had met Sydney Mercer before she did, or where the body's been kept for the last four decades."

"I agree with you, Detective. Which is why this case sucks, and it needs to go away. At most, going by your theory, Richard Mercer is guilty of helping to cover up a murder by not calling the police the minute he read his father's confession, along with tampering with evidence and possibly obstruction of a police investigation. I'm sure I could figure out more, but I think that's good enough. Otherwise, he is *still* helping to cover up the murder, but this time to protect his mother."

After a brief pause, the state's attorney said, "Look, Ben, I don't want to charge this guy with anything. At the end of the day, it looks like he's just a guy covering for something one of his parents did forty years ago. I'm not a mean guy. I don't want to punish someone just to make a point. If Sydney Mercer killed Lucy Martin, there's nothing we can do about it now. But if there's a slight chance Lillian could have been the one who killed her sister…we may need to take some time to look into that."

Ben was silently praying Richard Mercer had not thrown the confession into the fire. It was the one piece of evidence that would put an end to the case right then and there. So, Ben felt an incredible sense of relief when Mercer reached into his inside jacket pocket and laid an envelope on the table.

"When Mother said you called last night, I had a feeling you'd figured everything out. So, I brought this with me today. I just want all of this to be over."

Sliding the envelope across the table, Ben instantly felt a weight lift from his shoulders.

Chapter Sixty-Eight

"Y ou know you got lucky with the written confession," Chief Brent said to Ben while they stood in the second-floor breakroom pouring themselves a couple of cups of coffee.

"Yeah. But I knew there had to be some way Richard Mercer found out about the Fifth Street house and what was in it. And the way he spoke of his father when we first met him… There was something there. An anger. More than just the usual father-son tension. Something new and still raw. I had a hunch."

"So, you just made that jump?"

"Tommy thought it sounded reasonable," Ben offered, taking a sip of his coffee.

"Oh, yes. Because we want Detective Mason being the arbiter of what does and doesn't make sense. Tell me, Ben, at any point, did he suggest Lucy Martin was kidnapped by ninjas?"

"That doesn't make any sense," Tommy said, standing in the doorway to the break room. "Ninjas are assassins. I would have suggested ninjas *killed* Lucy Martin. Talking about kidnapping, strictly speaking, I would have gone with mercenaries."

"What are you wearing?" Ben asked, referring to the fedora sitting atop his partner's head.

Removing the hat and spinning it on his finger, Tommy said, "This? It's Uncle Fitz's hat. It was in with his stuff. I thought it looked good on me. I thought maybe I'd bring wearing hats back into style."

"You know, fedoras go with suits," Ben pointed out. "You'd have to wear a suit *every* day."

Tommy's face twisted into a sour expression.

Before he was able to respond with one of his own witty comebacks, Sergeant Shepherd came jogging into the breakroom. "Chief. Sarg. Sorry to interrupt, but we just got a call about a body found out at the old train yard. No one knows who the guy is or where he came from. Office LuCoco is requesting detectives on the scene."

"Dammit, LuCoco," Tommy said under his breath.

Ben looked to the chief who said, "You can finish up the paperwork on the Martin case later. It'll keep. Go see what this is all about."

"Yes, sir," Ben said, heading out the door behind Tommy.

"And keep me posted," Chief Brent hollered after them.

Chapter Sixty-Nine

1945 . . .

The Beaux-Arts style Baltimore Pennsylvania Station sat along North Charles Street in Baltimore, a little over a mile north of downtown and the harbor. On a bright day like today, the granite façade practically glimmered in the sun. Fitz stepped through the front doors with a throng of other passengers, happy he was home. The crowds of people reenergized him. He thrived on the hustle and bustle of the city.

A businessman in a dark brown suit rushed past him, nearly knocking him over.

"Sorry, Mack," the man said, barely breaking his stride.

Fitz smiled.

He'd spent the ride back on the train from Parker City considering what to do about Conrad Martin and Joe Grainger. The list he'd taken from under George Milford's bed didn't actually implicate either of the men. But, according to the file Jerry Hopkins had passed him from the War Department, they were already suspicious of Martin, they just didn't have enough to pursue an investigation. The list might be able to give them some new leads. With it looking like the war would be coming to an end in the not-too-distant future, Fitz didn't want to see the whole affair swept under the rug. But part of him understood that was the way the game was played, and a few stolen pieces of artwork, no matter how valuable, weren't enough to tarnish the reputation of the American Diplomatic Corps. Especially when the United States was going to have to be the one stepping up and leading the world in rebuilding after the last years of fighting and slaughter.

He figured he'd talk to Archibald Stride about the matter when he got back to the office. Fitz had good connections that he could hand the list off to, but Archie's contacts were the men to whom Fitz's connections' bosses answered.

When he'd telephoned the Stride Agency from the Parker station before leaving, Elaine Straitt said she'd have one of the other fellas from the office pick him up. So, he was surprised when a guy he didn't know, wearing a dark suit and matching hat, stepped up to him.

"Francis Mason?"

"One and the same."

"My boss was hoping to have a word with you," he said, gesturing toward a pair of black sedans parked by the curb. Another man dressed in an almost identical suit stood next to one of the cars. Fitz clocked the bulge under the first man's jacket. His own holster tended to do the same thing.

"Do I know your boss?" Fitz asked, not making a move toward the cars.

"You have nothing to worry about, Mr. Mason. We're all friends here."

"Well. If we're all such good friends, I guess you won't mind carrying this," Fitz said, thrusting his valises into the man's hands. At least if he was holding the suitcases, it would make it a little more difficult to reach for his gun.

As Fitz cautiously approached the cars, the second man, also concealing a gun under his jacket, opened the backdoor of the first car. There were two more men sitting in the front seat of the second car, their eyes glued on him.

Fitz, knowing he was taking a risk by getting into the car, slid into the backseat. As his eyes adjusted to the dimmer interior, he had a chance to look at the man sitting next to him. It was the uniform he noticed first. Then, the man wearing it. At which point Fitz relaxed, no longer on guard. A broad smile appeared on the face of the man who ran the War Department's Executive Procurement and Resources Office, Lieutenant Colonel Jerry Hopkins.

"How ya doin', Fitz?" his friend asked.

"You really know how to put on a show, Jerry. So much for trying to stay inconspicuous. Your boys out there are going to get you noticed."

"They're not my men," Hopkins corrected.

"No. They're mine," came a sharp voice from the front seat. When the bulldog-faced man turned around, his dark eyes wordlessly told Fitz he was a man who didn't mess around.

"Fitz Mason," Hopkins began, "this is J. Edgar Hoover. The Director of the Federal Bureau of Investigation."

"Director Hoover, um, it's nice to know you," Fitz said, hoping he didn't sound as surprised as he felt.

"Fitz," Hopkins continued, "for the first time, my office and the Bureau have intersecting operations, and we need someone with the smarts to take over and make sure things are done right. Someone we can all trust."

"The matter is highly confidential," Hoover added. "The lieutenant colonel here tells me you're the only man for the job."

"I'm flattered, gentlemen," Fitz said, a smile crossing his face, "but I would have to speak with my employer to see–"

"I've already spoken with Archie," Hopkins said. "You're all ours as long as we need you."

The officer then laid a file on Fitz's lap. "I think you're going to like this case."

Fitz opened the folder's cover and read the name of the operation. He smiled without even realizing it. OPERATION SILK TIE.

"Are you in?" Hoover demanded. The guy really had a way about him. Obviously, the stories were all true, Fitz thought.

"Director Hoover, I am always happy to help my country. And maybe you can help me with something," Fitz said, the smile on his face broadening as he removed the list of stolen artwork from his jacket pocket.

About the Author

When not sitting in his library devising new and clever ways to kill people (*for his mysteries*), Justin can usually be found at The Way Off Broadway Dinner Theatre, outside of Washington, DC, where he is one of the owners and producers. In addition to writing the Parker City Mysteries Series, which includes *Now & Then* (Finalist for the 2022 Silver Falchion Award for Best Investigator), *Vice & Virtue*, and *Fact & Fiction*, he is also the mastermind behind Marquee Mysteries, a series of interactive mystery events he has been writing and producing for over fifteen years. Justin and his wife, Jessica, live along Lake Linganore outside of Frederick, Maryland.

SOCIAL MEDIA HANDLES:
Facebook: @JMKiska
Instagram: @JMKiska
Goodreads: @JustinKiska
BookBub: @JMKiska

AUTHOR WEBSITE:

www.JustinKiska.com

Also by Justin M. Kiska

Now & Then

Vice & Virtue

Fact & Fiction